The Serpent & the Slave

Scott Hunter was born in Romford, Essex in 1956. He was educated at the now sadly defunct Douai Abbey School in Woolhampton, Berkshire. His writing career was kick-started after he won first prize in the Sunday Express short story competition in 1996. Scott's fantasy novel for children, 'The Ley Lines of Lushbury' was long-listed for the Times/Chicken House Children's novel competition in 2010. His adult thriller, 'The Trespass' is a *Kindle* bestseller. Scott combines a career in IT with a parallel career as a semi-professional drummer. Where he fits in the writing is anyone's guess. Scott lives in Berkshire with his wife and two youngest children.

Scott can be contacted via his website at:-

www.scott-hunter.net

The Serpent & the Slave

Scott Hunter

Myrtle Villa Publishing

The Serpent & the Slave
A Myrtle Villa Book

Originally published in Great Britain by Myrtle Villa
Publishing

A CIP record for this book is available from the British
Library

In this work of fiction, the characters, places and events
are either the product of the author's imagination or they
are used entirely fictitiously

ISBN 978-0-9561510-4-9

For Claire, Tom and Emily - and
the English teachers of Hutton Park Prep School 1966-
1969

Acknowledgements

My grateful thanks to Hilary Johnson for her sound advice and encouragement at the commencement of this project. Thanks too to my wife, Katherine, for reminding me that it needed finishing. . .

Cover Design:

Andrew Brown
Design for Writers
hello@designforwriters.com

*'A spirit goes along with every man
From birth, to guide him on the path of life.'
Menander (342 – 291 BC)*

Preface

By the time Valentinian 1 became emperor of the fourth century Roman world, the seeds of a dark future were already beginning to germinate. The land we know today as Great Britain had enjoyed almost fifty years of great prosperity and security under Constantius and his more famous son, Constantine. But by the middle of the century the tribes of Scotland, the Picts, and the warriors of Ireland, curiously known as *Scots*, *Scotti*, or *Atacotti* had begun to test Britain's frontier defences. From across the channel the Saxons had recommenced their raids on the shores of the eastern provinces.

It is a common misunderstanding that the inhabitants of late Roman Britain were a people oppressed by an occupying force, as in the early days of the Roman conquest. They were most certainly not. Over a period of centuries the prevailing culture had become almost completely 'Romanized' so as to be indistinguishable from the citizens of any other Roman province in custom and lifestyle. Britain was part of the 'Praefecture of the Gauls' and within this structure its provincial towns flourished to such a degree that we can be pretty sure the townsfolk enjoyed a reasonable standard of living. There was a well-defined infrastructure of government, now entirely separated from the military whose legions had been redeployed into mobile field armies and frontier units under the overall command of a *dux* (the *Dux Britanniarum*) and although the frontiers suffered regular harassment of one kind or another, no major invasion had threatened the island for decades.

Christianity had been granted full toleration by Constantine at the Edict of Milan in 313AD but despite the official blessing of the emperor, religion in Britain was still very much a mixture of old pagan tradition and superstition. Despite the fact that Valentinian was of Christian, not pagan, persuasion, the society in which Marius, the novel's main character, lived remained truly polytheistic. Hardly surprising then that, given this pot-pourri of deities, the citizens of Britain struggled with the concept that religion could have a personal application, rather than being a mere mechanical observance. Although there is little evidence in archaeological terms for a strong church in the provinces c.367AD, it is well attested that bishops and other church officials, although poor and living very much an ascetic lifestyle, went about their business without undue interference from the state. Archaeological finds in the South of England seem to confirm that Christianity was openly practised, especially in well-to-do households and country villas.

But Britain had not got off scot-free during the years leading up to the events described in this novel; the biggest upset experienced by mid-fourth century Britain had been the attempted usurpation of Magnentius, a man of British origin who made a bid for the seat of power and in the process requisitioned much of Britain's military strength for his overseas campaigns between 350 and 353AD. The reprisals administered by Valentinian's predecessor Constantius following Magnentius' defeat at Mons Seleucus in Gaul were masterminded by one *Paulus*, the man whose fearsome reputation earned him the nickname *Catena* - The Chain. The historian Ammianus tells us that

Paulus was eventually burned to death in Africa. Or was he?

Dramatis Personae

Marius Appius Scaevola	Main character, youngest member of the *curia*
Fraomar	*Alamanni* chieftain, slave and gladiator
Freia	Fraomar's sister, a slave in Drufidius' household
Lucius Septimius Tullio	Governor of *Britannia Prima*
Drufidius Sextus	Senior councillor, benefactor to Marius
Bernicca	Drufidius' wife
Barnabas	Itinerant Christian bishop
Romanus	Barnabas' protégé
Valentinian	The emperor of the west
Nipius	*Magister equitum*, sent by Valentinian to fetch Fraomar
Faelan	Irish war band leader
Iuillath	Irish magus
Scapulus	Leader of survivors - (Fullofaudes' *vexillatio)*
Crimthann	Irish High King
Terricula	Assistant to Nipius - rank unknown
Paulus *Catena*	Ex imperial notary, now leader of barbarian alliance
Gallio Velius Marsallas.	Member of the *Areani*, or *Arcani*, the emperor's frontier spy service
Caelius	Military leader of rebels under Paulus - rank unknown
Jovinus	Leader of task force, rank unknown, possibly *Dux Ripae* serving on the Rhine

Prologue I

Britannia – Praefecture of Gaul
Province of Britannia Prima, near Corinium. 353 AD

The sun is shining today, as it always shines in the dog days of childhood. Marius is seven years old and very happy. His garden is filled with flowers and the smell of freshly scythed grass hangs in the air. He can hear the clatter of dishes in the kitchen as his mother's household slaves go about their duties. He is a privileged child, the son of a wealthy landowner. His father is often away on business but today he is at home, working in his study. He has promised to take Marius to the field before bedtime to ride the new horse, a beautiful chestnut mare. Marius is so excited he can scarcely contain himself. But each time he re-enters the villa he is shooed back into the garden. His father will come out when he is ready. But adults take so long. Why can't they just come and have fun? It's a warm day and the garden has so many attractions. Marius loves to explore. He knows he is lucky to have this playground, because his mother always reminds him. Some boys, she says, have no gardens. They have to fetch and carry all day, with no playtime. Marius can't imagine that, but he tries to be grateful. Now he is a soldier, spinning around among the apple trees. Each tree is an enemy of Rome and each is killed with a single blow from his birthday present, a replica wooden sword. It's

1

perfect, right down to the last detail, and painted so cleverly you'd never know it wasn't the real thing. It scared Uncle out of his wits the other day when he came to visit. What was the boy doing with a weapon? His uncle had been cross. It made Marius giggle to remember his face, all red and twitchy. He said Marius should be at his books, not charging around frightening the living daylights out of his family. They shouldn't encourage him to use a weapon like that. But his mother had smiled sweetly and hugged his uncle. She told Uncle that he was only a boy, and boys needed to have fun.

Marius laughs as he remembers Uncle blowing and puffing. What was wrong with being a swordsman? When he grew up he would be a soldier like his cousin, Antonius. Marius swings his sword again and a barbarian apple loses the top of its head. But now a kitchen slave – the grumpy one – is calling from the house. Not the apples. They are for picking, not killing. And don't come into the house because there are important visitors. Marius calls back. He knows. He heard the clatter of their horses a while ago. It's boring. It will just make father even later. He sighs and chops at the short grass in frustration. Then he remembers the army horsemen he saw last week riding into Corinium. He snorts and jumps, runs off down the garden, turns the corner by the secret hedge and tethers his invisible mount to a convenient branch. This is the best place in the whole garden, the secret hedge. It's secret because you'd never know what was behind it, or even that there *was* anything there worth finding. Father had hired the best gardener and Mother said he was more like a magician than a gardener and they had both laughed. Marius had laughed too, although he didn't really understand why. Now Marius looks around to make sure no one is looking. That's what he always has to do, his father said. No one is to know. The thick foliage parts and reveals a narrow path. It's darker in here out of the sunlight, but Marius knows his way. The path leads to a small, square temple nestling against a backdrop of thick hedgerow. Marius climbs the wooden steps to the portico and enters by the wood-framed door. It's quiet, but Marius isn't scared. He's been here many times before. He especially loves coming in here with his father to pray together to the gods of the wood. Father says they are the family gods, special for them. They bring good, or if they're unhappy, bad luck. So it's important to keep them happy. Sometimes his father burns sweet herbs and incense that Marius can smell on his clothes for days afterwards.

Marius holds up his hands as his father has taught him and prays a special prayer. Please can father be ready soon? Please can his visitors go? Marius feels a little guilty about this prayer, but he is sure that the gods will hear him. Surely they want him to have fun? He hums a tune softly, one that his tutor has taught him. The gods like music, he's sure of that too. He finishes his song before the last verse because he can hear shouting. Probably one of the slaves has done something wrong. Marius slips back into the garden. As he does so, he sees his father coming out of the villa. Marius smiles but his father is waving him away. Someone comes behind his father and lifts his arm. His father is falling now, lying on the steps. Marius is frozen to the spot. He tries to speak but his mouth makes no sound. He hears another scream but the sound is cut off suddenly. There are other sounds too, tearing and smashing sounds, as if the house is being broken from inside. There are more people coming out. There is Procullus, the grumpy kitchen slave. He is shouting at the other people. Marius sees that they are soldiers. Procullus is being held by two of them. That's not fair. Marius looks at his wooden sword and wonders what to do. When he looks back, Procullus is falling, a red streak across his throat. Someone else is coming out. A tall man. He has no hair and his long, black cloak flaps around him like crows' wings. He looks out over the lawn, but Marius slips away – back into the secret place. His heart is pounding. He hears the clank of armour, gruff voices, then silence. But he knows that *the man* is listening, searching for him.

Marius is lying in the temple, against the far wall. He watches the door and waits for the shadow to appear.

Prologue II

The stars were brighter than usual tonight, Publius Albanus Tutor mused as he made his way down the colonnaded main street of Leptis. Funny how cold it could get after you'd spent the day baking under your armour. But he wasn't complaining. Compared to other postings, this was a good one. He pitied the legions freezing their jerkins off in Britannia. He had a friend on the northern wall who wrote occasionally and the stories he came out with made Publius even more grateful for the exotic climate of Africa. Sometimes he was assigned sentry duty on the long harbour breakwater; those were Publius' favourite nights, watching the moonlight sparkle on the dark sea, feeling the warm wind on your face; sharing a game of dice with comrades after a shift. Publius smiled to himself. Life was pretty good here, even if the local tribes were getting a bit restless; he'd been south a couple of times to teach them who their masters were and, despite their legendary ferocity, they'd received a good beating from Rome's finest. There hadn't been any trouble since. Not since last full moon. Publius glanced up and watched a wisp of cloud pass over the face of the shining orb. Besides, he mused, while the great walls of Leptis stood what hope did the tribesmen have? Wasting their time, Publius smiled to himself. Rome was Rome, and no one could touch it. Not even here.

Publius lengthened his stride down the wide thoroughfare, breathing in the exotic smells of night time

Leptis. He stopped at a stall to buy a skewer of roast meat, flavoured with fish sauce and spices. The boy smiled at him as he plucked the skewer expertly from the flames and winked. Publius followed the boy's pointing finger and caught sight of a group of young girls loitering by the pillars. They giggled and whispered amongst themselves as the soldier scrutinized them, but their excitement turned to jibes of disappointment as Publius shook his head and paid for his food with a grimy coin. No time for that tonight, business to get on with. And a bad business for someone, he ruminated, munching a piece of meat. Tonight he was on execution duty and they were expecting a large crowd to witness the burning of two of the Empire's most hated figures: Paulus 'Catena', head of the *agentes in rebus* and one Apodemius, also involved in treason trials under Constantius and judged guilty himself under the Emperor Julian's new regime. Publius was an experienced executioner, but there was something about burnings even a hardened veteran like himself found detestable. Still, orders were orders. He turned into the main square and found as predicted, a hundred or so citizens already gathered. The mood was expectant, an almost carnival atmosphere as people jostled for position or gossiped together in small groups whilst they waited for the main event. Street vendors and entertainers mingled with the crowd, weaving their way expertly in and out as they dispensed their tricks and consumables. Publius pushed his way to the middle of the square where the two stakes stood erect, surrounded by the cut logs and brushwood of his unit's earlier preparations.

'*Salve* Publius. Bit late, aren't you?' A lugubrious officer raised his hand in half-hearted greeting.

'Held up at the harbour. Everything ready?'

'Ready as it'll ever be. 'Let's get the torches lit.'

Placed at intervals around the pyre were a number of torches set upon tall poles. Each would be allocated to an attending soldier, who at a given signal would reach into the brushwood and ignite it.

'Orders the same?' the officer asked him.

'No change, Quintus,' Publius replied, 'they've obviously upset Julian a lot.'

'I pity them. This is the worst way to die.' Quintus took the first pole and lit the torch from the brazier. He replaced the pole in its locating socket and moved to the next. Other members of the unit followed suit and soon the circle of fire was complete. The crowd watched the proceedings and when the final torch was lit a loud cheer went up, the echo slapping back from the stone walls of the buildings surrounding the square.

Publius approached the pyre to make his final checks. He mentally ticked off each check as he completed it. Stakes secure, wood dry. No sign of tampering. Air channel unblocked. No rope. He felt an uncharacteristic stab of compassion for the victims. The addition of a neck rope would be a mercy, enabling the condemned men to be strangled before the flames took them. But their orders had contained no such lenience; the victims would burn alive. Publius shook his head ruefully and stepped back to review his handiwork Now all they had to do was await the execution squad and keep the crowd under control. Publius accepted a cup of wine and walked slowly around the pyre in his usual thorough manner. Any technical problems would rest fairly and squarely on his shoulders and the last thing Publius wanted was to put his reputation in jeopardy. He'd done a good job here in

Africa and the end of his assignment was only a few moons away, after which retirement beckoned. A quiet life in the foothills somewhere south of Rome. A vineyard, maybe some livestock, one or two young slaves. All he had to do was keep his nose clean. Publius knew how swiftly a fall from grace could occur. Case in point tonight. Paulus, favourite of the Emperor Constantius. Couldn't put a foot wrong at first, then got too ahead of himself. Started to take the law into his own hands. Even had a go at Britannia's *vicarius*. It was no good being in with the emperor if everyone else hated you, Publius reckoned. Emperors came and went, but people had long memories. And tonight's other victim, Apodemius, he knew less about. But the same principle applied: overstep the mark and watch your fortunes crumble.

He swore under his breath and bent to adjust a clump of brushwood that had become detached from the rest. There'd be political heavyweights here this evening. Everything had to be right or he'd feel the wrath of his commanding officer, a man not known for his tolerance. Publius wiped a bead of perspiration from his forehead and stamped the wood back into place with a hob-nailed sandal. That was better. He rejoined his comrades and refilled his cup. There was a strange smell about tonight. He sniffed the air and frowned. Had someone planted something in the pyre? Sabotage attempts were not unknown, particularly for high profile executions such as this. Who knew how many followers these men had? Publius repeated his careful inspection and drew a blank. He shrugged his shoulders and gave the thumbs up to his colleagues

The crowd had quietened in the pre-emptive lull before the appearance of the prisoners, then a louder cheer went up as the execution party appeared and advanced with measured stride across the square. Necks craned as the prisoners drew near to the centre. Publius stood back to watch. His job was done. He wondered how these men would die. Some died bravely. With scarcely a word. Others – well, others fought and screamed to the last. The escort fell back to reveal two men, manacled together. The first, unremarkable. Slightly overweight, reddish hair matted with sweat. Trembling. The other: he was different. Tall, still, almost confident. That must be Paulus. He was bald, with a long, almost pointed skull. His lips wore a faint smile and he surveyed the crowd with such studied casualness it was as if he imagined himself to be attending a banquet in his honour or a day at the races rather than his last moments on earth. The men were quickly bound to the stakes and Publius wrinkled his nose as he saw a gush of liquid spray from the first prisoner's breeches and trickle down his leg. He took a swig of wine. Couldn't blame the man. Next to crucifixion this sort of death was the worst imaginable.

'Squad. Torches!' the commander barked. The poles were retrieved and hoisted skywards. The commander paused momentarily, then announced: 'The charges are treason for both.' He turned to the crowd. 'Are you ready to see Roman justice?'

They knew the responses and bayed back at him: 'Justice! Justice! Roman Justice!'

Publius winced as the torches were applied and the first orange flames licked the feet of the victims. He stood back a few paces. Gods, what *was* that smell? Not the usual smell, which never failed to turn Publius'

13

stomach however many burnings he attended. Something else. Sickly. He stepped back a few more paces to give his nostrils some relief. Greyish black smoke was beginning to rise and they heard the first screams begin. Apodemius, begging for mercy. Nothing yet from the other figure in the flames. And then he looked again. Something was stirring. He could see the slumped figure of Apodemius whose hopeless cries had tailed off. But Paulus? Publius shielded his eyes with one hand and took a step forward. There was movement, a snake-like writhing. And then he saw, piercing the smoke like beacons, two slits of green malevolence staring out of the fire. The noise of the crowd receded and his only focus became the eyes. They were all that was important. He no longer felt the heat of the fire and felt no pain at all when he stepped forward again and raised his arm. Of course he would come, he replied to the simple question posed by the eyes. There was nothing to stop him. He was vaguely aware of other voices calling him, and at one point felt an arm on his shoulder. He smiled as he heard it withdrawn with a cry of pain. Publius knew they couldn't stop him. He was still smiling as he fell forward into the flames and embraced the stake. It felt good to be here. And then he realized that the eyes no longer held him. He turned his head slightly to look for them. Surely they wouldn't leave him? And then the pain seared through his body, welding him to the stake in a contortion of agony. His last conscious thought was that he was alone; whoever had invited him to share the flames had lied.

Part One

Catena

Chapter 1

Calleva – formerly Calleva Atrebatum, Province of Britannia Prima. 367AD

Six years later

A hush fell over the arena as if every man, woman and child had taken one collective breath and held it. All eyes were focused on the two men who had fought for one purpose: to live. But for one the unthinkable had happened. Disarmed and prostrate, he faced a bloody end.

From his vantage point in the dignitaries seating, Marius Appius Scaevola turned his head away, stomach tightening in distaste. Even at his youthful age he had witnessed similar scenes many times and they sickened him to the very core of his being. Games to the death should be banned – but who would risk speaking against them here in Britannia? Marius glanced at his mentor. Not Drufidius, that was for sure; he was old empire through and through. Marius studied the man from the corner of his eye. Sallow complexion. Cropped beard. Hint of grey. Drufidius' chin was thrust forward aggressively in anticipation of the kill. Feeling Marius' eyes upon him, he risked a sideways look. 'Splendid fellow, eh Marius? My money was on him from the start,' he chuckled to himself. Reluctantly, Marius returned his attention to the arena and the object of his companion's enthusiasm. He had to agree. The gladiator

17

straddling his fallen adversary stood a full six feet tall. His naked torso gleamed with oil and sweat, enhancing his physique and lending the man a sculpted, athletic appearance. He swayed confidently on his heavily muscled legs, rotating the point of his spear above his opponent's exposed stomach. In Jupiter's name, thought Marius, *get it over with.*

The fallen man lay spreadeagled on the sand. The spear ceased its rotation as the victor elect raised his head to seek confirmation of the death sentence. As Marius watched it seemed in the moments that followed as if the world had slowed to a fraction of its normal speed. He saw the prostrate man's arm bend and swing in an easy motion, the razor edge of his sword catching the weak autumn sunlight as it tore through bone and sinew before returning in a deadly vertical arc, slicing the spear neatly in half and opening the stomach of the victor elect who was dead before his body met the arena floor.

Marius stared in wonder as the gladiator sprang, catlike, to his feet, bowed and made his way towards the exit tunnel. The crowd broke into spontaneous applause at this spectacular reversal of fortune. Marius found himself clapping with them. He looked at his companion, and noted that his mood had changed.

'By all the gods! Marius – did you see that? My fellow wasn't even looking. How unsporting can you get? Foul play, f–foul play!' Drufidius yelled into the arena, shaking his fist.

Marius had to shout to make himself heard: 'It looked fair to me. Your man was caught napping.' They watched the victor leaving the arena to loud acclaim. Some threw wild flowers in his path from the ringside seats; others cast coins that fell ungathered in the dust. The victor ignored their entreaties, walking purposefully to the exit tunnel with long, loping strides until he eventually disappeared from view.

Drufidius took Marius' arm and pointed. 'The Praeses is on the move – thank the gods there are no more contests today – at this rate I shall be b–bankrupt before we get to the Corinium g–games. Come on – best not keep him waiting.'

Marius looked towards the seats of honour where the Praeses was smiling and nodding with evident satisfaction. Now there was a man of considerable charisma: Lucius Septimius Tullio, governor of Britannia Prima. He saw them and beckoned. Marius followed Drufidius as he pressed through the crowd and joined Lucius and his entourage. Drufidius inclined his head in a gesture of submission. 'Ready to leave, Praeses? I hope you enjoyed the show.'

The governor beamed. 'Enjoyed? It was magnificent, Drufidius. And I want to reward the victor personally. Get me his name, would you? All the details, mind – none of your usual sketchy stuff.'

Drufidius bowed stiffly. 'With pleasure, Praeses. I will ensure that the gladiator is b–brought before you to doubtless benefit from your great generosity.'

Marius looked away in embarrassment. Marius watched for the Praeses' reaction and caught it in the imperceptible curling of the lip, the slight darkening of the eyes. Lucius turned his attention to Marius. 'Ah, young Marius. I hope Drufidius is setting a good example for you? We'll catch up later over dinner, eh?'

'It will be an honour, sir,' Marius replied, hoping his face didn't give away his reluctance. The last thing he wanted was a dull evening at Drufidius' table.

'Drufidius has the best kitchen staff in Calleva and what's more– ' the Praeses raised a large hand to hide his face from Drufidius, '– a wife who is able and willing,' he stage-whispered. He let his hand fall, winked and in a normal voice said: 'Perhaps we can digest some useful information together.'

Marius felt himself flush but managed a smile. 'I look forward to it, Praeses.'

Lucius Septimius barked several orders in rapid succession before moving towards the amphitheatre exit. An armed escort led the way, giving the procession precedence over members of the public. Drufidius turned to Marius. 'Now young man, allow me to put my carriage at your disposal.. My slave, Pelio, awaits you at the east exit. No doubt you will wish to refresh yourself before we dine with the Praeses this evening. In the meantime it seems that I must extend an invitation to that gladiatorial barbarian who has pleased the Praeses so much but who has caused me an equal measure of f–financial distress. Please excuse me.'

Relief shot through Marius. At last: some time to himself. 'Of course. I'll catch up with you later.'

Drufidius disappeared into the thinning crowd and Marius watched the amphitheatre empty. Two slaves were clearing the body of the dead gladiator from the arena. One of them raked over the earth where the man had fallen. Marius wondered how much more blood would be spilled in the guise of entertainment before the world came to its senses. He looked at the sky, grey and overcast. A flight of wild geese flew overhead in perfect formation, skimming the treetops surrounding the arena. An omen. But was it for good or ill? Whichever, the contrast between nature's raw beauty and the orchestrated barbarism of the amphitheatre struck him afresh. Several large spots of rain landed on his upturned face followed by a cold gust of wind that blew bitingly across the arena, chilling him to the bone. Marius shivered and, wrapping his cloak tightly around him, made quickly for the exit to find Pelio.

The journey to Drufidius' house would usually have taken only a short time as the amphitheatre was situated on the outskirts of Calleva, beyond the defensive wall but within walking distance for the general public. Today however, the crowd returning from the amphitheatre together with the market traders on either side of the approach to the east gate clogged the road. From within the carriage, a simple horse-drawn wagon, Marius watched the townsfolk of Calleva bustle past. A real mixture of civilian and military – the latter mainly from the ranks of the local militia – but there were also troops camped nearby on their way to Londinium from the west country. There were more comings and goings of the military these days, Marius thought enviously, as the carriage bumped along the narrow approach to the town gate; ever since the barbarian raids in the north had worsened. There had been rumours of raiders from north of the Great Wall uniting with the Irish whose inland forays were becoming ever bolder. But the *dux Britanniarum* – a man named Fullofaudes, commander of the northern forces, reportedly had the situation firmly under control. How successful this control was Marius didn't know but the *dux* was considered a capable military leader, certainly more than able to contain the raiding barbarians. Stories of valour from Britannia's northern frontier had Marius seething with envy but he knew there was little chance of such excitement coming his way. Marius sighed. Coming of age was supposed to be a manly thing, something to be proud of. What pride could he take in municipal fund deficits, tax evasion and interminable meetings? Not for the first time Marius cursed the fates who had aligned his destiny not with a great military family but with the land owning gentry.

Eventually the carriage squeezed through the gates and they were waved through by a harassed-looking soldier, his face scarlet from yelling at the pedestrians to make room. But why hurry? Marius sighed. The week stretched ahead like a prison sentence; meetings, meetings, meetings. All he could hope for was brevity, but there was precious little of that when Lucius and Drufidius got together. Marius itched to return to his villa and his fencing practice - Saturnus, the household slave, was an expert with the *spatha*, the favoured weapon of the Roman legionary and Marius was anxious to pick up as many tips as he could. He longed for a commission but his inherited duties made it highly improbable that he would ever fulfill his dream. He'd begged his uncle, Lactantius, to pull strings but to no avail. His path, Lactantius said, had been decreed long ago; he was to serve as a member of the *Curia*, Britannia Prima's governing body – *It's what your father would have wanted*, Lactantius had often told him, and no amount of begging on Marius' part had ever changed his uncle's mind.

The carriage jolted on, passing the temple on the right and the many familiar buildings of Calleva. Eventually they turned off the main street into the lane that Marius remembered led to Drufidius' house. The house was built in an inverted 'U', its open end protected by a large gate. The two wings were a later addition to the property, born of necessity as Drufidius had increased his staff and greater demands had been made on his accommodation. The west wing housed the stables, and having entered the gate leading into the central courtyard, Pelio guided the carriage towards them. Marius watched the space above the stable gate as they approached and was rewarded by the appearance of a familiar maned head. He climbed down from the carriage and reached up to pat his horse's muzzle. Pelio watched him while he unhitched the carriage horses.

'Thanks for looking after him, Pelio. He's had an idle afternoon, and he thinks we should be heading for home. There now, boy,' Marius comforted the restless animal, 'I want to go home too, but we've got to stay awhile. Pelio will exercise you well enough, won't you Pelio?' Pelio grinned in reply, and walked his charges through to the adjacent stable. Marius remained with his horse, soothing the beast and stroking his nose. The sun was setting, casting a deep orange glow across the yard. In the distance, the clatter of the town could be heard as it carried its holiday mood into the early evening. Voices were raised momentarily in song above the general hubbub before being whipped away by the autumn wind. Marius felt a sudden sense of foreboding, as if a dark hand had reached into his heart. The horse whinnied and shifted uncomfortably in its stall. He patted the brown flank and frowned. 'Patience, old friend, patience. We'll be home soon enough.'

Chapter 2

Marius had remained in his guest room for as long as politeness permitted but he knew he couldn't put the evening off any longer. Having changed into a fresh toga he walked quickly across the marble floor of the hall to the dining room where he was met by a young female slave. Her fair hair fell over the whiteness of her bare shoulders as she bowed a greeting, opened the door and stood respectfully to one side. Marius was struck by her bearing and beauty and he found it hard not to stare as she ushered him into the dining room. Inside, Drufidius was bustling about, making final preparations and issuing terse instructions to his catering slaves.

'Marius, my boy – come in, come in. Are you rested? Good.' Drufidius went on without waiting for a reply. 'We shall dine like the gods tonight! All is ready!' He gripped a slave by the elbow and steered him towards the door, whilst motioning urgently to the other. 'Out, out. Begone. Your duties are done – and they had better be done well, or you shall answer to the Praeses himself! Now then Marius, do make yourself comfortable. I'll be back in an instant – Bernicca is late – as usual. And the P–Praeses due at any time–' He trailed off, nervously smoothing his toga with his hands.

Marius raised his hand politely. 'I'll enjoy a cup of wine until you return.' He resisted the urge to add *and don't hurry back. . .*

Drufidius clapped a hand to his forehead. 'Oh, may the *Lares* forgive me.' He clicked his fingers. A slave magically appeared at the door. 'Quickly – wine for our guest.' The slave raised an eyebrow, seeking more specific information. Drufidius offered none and waved him away: 'Go on man, go on.' The slave vanished, followed swiftly by his host. The door closed and silence reigned. Marius shook his head wearily. Why Drufidius was so agitated about receiving the Praeses was beyond him. Lucius was a bully and a bore. But he was also powerful, and Drufidius was ever keen to impress those of high rank. The door opened and the slave girl who had previously greeted him entered carrying a tray on which was balanced a pewter goblet. Marius watched her with fascination; she really was very attractive and he felt a sudden urge to find out more about her. 'I haven't seen you before,' he heard himself say. 'Are you new?'

The girl looked up in surprise and shook her head. Her eyes were a steely blue, her skin so pale it was almost translucent.

'Well then, I must have missed you on previous visits,' he said awkwardly, regretting his impulsiveness.

'I served in the kitchens when I arrived,' she replied, 'but the master has allowed me to serve his guests.'

'Where are you from?' Marius asked, struck by her bearing and confidence.

'From Germania, sir.'

'From which tribe?'

The girl raised her chin a fraction. 'The *Alamanni*.'

'Do you like it here?' *What a stupid question, Marius you idiot. Of course she doesn't like it. She's a slave…*

'The master and mistress look after me well enough,' she bent and dabbed at his table to remove a stray droplet of wine. 'I cannot talk any more. I must return to my duties. Please excuse me.' She looked him in the eye and Marius felt his stomach flutter as if a flight of butterflies had been released in his heart.

He watched her leave, his brain whirling with confused thoughts. *Why didn't I say something sensible? How can a girl have such an effect on me?* Marius took a sip of wine to calm himself and made a mental note to query Drufidius later on. Somehow he would find out more without giving himself away.

He heard a commotion outside, a clatter of hooves followed by footsteps on the front steps. Voices echoed in the hall. Drufidius' voice raised in greeting. Another, unmistakeably Lucius Septimius. Savouring his last seconds of peace, Marius took a deep breath. Drufidius came first, followed by Bernicca and two attendant male slaves. The Praeses followed, an imposing figure in full civil uniform. The procession was supported by two of his personal guard, who took up position at either side of the door. Marius bowed formally to Drufidius and Bernicca and saluted the Praeses. Lucius Septimius waved it away. 'Save the formalities for the Forum, Marius. Tonight is a night to relax. I'm sure the meal will be up to our hosts' usual standards.'

Bernicca made a great show of transparently fake embarrassment, inclining her head like a young maid, patting her extravagant hairstyle and simpering until Marius felt he would be ill. Drufidius interrupted his wife's theatrics with a short speech during which the male slaves quietly and efficiently replaced the guest's footwear with sandals. By and by Drufidius concluded with a toast to the household gods. Marius dutifully and gratefully drank. *It's going to be a long evening*, he thought gloomily.

The first course arrived and gave a fair indication of Drufidius' desire to impress. A Corinthian bronze statuette of a horse carrying twin baskets set upon a tray of relishes was placed carefully on the central table between their individual couches. One basket was filled with black olives, the other with green. Silver salvers inscribed with Drufidius' name and containing seasoned dormice were placed on each guest's table. The next moment two tall African slaves swept into the room carrying a gridiron of sizzling sausages beneath which rested what looked to be plums mixed with pomegranate seeds. Drufidius beamed with pleasure at each fresh culinary revelation. Finally a tray was placed on the groaning table containing a basket in which was placed rather oddly, as if sitting on a nest, what seemed to be a carved wooden hen. The slaves then revealed that the nest was filled with pea-fowl eggs and distributed them to each diner. Marius eyed his portion suspiciously. 'Go on, try it, try it!' Drufidius encouraged them enthusiastically. Marius broke his gingerly and exclaimed in surprise. They were made of a very light pastry and hidden within the yolks were tiny spiced garden warblers.

'What do you think?' Drufidius asked with barely suppressed glee. Marius smiled weakly. He would have settled for a plate of snails and garlic rather than sit through this over exuberant show. Lucius was indulging his appetite with abandon, recounting some lewd story which involved many winks and, Marius noticed, much contact with Bernicca's leg which dangled just within range of the Praeses' large hand. *Surprise surprise*, Marius thought to himself; Bernicca's dalliance with the Praeses was common knowledge. If Drufidius was aware – and Marius was sure he must be – his mentor didn't seem that bothered.

Beside each couch hovered a slave, keeping their cups topped up with rich red Gallic wine, too dry for Marius' taste but refreshing enough. 'You like it, Marius?' the host enquired, draining his goblet noisily, 'Fifty years old, I swear, from the cellars of Constantine himself. Cost the earth, but – well, why not?' Drufidius made an inclusive gesture as if to suggest that money was no barrier to his hospitality.

'I fear, my dear Drufidius,' Lucius Septimius broke off his conversation with a glint in his eye, 'that your gladiator was not as good a choice as you led me to believe.'

Drufidius eyed the Praeses warily. 'He was a d–disappointment, Praeses, a careless oaf. I have had ill luck with my tips recently, despite painstaking research.'

Lucius Septimius supped deeply from his goblet. 'You are wretchedly ill-advised Drufidius, as always. Now take that blond fellow, the one I backed. He'll go far, mark my words. Something about him. A keen spirit.'

Drufidius smiled indulgently. Marius made no comment. He hoped that Lucius would not spend the remainder of the evening baiting the luckless Drufidius. Marius liked the councillor, despite his weaknesses; and he had good reason for his affection: Drufidius had stepped in after his mother and father's murder and made all the necessary arrangements for his cousin to act *in loco parentis*; this cousin was Marius' much loved 'Uncle' Lactantius.

The slaves resumed their duties, handing out little pastry sucking pigs which Marius left untasted. He watched as one of the slaves drew a hunting knife from within his tunic and slit the boar's belly. Instead of entrails and blood a number of thrushes flew out of the opening to be caught in nets by the slaves and offered to the guests. Marius chewed unenthusiastically, racking his brains for a plausible excuse to leave the dinner party early. Presently there was a sharp knock at the door. One of the guards entered, saluted Lucius Septimius and addressed Drufidius briskly.

'The gladiator is here, councillor. He is unarmed and chained. He will be brought in at your word.'

Drufidius nodded and turned to Lucius. 'As you desired, Praeses. The winner is here for your inspection.'

Marius sat up. Here at last was something of interest.

'Well then, bring him in!' Lucius ordered, licking his lips with anticipation.

The guard withdrew and the man Marius recognised from the amphitheatre took his place, filling the door frame with his bulk. He was dressed in a standard *tunica*, worn loosely belted at the waist. He looked fit and well fed, unlike other gladiators Marius had seen at close quarters. His expression was proud and confident, his eyes keen. He fixed them first on Marius, then Drufidius and finally his steely gaze rested upon Bernicca. A manacle was fastened round his ankle, attached at its opposite end to the arm of a soldier of centurion rank. The centurion noticed Bernicca's unease.

'He'll not harm you, my lady. He knows his place.'

Bernicca shifted uncomfortably on her couch but Marius could see that she was fascinated, just as he was.

'Thank you, centurion,' Drufidius said, 'Please c–come forward.' He spoke directly to the gladiator. 'You are here because the provincial governor, Lucius Septimius has requested your presence. You have the honour of winning today and the Praeses is pleased with you. You may relax and speak when you are spoken to. Do you understand?'

The gladiator nodded. Drufidius was not satisfied. He repeated the question. Again, the nod. Lucius interrupted impatiently, rising to his feet. 'Answer him, man. Have you lost your tongue? By Jupiter, I shall help you find it.' He faced the chained man, his nose an inch from the gladiator's face. 'My pleasure with you may be short-lived. Now *answer*.'

The man regarded Lucius calmly, 'I have no desire to offend,' replied the gladiator in an even voice, 'and I do understand.'

Lucius grunted and returned to his couch. He lay back on the cushions and picked up his goblet.

'So. What is your name?'

'My name is Fraomar.'

'Where are you from? You don't look like a native of Britannia.'

'I belong to the *Alamanni*.'

Marius raised an eyebrow. Coincidence, surely. Slaves came from all over the Empire. But two from the same tribe in one evening?

The Praeses was warming to his interrogation. 'Hm. A troublesome people. A *fighting* people. I acknowledge that it is a discipline in which you excel.'

Fraomar nodded. 'I was trained to fight from birth.'

'You were trained well.'

Fraomar smiled faintly. 'It is a matter of survival. To die is not as honourable as your poets suggest.'

The Praeses scrutinized him. 'So, you are a man of honour and learning. Tell me: how long have you been a gladiator?'

'Five winters have passed.'

Marius' eyes widened. Five years was a long time to survive as a gladiator. It meant that this man had endured not only hundreds of arena encounters but also the most rigorously demanding lifestyle. Many provincial gladiators, unlike their celebrity counterparts in Rome, died in practice sessions as violent as the real thing or perished through disease or malnutrition. Statistically it was an impressive feat and he said so.

Lucius rose to his feet again. He faced Fraomar, circling him slowly. 'Built to last, eh Drufidius?' Drufidius smiled weakly and Lucius went on, speaking to Fraomar's back: 'What would you do if you were freed, I wonder?'

If the gladiator was fazed by such directness, he did not show it. 'I would deliver justice to my enemies, reunite my family, return to my people.'

The Praeses pounced. 'And who are your enemies?' His eyes narrowed. 'Would you yet have Rome as your enemy, after your people have suffered so many defeats at the hands of our generals?'

'Our people seek only to live in peace. We do not choose to make war – it is forced upon us. We merely wish to continue our way of life, our traditions.'

'And to extract the maximum tribute from the emperor, so I've heard. And now you have another war. You barbarians don't know what's good for you. You don't know when you're beaten.' Lucius stroked his chin as he continued his appraisal. After a moment he asked the centurion: 'How much?'

The centurion was visibly taken aback. 'Well, he's not really for sale, Praeses. This is a dangerous man.'

'I need dangerous men in my guardroom.'

'If I might m–m–make a suggestion, Praeses –' Drufidius began.

Lucius waved away his interruption, as if swatting a gnat. 'What do you think, Marius?'

Marius opted for a diplomatic reply. 'Well,' he began carefully, 'it may be best to obtain further information before– '

'By Mithras, man, what do you think I've been doing these last ten minutes?'

Defeated, Marius shrugged his shoulders. The Praeses was a difficult man. If he wanted something he usually got it. Bernicca made an excuse and got up to leave. The door opened before she reached it and the slave girl entered, carrying further savouries. As she passed Lucius her foot caught against a table leg and she stumbled awkwardly against him, catching hold of his arm to steady herself. Lucius flew round, striking the girl across the face. He eyes blazed. 'You presume to touch me, girl? You'll feel a whip across your back before this night is over.' He raised his hand to strike again but Marius saw the gladiator lunge towards the Praeses, the sudden movement catching his guardian unawares. Lucius was an agile man, despite his size and he spun to face the threat, reaching for the short dagger at his side. The gladiator was faster. Before the centurion could restrain him he had launched himself at Lucius, knocking him off balance and sending them both crashing against the table, scattering dishes and food across the mosaic. Recovering his wits, the centurion hauled at the chain in an effort to pull the gladiator back. He wrenched the chain a second time and shoved Fraomar hard against the wall, driving the butt of his sword across the Alamann's neck. Lucius' men positioned their weapons at the gladiator's stomach. Breathing heavily the Praeses rose to his feet, face red and eyes murderous.

'So, you dare to lay hands on a provincial governor. Barbarian scum.' He approached Fraomar slowly, menacingly.

Drufidius reappeared from behind his couch. 'Praeses, I would be g–grateful if– '

Be silent!' Lucius roared. He stood before Fraomar. When he spoke again it was in a lower voice that somehow carried greater threat. 'Well my honourable friend, tell me. What is the girl to you?'

Marius glanced across at the slave girl. She was standing next to Bernicca and had lost none of her poise. Fraomar remained silent, his expression unreadable.

'Are you champion of the female species as well as the arena? Or is there more to this than meets the eye?' Lucius persisted.

Fraomar's eyes were fixed on some point in the distance, at the lamp stand in the far corner of the room.

Lucius continued, 'Do you realise I have the power to set you free or to condemn you?'

Silence.

The Praeses addressed the centurion. 'Very well. Get him out of my sight. Tomorrow I will instruct you as to my preferred method of execution.'

The centurion's face betrayed his discomfort. Marius could almost hear the man's mind working. The gladiator was his responsibility, but not his property. Neither was he the property of the Praeses. Lucius had no authority to condemn Fraomar, yet he had certainly been the victim of an assault. The silence was uncomfortable. It was Drufidius who eventually spoke.

'Praeses, this is most regrettable. An unfortunate incident. I am sure that no harm was intended, and indeed none has been d–done. You said yourself that a man like this could be of some use. Such f–fire! Perhaps, in view of this afternoon's games and the skill which, after all, b–brought you a good return, I can encourage you to reconsider?'

Lucius regarded Drufidius carefully. His breathing was still laboured following the scuffle but the councillor's words seemed to have a calming effect. 'A second chance, hmm? Well then, let us see.'

Lucius approached Fraomar and let his dagger trace the outline of a small tattoo on the gladiator's neck. 'What's this? What does the mark signify?'

Marius watched the gladiator stiffen as the Praeses pressed harder into the man's flesh.

And then the centurion spoke up. 'I know its meaning, Praeses.'

Lucius let his arm drop and turned to the centurion. 'Well?'

'He's one of their chieftain's. A king of sorts.'

'A king? Is he indeed? And how do you come by this information, soldier?'

'I fought in the Rhine campaigns under Valentinian in 360 and 365, sir. I got to know their rankings and their ways. The *Alamanni*, I mean.'

'Did you now? Did you really?' The Praeses stood back and regarded Fraomar proprietarily. 'And you didn't think to mention this before?'

'I'm just a soldier, sir. I do what I'm told. It didn't seem important.'

Lucius turned on him. 'I'll decide what's important, your moronic foot-slogger!' he roared into the centurion's face, then turned to Marius. 'Damned army. Brains in their backsides.' The Praeses returned to his couch, shaking his head in disbelief. After a restorative gulp of wine he was able to address the officer again. 'Take him away centurion – and look after him. We'll sort this out tomorrow.'

The centurion, relieved in more senses than one, escorted Fraomar from the room, followed closely by the guards. Bernicca went out too, an arm around the slave girl's shoulder, casting a backward accusing glance at Drufidius. Marius coughed and covered a smile with his goblet – words would no doubt be exchanged later between his host and hostess. As the two slaves righted the table and replaced items of food and drink, Marius engineered a change of subject.

'The agenda tomorrow, Praeses. Might I have your ear concerning certain urgent matters?'

Drufidius shot Marius a grateful look. A change in atmosphere was badly needed.

Lucius settled back on his couch. 'What's on your mind, Marius?'

'My concerns are financial, Praeses. The municipal funds are, as you know, severely depleted. I strongly feel that a system of priorities should be drawn up to unify expenditure on public amenities throughout the province. We badly need guidelines. If we maintain our current system we risk a steady decline in basic standards.' It was true. One of the first things Uncle Lactantius had pointed out to Marius during his pre-curial studies was the dire financial situation.

Lucius nodded. 'Go on.'

It was obvious to Marius that the Praeses' thoughts were elsewhere, but he went on anyway. 'The towns' individual budgets are meaningless without hard cash in the coffers. I believe that we need to administer each town's requirements from one fund.'

'Then how is it to be decided which town's need is greater? Is the repair of sewers of greater import in Calleva than, say, refurbishments to the temple in Aquae Sulis? In any case, a central fund will spread the sauce too thinly,' Lucius replied dismissively.

'We'll need a system of priorities.'

'Difficult to manage. In any case, if the need is pressing then that town should look to its own decurions for funding, as you well know Marius,' Lucius said sternly.

Marius had suspected that was coming. All right, he was wealthy, but it was unreasonable for the governor to expect the landowners to cover *all* the costs. He felt himself colour. 'But our reserves are not bottomless. We're hard pressed to maintain our own financial security. If the councillors are bankrupted the decline within the towns will continue, only much faster.'

'It will take a long time to plumb Drufidius' resources,' Lucius laughed humourlessly, 'I suggest you start there, my young *curiales*. Your father left you a very rich man, Marius, so I'm surprised at your concern.'

'But surely, Praeses,' Drufidius broke in, 'The upkeep of our towns is of p–prime importance. The infrastructure of our society depends on it.'

'Yes, of course it does,' Lucius said, 'but it also depends on the stability afforded by peace – and that is bought at a price. So clearly the financial priority lies with the military.'

'There has been p–peace for some years now,' said Drufidius. 'Why should the army still insist on the lion's share?'

The Praeses leaned forward. 'Do you realise on how many fronts we are pressed? The campaigns across the channel require a bottomless reserve of supplies, arms, equipment,' he ticked the items off on his fingers, 'not to mention the garrisons of the northern wall. The Roman army is the best equipped fighting force the world has ever

36

known. It is only by maintaining that position that the Empire stands. What do you think Valentinian is doing at this moment? He's knocking two shades of purple out of the Germans on the Rhine, that's what he's doing. And it all costs *money*.'

'Is the emperor aware of our financial predicament?' Marius asked.

Lucius guffawed. 'My dear Marius, he's the author of it.'

'So that's it? It's down to us?'

'There may be other options. Remember, my interests are served by the efficient running of this province, Marius. The matter is a subject close to my heart. We shall raise it at the Basilica tomorrow where we may hear the common view of our colleagues here in Calleva.'

Marius had his own view of what served Lucius' interests but he held his tongue.

'I fear that the *Curia* is dispirited, Praeses,' Drufidius said, 'the burden is too great.'

'Then, Drufidius, I shall rely on you to raise their morale.'

That effectively brought the conversation to a close and their attention was subsequently diverted by the arrival of the evening's entertainment: two coal-black dancers from Africa, who swayed erotically around the room to the accompaniment of pipes, flutes and drums.

Later, as Lucius was leaving, he called Marius aside.

'That barbarian, Marius. He could be useful. In fact, I want *you* to look after him.'

Marius was stunned. 'Me? Why–'

'Because he's gold dust, lad, that's why – and because I trust you. Besides it'll be good experience. You wanted some action, didn't you? All this council talk isn't really your cup of wine – I know that, boy. Listen,' he leaned closer so that Marius could smell the drink on his breath, 'what d'you think the emperor will give for him, eh? An Alamannic king? His political value is enormous. Think about it!'

Marius frowned. 'It's odd that he wasn't spotted as a VIP before. When he was captured, I mean.'

'You're right. As I said, the army's brains are in their backsides, but we've got him now, eh? So let's keep him safe; no more fighting, all right? Talk to his owners, negotiate a price. I'll sort the money out, don't worry. And let me know as soon as you can.' Lucius turned and signalled to his escort, who helped him into his saddle, then enclosed him within their ranks, marching swiftly away leaving Marius staring after them into the night. He felt a hand on his shoulder.

'Come, Marius. It's cold.' Drufidius smiled nervously. As they walked back into the house, Drufidius said 'Thank the gods that his temper improved. I thought someone was really going to g–get it in the neck tonight.'

'It could have been anyone, the mood he was in,' Marius laughed. 'The gladiator had a close call. But who is the girl? They seemed to know each other – and they're from the same people group – the *Alamanni?*'

Drufidius grinned. 'Taken a s–shine to her, have you Marius? Well, by the gods I don't blame you. Listen, they're brother and sister, separated during the 360 campaign. She was b–brought to this country a year ago. I discovered only today that the gladiator was her brother. My wife has the girl's confidence, you see, and she heard the whole story. Well, women talk to each other don't they? The girl didn't know if her brother was alive or dead,

38

but yesterday when on an errand she saw him arrive with the gladiator school.'

Marius felt his heart beating with excitement; as Lucius had given him responsibility for Fraomar's wellbeing he would have a perfect excuse to talk to the girl.. But there was one question he needed to ask. 'And her name? Do you know it, Drufidius?'

'Of course I know it you n–numbskull,' Drufidius shook his head good-naturedly. 'Her name is Freia.'

Marius couldn't sleep. When he closed his eyes he could see only Freia's beautiful face. It was no good. He knew what he had to do. He got up, retrieved wine and incense from his pack, and after unslotting a glowing torch from the corridor, let himself quietly into the garden. It was the night of the full moon. An autumnal breeze rustled the leaves above him and there came a muffled neigh from the stables. Apart from this, the night was still. In one corner of the garden Drufidius had installed an altar. Marius found his way to where the stone monument stood on its fluted column, gleaming like bone in the moonlight. He unstoppered the wine - the best of last year's harvest - and laid the jar down carefully. He then spread a generous portion of incense in the altar's bowl and fired the incense with a burning fragment from the torch. He paused for a moment until the sweet smell reached his nostrils. 'Father Ianus, doorkeeper of the heavens, in offering this incense to you I pray good prayers so that you may be propitious to me and my offspring, such as they may be, and to my house and my household.'

Marius then carefully poured the wine over the *focus*. 'Father Ianus, as in offering to you the incense, virtuous prayers were well prayed, so for the sake of this be honoured by this wine, offered in libation. O god of beginnings, go before me and prosper my future, whatever it may hold.' Marius bowed his head.

'To whom are you praying?' A voice spoke softly behind him.

Marius spun on his heels to see the object of his sleepless night, Freia, standing a few paces away. She was dressed in a long woven tunic and her feet were bare.

'Gods, but you made me jump,' Marius said. 'What are you doing sneaking about at this time of night?'

'I cannot sleep,' she smiled and shrugged. 'That's all.'

Marius' heart did a back flip. 'Well, you scared me half to death,' he grinned ruefully.

'You haven't answered my question, *dominus*,' Freia said.

Marius' upbringing whispered to him that a slave should not be so bold as to address a Roman citizen without being prompted to do so. But what did he care for such social niceties at this moment? They were alone, weren't they? 'Well,' he said, choosing his words carefully, 'I am making a sacrifice to Ianus, the god of beginnings, for my future.' *And for my prospective fortunes with you*, he wanted to add.

'Does he answer your prayers?' Freia asked, moving closer to inspect the altar.

'I believe he does, yes,' Marius replied. He could smell her fragrance over the incense, something darker, muskier.

'Well then,' she said. 'I will also pray for your beginnings, whatever they may be.'

'And whom do you pray to?' Marius asked and, fearing that she was about to turn away, grasped her wrist impulsively.

Freia made no effort to disengage. She brought her face close to his. 'I cannot say. A god who is personal to me.'

'Too personal to share?' Marius' heart was thumping at her closeness.

'Too dangerous to share,' she said quietly and looked at the ground, a stray lock of hair falling across her face. 'Like many things in your Roman world.'

'Ah. I see.' That could only mean the Christian god. He elected not to pursue the line of conversation, but to try to move it instead in a more amorous direction. 'Are you recovered from this evening's ill fortune?' he asked. 'Your face is a little bruised.' He wanted to reach out, stroke her cheek. Her scent was intoxicating.

'I am all right; thank you for your concern.' Freia pulled her hand free. 'I am more concerned about my brother.'

Marius nodded. 'Yes, I understand. Well then, you must take comfort. I have been asked to accompany Fraomar to Corinium. He will not compete,' Marius added quickly. 'But I am afraid he is likely to be summoned by the emperor, the outcome of which I cannot guess at.'

Freia bit her lip. 'I am glad you have told me this.' She reached out and touched his shoulder. Marius was about to cover her hand with his when a hiss from the shadows made them both jump.

'Freia? Come, quickly, the mistress calls for you.'

Cassipor, the kitchen slave, appeared, holding a tallow. 'Hurry up! She's looking for you all over. She wants you to massage her back - she cannot sleep.'

She's not the only one Marius thought, cursing the slave for his interruption.

Freia gave Marius a lingering look, then turned and hurried back into the villa after Cassipor.

Marius stood by the altar for a long time after she had gone, trying not to think about massage. It was hopeless. Freia's perfume still hung in the air like a sweet memory and his prayerful thoughts had vanished like the dawn mist. He gave up and went back to bed. Sleep was a long time coming.

Chapter 3

For the third time that morning, Marius cursed Drufidius and his cooks. He cursed them inventively and he cursed them thoroughly as the cramps in his gut returned with a vengeance. He vowed never to set foot in his benefactor's dining room again. The smells floating up from the cellars did nothing to ease his nausea. He folded the sleeve of his toga over his face and tried breathing through his mouth. It didn't help. How could they keep men in such conditions, slaves or otherwise? Marius steadied himself against the wall. It was moist and cold. His stomach yawed in protest.

'Down 'ere. Come on down, and mind the steps – they're slippery.' The voice of the *lanista* floated up the stairwell from the depths of the keep. Marius gingerly placed a foot on the first step. *Gods, what a life*. He followed the dim shape and the jangling keys down a further flight of stairs until they reached a narrow corridor where the man paused and turned. 'Shouldn't be no trouble, but you'd better take this in case.' Marius accepted the short sword and stood back as the cell door was opened.

'Now then Fraomar, let's be having you, nice and easy. You've got yourself a pass out of here, my lad. Don't ask me how or why, but the price is good enough for old Nennius, and that's all you need to know.' Fraomar's large figure appeared, stooping under the low cell door and standing at ease, eyes ever watchful. His hands were manacled, with sturdy chains connecting to circlets of iron around his ankles. 'But we'll miss 'im, that's for sure,' Nennius stroked his oiled beard thoughtfully. 'Could always count on you to put up a good show, lad, mmm? Mind you –' Nennius leaned in close, sharing his hop-laden breath, 'always felt sorry for his opponents. Didn't stand a chance in Hades – any of 'em!' Nennius rapped the gladiator sharply on the chest with a beringed fist. 'Fast Fraomar, that's what they call you, eh?' the *lanista* cackled and turned to share the nickname with Marius. 'Oh, and a word of warning. Just watch his 'ead,' Nennius advised. 'Lost count of the number of noses he's fractured or heads he's broken since I've had 'im. Only when summun upsets 'im, like. Good as gold most of the time.' He stood aside to allow Marius a clear view.

Marius cleared his throat self-consciously. 'You have been given into my care,' Marius said. 'My name is Marius of Corinium but you are now the property of Lucius Septimius Tullio, Governor of Britannia Prima. You are in my custody until further notice. You are no longer expected to compete in gladiatorial combat. Is that clear?'

Fraomar inclined his head minutely, as he had done during his interview with Lucius. Marius relaxed his grip on the borrowed sword, aware that his hands were sweating. But Fraomar, for the moment at least, seemed fully compliant.

Drufidius met them outside, accompanied by a squad of soldiers assigned as Fraomar's escort. Nennius received his fee with much hand rubbing and nodding – it was a generous deal. Marius gratefully drew the clean air into his lungs, and waited for the transaction to be completed. The day was mild, with a light wind that carried with it the smells of harvest. Wagons clopped past on the narrow street, laden with the produce of surrounding fields. It was a good time of year, a time to thank the gods for the prosperity of the province, yet Marius still felt strangely uneasy.

'Ready, councillor?' The officer in charge stood to attention.

'Yes, of course.' Marius accepted Drufidius' invitation to climb into the waiting carriage, but hesitated as his stomach once again reminded him of the previous evening's excesses.

Drufidius raised his eyebrows. 'Problem, Marius?'

'I think I'll walk, if you don't mind. I need to clear my head.'

'You must learn to manage your wine, Marius my boy.' Drufidius wagged a finger as he waved his assent, 'I shall expect you at the council session, at midday. Don't be late.' He signalled to the officer who set off at a brisk pace, Fraomar manacled securely in their midst.

Marius watched the foot soldiers and carriage move off before turning and making his way through the back streets onto the main thoroughfare. By the time he had covered half the distance to the Forum he was beginning to feel better. From a small building situated on the approaching crossways came the sound of voices raised in song. Marius hesitated, curiosity replacing his sense of unease. Above the entrance to the small, unremarkable looking building was an odd sign he had noticed on several occasions, a *Chi–Rho*, a Christian symbol. Unable to resist, he stepped into the building and found a seat just inside the entrance. Twenty or more townsfolk were crammed into the tiny area. Marius was captivated by the hymn they were singing. It was a simple melody, but it was the repetitive refrain that Marius was to remember in days to come:

'God made man; God became man,
God saved us in Yeshua,
Christos, who is God'

The last notes died away and a man rose from his seat at the far end of the building, turned and faced the expectant gathering. He looked, so it seemed, directly at Marius, raised his hands above his head and intoned, 'Yeshua is Lord. He is Lord of all.' The people responded together, repeating the words. Marius found himself mouthing the response, fascinated by the appearance of the man leading the worship. Although, with his shaven head and simple clothing he looked every bit the ascetic Christian official, his expression was serene. One by one the worshippers formed a queue before the leader who touched each head and muttered a word of blessing. Marius stood aside as the worshippers filed out of the building, heads bowed in devotion. Soon there was only the master of ceremonies and one other remaining. Marius was beginning to feel like a trespasser but something kept him from leaving. The last worshipper eventually hurried towards the exit. Marius could tell from her clothing that she was a slave and then his heart leapt. It was the girl, Freia. Startled by his presence she quickly bowed her head and drew her cloak tighter around her body. Marius took her arm.

'Wait.'

The girl hesitated, but as a slave she had no option but to obey.

Once again Marius found himself tongue-tied. Now he could see her in broad daylight and by the gods, she was a real beauty; not even her dowdy cloak and shawl could hide that. 'I enjoyed our meeting last night,' he blurted, cursing his stumbling tongue.

'As did I,' Freia said, her eyes downcast in customary supplication.

He wanted to tip her chin up, to see that radiant smile again. 'Look, I will see to it that your brother has the best care—'

'Care? What *care* have my people ever received from a Roman?' Freia's lips compressed in a hard line.

Marius couldn't bear her to look at him like that. 'He is a brave warrior,' he said, ignoring the slight. 'And I respect him as such. As I told you, he will not fight in the arena again. You mustn't worry.' It sounded weak, he knew. How could you not worry about close members of your *familia?*

Freia's face softened and for a moment she looked as though she might cry. 'Thank you,' she looked down at her sandals. 'I never thought I'd see him again,' she said in a whisper. 'You are kind. I did not mean to be so rude.'

'That's all right,' Marius smiled. 'I understand. I would feel the same if I were in your position.'

Now Freia returned his smile and once again Marius thought he'd never seen such an extraordinary expression on anyone's face. Her blue eyes sparkled as her smile widened; it seemed to light up her whole face, giving her the countenance of a goddess. Marius was overwhelmed with desire and found that he could neither speak nor move. All he could do was repeat to himself over and over, again and again, like an enchanted prayer: *beauty . . . I have never seen such. . . beauty. . .*

But Freia had already hurried away, closing the door of the church behind her without a backward glance.

The Forum Basilica was the largest building in Calleva. Tall columns supported the massive external elevations, whilst imposing bronze statues delimited the four corners of the central courtyard. Within this boundary the busy market was in full swing. Traders touted bargain prices and held up their wares for scrutiny whilst merchants jostled for attention and hard cash. Children ran between the awnings and barrows of the many shops ranged around the perimeter of the market. The adjacent cattle market contributed to the general noise and hubbub and the air hung heavy with the smells of a hundred meats, spices and perfumes. Marius shouldered his way through the crowds, carefully avoiding the attentions of an obstructive stray dog and wondering why in the name of Jupiter the offices of civil administration were bound up with this turmoil of bartering humanity. He trod on something soft and swore under his breath, pausing to scrape his sandal against a convenient stall. As he slipped his foot into his sandal he caught another glimpse of Freia. This time a slender young man accompanied her, by his appearance also a slave. She was holding up a sheet of linen for his approval and from the tactile nature of their body language, it was clear that this was more than a casual acquaintance. Marius' heart sank.

'Looks like she's already spoken for, more's the pity for you.'

Marius turned to see a fellow councillor eyeing him with amusement from the steps leading to the council chambers. 'Just curious, Carullus, that's all.'

'Oh, really,' Carullus smirked. 'Tell me another.'

They watched the girl and her companion move off amongst the stalls. Carullus grunted with approval. 'She's a pretty one, eh?'

'She belongs to Drufidius – caused a bit of an upset at his place last night.'

'So I heard.' Carullus descended from his vantage point. 'The old rogue knows how to choose his slaves all right, but he's a little on the tactless side when it comes to people management.'

'I believe the girl was Bernicca's choice. But yes, it was a bit awkward – and I'm the one who's cleaning up as usual. I now have a gladiator to worry about on top of everything else.'

'Aha. Let me guess. He's a big shot of some sort, eh? A chieftain?'

Marius nodded. There was no point in hiding it. The news would be all over Calleva by now anyway. 'You're right. Lucius has sent word to Valentinian that we have an Alamannic king in custody. I expect he'll be escorted across the channel in due course and used as the emperor sees fit. Until then, he's my responsibility.'

'And a big responsibility for a young lad to take on,' Carullus stroked his short beard. 'Let me know if you can't handle it – I could use a bit of *kudos* these days.'

Marius flushed. 'I can handle it well enough, thank you.' If this was what working for the council was going to be like, Marius thought, I'd rather be a slave. The thought of spending his life in the company of men like Carullus, always having to watch your back whilst trying to score political favour in every situation, filled him with frustration and horror. But he'd promised his uncle that he would make his career in the *Curia*. And how could he let his uncle down when he had done so much for him?

They ascended the wide steps of the Basilica and joined the queue forming in the portico leading to the council chambers. Marius felt his stomach churn as it continued its digestive struggle. *Oh no, not now – not before my first meeting* . . . The public latrines beside the Forum beckoned. It had to be done; Lucius would have to wait. Carullus shot him a startled look as Marius fled down the steps two at a time, the iron doors of the *Curia* clanging shut behind him.

After the meeting, Marius tried to make the door before the Praeses had a chance to intercept him but Lucius was already bearing down like a bird of prey.

'Try to arrive promptly next time, Marius, would you?'

Marius opened his mouth to excuse his late arrival but was interrupted by one of the guards as they made their way from the curial chambers to the Forum's airy lobby. 'Praeses? A word?'

Lucius swept on towards the exit, forcing the man to trot alongside. 'There's someone to see you,' the guard persisted.

'He's wasted his time.' Lucius' stride continued unbroken.

'But Praeses, he insists.'

'I do indeed.' A man blocked their path. His face was sweat-stained and weatherworn. 'A matter of urgency, *Praeses*.' Marius noticed the slight inflexion, a hint of disrespect.

'And you are?' Lucius squared his shoulders.

'My name is unimportant, but I have news of interest.'

'I doubt it.'

'Perhaps I should explain. I have been gathering intelligence in the Welsh borderlands.'

'Tell the army, not me. Now let us pass or I'll have you thrown out.' Lucius' face turned a darker shade.

'I am instructed to make the offer to *you*, not the army.'

Marius studied the man with interest. He looked as if he'd been living rough for a long time. His face was caked with dirt and his clothing reeked of sweat. Marius guessed he was one of the *Areani*, a borderland scout, paid by the emperor to gather and pass on information.

'Offer? What sort of offer?' Lucius barked.

'Please,' the man gestured, 'perhaps a little privacy– '

'Privacy? I'll give you the privacy of a comfortable cell if you don't step aside.'

Marius laid a cautious hand on Lucius' arm. 'Maybe we'd better give him a few minutes.' Something about the man had fired Marius' curiosity. If he had a story to tell it looked as if it might be worth hearing. After the tedium of the curial meeting Marius was hungry for any stimulation. He'd spent most of the meeting daydreaming about Freia. He could still see her eyes, that smile. . .

The visitor spoke again: 'No. Just you, Praeses. Alone.'

'Don't push your luck. Both of us or nothing.'

'Very well.'

They entered a small side room and closed the door. The room was for use by the council scribes and contained only a table and several chairs.

'Make it quick.' Lucius sat down and leaned forward, eyebrows arching suspiciously.

'I have been instructed by my employer to tell you of trouble brewing in the west. The Irish are restless and there may be a consequence– '

'Speak plainly. Stop shilly-shallying around.' Lucius glared.

'The provinces may be rather – unsettled – over the coming months. My employer thought you might appreciate the opportunity to contribute a few – facts and figures . . .'

Lucius looked at Marius. 'What's this idiot talking about?' He frowned and glared at the scout. 'This is your final chance. Speak plainly or not at all.'

'My superior – you have heard the name *Paulus?*'

'Paulus? What is this – a cursed guessing game?' said Lucius, banging his fist on the table.

The man licked his lips. 'Perhaps then you may know him by another name. *'Catena'* – ?'

Lucius looked at Marius, but Marius had gasped aloud. 'Paulus *Catena?* The Chain? But he's dead. He was executed in Africa years ago.' Marius' heart pounded. *His parents' killer. Alive?*

'The bloody notary,' Lucius nodded, 'The scourge of Britannia after Magnentius was defeated? I met him once and that was enough. Constantius should have had *him* locked up and done everybody a favour.'

The visitor spoke again. 'He is very much alive. He sends his greetings and asks if you will provide some information in return for, well, whatever you would like. Name your price.'

'What sort of information?' Lucius growled.

The man bent forward and placed his hands on the table. The rancid smell wafted across with the slight movement of air. 'It's only a matter of time before the rich pickings of the south are harvested. Better make something for yourselves while you can. Paulus is ready to act. He has allies, many allies. But there are certain things he needs to know.'

Marius glanced at Lucius who appeared to be struggling to speak.

The man continued: 'You have access, I believe, to intelligence regarding army supply chains, particularly for the coastal regions in the south-east?'

Lucius had risen to his feet. 'Am I hearing this correctly?' The governor's fists clenched and unclenched involuntarily at his side, then one large hand made its way slowly to the hilt of his dagger. 'You want *me* to give *you* classified information regarding the security of this province? Are you completely insane?'

'Before you act rashly, I suggest you hear the offer.'

'Offer?' Now the fist had closed around the dagger's hilt.

The stranger reached for his belt pouch and shook out the contents into his open palm. 'I needn't tell you how much these are worth. You can see the quality for yourselves.' He held out his hand for inspection. In his palm gleamed three of the largest opals Marius had ever seen. 'Beautiful, yes?' the man went on, 'but these are only a sample – if you would care to name your price I can show you the rest– '

Lucius roared. 'My price is your scrawny head – on a platter.' The Praeses lunged, The visitor, startled at the reaction, leapt backwards whilst attempting to replace the stones in his pouch. He was partially successful, but the smallest stone fell and rolled towards Marius who scooped it up as the man half-stumbled towards the door, a stumble that saved him from the whickering point of the governor's dagger. Recovering his balance, he skirted the table with a deft movement and was out of the door like a ferret. By the time Marius reached the Forum steps the man was barging his way through the market place. Soon he turned a corner and was gone. Lucius, breathing heavily, joined Marius on the steps. The governor waved his fist and yelled out across the market place 'You double-dealing, rat-faced turd! I'll have your weasel-head off your shoulders in a second if I catch you!' This oath drew some attention from the late market shoppers and within a few moments a small crowd had gathered. The duty officer approached, waving them away. 'Everything all right, Praeses?'

Marius nodded. 'I think so. We are unharmed.'

'No. Everything is *not* all right soldier.' Lucius gave Marius a severe look. 'A frontier runner comes walking in here, offers a bribe to the governor and you and your useless squaddies just stand there picking your noses? I should put you on a charge.'

'We didn't know his business, Praeses.'

'It's your damned business to know people's business.' Lucius fumed.

Marius held out his hand. The stray opal gleamed in the early evening sun, causing a sharp intake of breath from the duty officer. 'The *Areani* are used to slipping in and out unseen. But you need to find this one. If there's a grain of truth in what he said the military command centres must be informed.' Marius' mind was racing. Could it be true? Paulus Catena, the man responsible for his parents' death, was alive? And moreover in Britannia?

'We'll find him, councillor, don't worry.' The officer saluted and moved off to rally the Forum guard. They watched as the crowd moved respectfully aside to let the soldiers pass. Lucius grunted and turned back into the building. 'Now, where has Drufidius got to? Blast the man, surely he hasn't left for the baths already?'

Chapter 4

Freia rushed through the courtyard and into the villa's marbled hall. There was no sign of Drufidius. That was good. Her errands had taken longer than she'd expected but her timing had allowed for that possibility. In fact, everything had gone to plan except for one thing: the young councillor at the church. Freia knew that Bernicca tolerated her devotion to the Christian god, but she had advised her to keep her church attendance quiet – certainly not to mention it to Drufidius. And now, her secret was out – or at least it might be. But the councillor, Marius, seemed different somehow. He had taken the trouble to allay her fears about her brother. And he had spoken kindly to her. Not only that, but she had felt something else, something special when she had looked into his clear brown eyes. He liked her. That was obvious. So, she reasoned, perhaps he wouldn't give away her secret after all.

Her emotions were all over the place – ever since she had caught sight of her brother. At first she was in shock. Could it really be him? And impossibly, it was. It was a full two years since she had last set eyes on her dear Fraomar. She had almost lost control and run to him but had made herself wait at the roadside as the gladiatorial entourage passed by on its way to the town keep. He had seen her, she knew. His blue eyes had widened with surprise and pleasure but he had received a blow from one of the watchful guards for letting his eyes wander. She had bitten her tongue then, drawing blood, feeling helpless as he walked on, his chains dragging on the cobbles. But his presence was an answer to prayer. He was still alive. He was unhurt. And to think that last night she had almost ruined everything. Freia clenched her fists at the memory. But for the moment, thanks to Drufidius' intervention, Fraomar was safe.

She took a deep breath and wended her way to the kitchens, depositing her purchases on the stone floor. The kitchen was filled with smoke from the large griddle set in the corner of the room. A joint of pork turned slowly on the spit, sizzling fat dropping and hissing onto the hot embers beneath. The cooks were busy, grinding spices, chopping herbs, preparing their creations for the delight of the evening diners. Drufidius was proud of his kitchen and everyone benefitted from his choice of staff. The senior cook, a short dark-skinned native of Gaul made sure that the quality of the food shared amongst the slaves equalled that of the food served to the main household, even if it was served in a plainer fashion.

'Greetings, my pretty one,' a passing kitchen hand aimed a slap at her rump. Freia dodged to one side. 'How's your boyfriend? We've heard the rumours . . .'

'I don't know what you mean.' Freia turned to make a quick exit. The daily banter with Cassipor was usually fun but she wasn't in the mood.

Trophimus, the head cook, cocked his head towards the delivery door. 'There's a panic on tonight – the military's out in force. They're stopping people in the streets – it's a good job you're back. Where have you been?'

'Shopping. Running errands,' Freia said, unpacking her purchases.

'Really,' said Trophimus, 'is that so? Well, whoever the fugitive is, they want him badly,' the cook said. 'I heard he was nearly caught fleeing from the Basilica. He's probably miles away by now.'

'Maybe you can catch him and get a reward, Troph,' Cassipor suggested, spooning some fat onto the pork carcass.

'I'll reward you with a kick up the backside if you burn that pig,' Trophimus threatened, waving a cleaver in his meaty hand. 'And you, Freia my girl, the master wants you *now*. There's an important guest, apparently.'

Freia gasped. 'But I thought the master was out!' She abandoned her groceries and hurried from the kitchen to report to Drufidius.

Freia waited patiently by the visitor's side. So far, he had left his wine untouched. The master was asking the man a question, but Freia was barely listening. Her thoughts flitted from her brother to the handsome young councillor, Marius. Could she trust him? Or was he like all the others?

'I hope the toga fits you well enough,' Drufidius addressed the guest, shaking his head ruefully. 'Most unfortunate to have your clothes stolen. I remember the days when you could safely leave your purse on display when bathing and be sure of its safety. Now it seems not even one's clothes are secure. I w–would recommend a curse to plague the thief – I know a g–good scribe at the baths who– '

The man interrupted with a raised hand. 'No need for a curse, my friend. I have proven ways and means of exacting revenge.'

'You do? Oh g–good.' Drufidius scratched his head and shrugged. He was a great believer in the value of curses. Still, it was up to this fellow how he went about his business. 'So,' he said eventually. 'There's trouble afoot is there? And what form is this trouble to take, I wonder?'

The man lifted his cup to drink and Freia noticed a small tattoo on his forearm, a snake coiled within a circle.

'Barbarians,' the visitor answered. 'An invasion, no less. And I'm not talking about the odd coastal raid here and there. This is the real thing. From all points of the compass. The provinces are going to be caught with their pants down. But–' the visitor sniffed at his cup, as if savouring the wine's fragrance before he tasted it. 'I have a proposition. Why should you not benefit from circumstances, Drufidius? A man in your position should be, how can I put it, ahead of the game.' He smiled, revealing a set of yellowed teeth.

Drufidius frowned. 'Forgive me, the steam has, as usual, dulled my mind. I don't quite follow.'

Bernicca appeared and wafted past on a cloud of scent. She sat opposite Drufidius and smiled at the visitor. Freia made sure the man's cup was full before pouring Bernicca her own measure.

'My rose petal,' Drufidius addressed Bernicca, 'allow me to introduce Gallio Velius Marsallas. He is in the intelligence business, from Wales.'

'A pleasure.' Freia noted Bernicca's appraising eye roving across Marsallas' body. The man was lithe and fit; he reminded Freia of a cat, sitting at ease but ready to pounce. He acknowledged Bernicca with a nod and continued. 'No doubt, councillor, you will recall the unfortunate episode of Magnentius?'

Drufidius sipped his wine. 'Well, it's almost fifteen years ago, but yes, I do indeed. Turbulent times.'

'You will also recall Constantius' servant, Paulus. A very thorough man in many ways. He was able to – 'clean up' Magnentius' supporters.'

'Yes, I believe he was, as you say, very thorough.'

'And still is,' Marsallas said carefully. 'And it is from him that I bring you an offer.'

'He is alive?'

'Very much so. But saddened by the turn of events in the Empire. He was not, how shall I put it, as *appreciated* as he should have been. In fact an attempt was made on his life in Africa by the emperor himself.'

'Yes. Yes, I believe I heard something about that.'

'Good. So it will come as no surprise to you that he has been busy.' Velius Marsallas leaned forward on his couch. 'Busy making allies in the right places.' He clicked his fingers and Freia moved forward. Marsallas gave her his cup. 'Would you taste this for me, my dear?'

Freia was taken aback and looked to Drufidius for confirmation.

'No offence,' Marsallas said, 'just a normal precaution. I have learned to be careful.'

'Yes, yes of course.' Drufidius motioned to Freia who sipped the wine suspiciously then replaced the cup on Marsallas' table.

'From the cellars of C–Constantine himself, you know,' Drufidius said. 'Quite safe,' he added quietly.

Marsallas reached inside the folds of his borrowed toga and produced a small bag. He untied the neck string and let the contents spill out onto his palm. 'As I was saying, Paulus has been busy, securing such wealth as you can only dream of here in Britannia Prima.'

Freia was transfixed. They were beautiful gemstones, opals and emeralds, the largest and clearest she had seen. She unconsciously moved in for a closer look.

'They would look pretty on you, my dear.' Marsallas held out his hand to Freia then closed his fingers sharply around the gems, 'ah ah.' He shook his head, 'I think perhaps the lady of the house would suit them better.'

Bernicca flushed with pleasure at the compliment and Freia stepped out of the lamplight, alarmed that she had acted inappropriately.

Drufidius cleared his throat. 'I think we require a little elaboration, Marsallas. What exactly do you want?'

'Just a little information.' Marsallas smiled. 'Quite painless, really.'

'No, no, no!' Drufidius repeated. 'Are you out of your mind?'

Freia glanced anxiously at Bernicca for her reaction. Marsallas had left before dinner, declining the master's invitation on account of a pressing business engagement. From the exchanges Freia had already heard that evening she suspected this business to be something other than official, but that really wasn't her problem. A row was brewing between the master and the mistress and Freia had been trying to catch Bernicca's eye to request a dismissal, but the couple were locked in heated debate.

'You're weak. That's your trouble,' Bernicca hissed.

Drufidius shot a worried look in Freia's direction.

'Don't worry about the girl. She can be trusted.' Bernicca said, 'but I can never trust you to take an opportunity when it comes your way on a silver plate.'

Drufidius raised himself unsteadily to his feet. Freia had lost count of the times he had requested a refill.

'Woman,' he replied testily, 'you have no idea of the implications. He has requested c–confidential information which may put the lives of our field army at risk.'

'From what he was saying,' Bernicca responded, 'they're at risk anyway.'

'What he is asking is illegal. And d–dangerous.'

'Illegal's never stopped you before.'

'By the god's woman. I will not be spoken to like this.' Drufidius advanced on Bernicca and Freia, alarmed, pretended to inspect her sandals, praying that she would be dismissed before she witnessed bloodshed.

'Go on then. Strike me if you want. It won't change anything.'

When Freia dared to look up she saw that Drufidius had retreated and was sitting dejectedly on the end of his couch. The lamplight played with his shadow as it flickered, elongating and then contracting his profile.

'You let Lucius walk all over you,' Bernicca raged on. 'He's draining our money away. And now, when we have a golden opportunity to put things right you go all patriotic on me.'

'It's a question of safety,' Drufidius said slowly. 'If anything happens to our army – and it *has* happened before – the c–consequences could be catacly – cataclis – ' He tried again and failed, 'very bad, anyway. Besides, I haven't got the d–details he wants. All supply information is filed with the *vicarius'* office in Londinium,' he finished weakly, reaching again for his cup, which slipped from his grasp and fell to the floor with a clatter.

'Gods, you're pathetic,' Bernicca spat. 'At least Lucius is a real man. Not some sad excuse for one.' She banged down her goblet and left the room, calling Freia to follow her.

Freia did so with relief but it was only when unbraiding Bernicca's hair later that evening that she saw the glint in her mistresses' eye.

Chapter 5

The Rhine Frontier, Gaul – Sept 367AD

In the headquarters tent of the Rhine campaign, the Emperor Valentinian, arguably the most powerful man in the known world, leaned back with some discomfort on the *curule*, an elaborately carved oak seat inlaid with ivory. The chair had been especially commissioned for his imperial behind, and was the only obvious indication of his status, except perhaps for the imperial purple of his cloak. The emperor's back was playing up again and he was not in a good mood. 'Well?' He barked at the tribune.

The tribune moistened his lips, 'Nipius Quintilius is here at your command, Caesar.'

'Well, don't just stand there like a wilting vine, man. Show him in!'

'*Caesar.*' The tribune saluted and signalled to the tent guard.

The tent flap opened and a man entered. He had a pinched, hunted appearance in marked contrast to his speech, which was direct and confident. 'You sent for me, Caesar?'

'I did.' The emperor stood up carefully with a grimace of pain. The seat was murdering his vertebrae. He drew a hand wearily across his eyes. 'Nipius. I seem to remember that you had a hankering for foreign travel.'

'Caesar?' Nipius frowned.

'I've had an interesting communication from Britannia. From Septimius in Corinium.'

Nipius raised an eyebrow quizzically.

'They have, apparently, in custody a member of the royal *Alamannic* line. One named Fraomar. Ring any bells?'

'Chnodomar's brother. Went missing after Strasbourg.'

Valentinian nodded approvingly. 'The same.'

'We were outnumbered three to one,' Nipius recalled, 'but Julian led us to a great victory.'

Valentinian allowed himself a smile. 'His gods certainly seemed to be with him that day. But I heard it was the *Magister Equitum* who deserves the credit for the victory.'

Nipius bowed stiffly. 'Caesar is too kind.'

'A shame that the victory of Strasbourg was marred by Fraomar's escape.'

For the first time, Nipius seemed uncomfortable. Rain began to drum softly on the leather covering of the tent roof as Valentinian continued:

'But you are a popular man, Nipius. Your exploits are legendary. You have – what can I say– ' Valentinian stroked his chin thoughtfully, 'a loyal following?'

'I am fortunate enough to have the respect of my men, yes Caesar.'

Valentinian grunted. 'Well, naturally I thought of you for this little job.'

'What does Caesar command?'

'A simple 'go fetch' job, nothing more. Give you a break. God knows you probably need one. And a chance to set the record straight.'

Nipius smiled thinly. 'I am most grateful to Caesar.'

Valentinian's eyes narrowed. 'I'm sure.'

Nipius cleared his throat. 'If I may, Caesar, what are your intentions on our return?'

Valentinian sighed. 'A little bargaining is in order, Nipius. At last I shall have a useful lever to negotiate a settlement with these wretched barbarians. But I need this fellow Fraomar quickly – no mistakes. Understood?'

'Of course.' Nipius saluted and turned to leave the tent. He had one hand on the flap when Valentinian called him back. 'Nipius?'

'Caesar?'

'One more thing.' The emperor clicked a finger and Nipius stood to one side as a newcomer entered the tent carrying a blast of icy wind and rain before him. He removed his helmet and wiped the water droplets from a face scarred and studded by deep pockmarks.

'This is Terricula. I have assigned him to your unit for the Britannia trip.'

'But I have no need– '

'He's a useful fellow. He has a persuasive touch. You can't put too high a price on that, can you Terricula?'

Terricula grinned. 'Delighted to be of assistance, Caesar.' The voice was smooth and cultured, contrasting with the ravaged complexion.

Nipius nodded. 'Very well. I'll introduce you to the men.'

Valentinian waved his hand in dismissal. 'Anything you need, let me know.'

Nipius took his cue and left the tent, Terricula following closely behind.

Chapter 6

As Freia made her way to the dining room carrying a tray of Trophimus' delicacies she heard her mistress call. Bernicca had been keeping a low profile since her return from Londinium and was resting in her chamber. Freia thrust the tray into Cassipor's protesting arms as he passed and hurried up the stairs, feeling the slats give slightly under her sandalled feet as she climbed. Her legs ached as they always did at this hour, but it was her pride that was hurting more. That pig of a governor, Lucius, had been treating her like dirt since his arrival. Even Drufidius showed *some* kindness, if only in a stern, proprietorial way, but the Praeses was arrogant and demanding. Thankfully he was leaving for Corinium tomorrow and normality would at last be restored. Her prayers had been answered more than once these last days, she thought to herself as she approached Bernicca's bedroom. Lucius had brought no charges against Fraomar and her brother was to be spared further fighting in the arena. Moreover Marius, the kind councillor, had been forthright in protecting her from Lucius while Drufidius and Bernicca were visiting the *vicarius*. It was obvious that Marius disliked Lucius almost as much as she did but he was good at hiding his distaste and an expert at sidelining the governor into other avenues of conversation.

Bernicca looked tired, the crow's feet at the corners of her eyes scarcely camouflaged by the generous application of blue tint. Her hair was down, hanging in lank ringlets about her neck. 'Freia, my dear. I've missed you.' She gave Freia a perfumed hug, then ushered her into the chamber. 'Londinium is such an uncivilized town. Too busy, too serious. Full of men.' Bernicca sat on her wicker chair and let Freia attend to her unruly tresses. 'Mind you, the *vicarius* is rather good looking,' she half turned and looked up at Freia. 'I think he was quite taken with me.'

Freia smiled obligingly as she smoothed and plaited. She'd heard this sort of thing many times before.

'Do you know, he showed me around his library? My dear, I have never seen so many manuscripts. I said I was a simple woman – all those complicated words would be utterly wasted on me.'

Freia caught something covert in Bernicca's expression but her mistress, perhaps distracted by the progress of her hair preparation, declined to give any further information about her Londinium trip. After a few minutes Freia stood back to assess her handiwork. It was the best she could do. Bernicca's hair was thinning and had become brittle with the various potions she insisted on using. Soon, Freia surmised, her mistress would take to wearing a wig, as did many of her female companions; it was only a matter of time.

'Thank you my child.' Bernicca checked her reflection and clucked with satisfaction. 'You're the only one I trust, do you know that?'

'Yes, mistress.' Freia replied. 'Thank you,' she added quickly, feeling that a measure of gratitude was expected for such an honour.

'Well, I am going to ask you to do something for me. Something important. But you mustn't breathe a word.'

'I won't, mistress.' Freia's heart sank. Now what?

Bernicca went to the window and looked over the tiled roofs of Calleva. Dusk was beginning to settle on the town and the streets were dotted here and there with amber torchlight.

'Do you remember our guest, Gallio Velius Marsallas?'

Freia recalled the wine-tasting episode and failed to conceal a frown. 'I remember him, mistress.'

Bernicca laughed. 'You didn't like him much did you, Freia? Well, no matter. I want you to find him and give him this.' Bernicca slid a wooden chest from an alcove beside her dressing table. She opened it and retrieved a scroll bound with thin leather straps, bearing an official seal which had clearly been broken. Bernicca tutted, 'No, no, not this one.' She reached into the chest again and found another document which she unrolled and scanned, her tongue protruding in concentration as she read. Satisfied, she rolled the document and reattached the vellum title strip, which, Freia noticed, had been left incomplete.

'Take this to Marsallas, child. He is expecting you, but his appearance may be – altered.'

Freia was unable to hide her discomfort. 'Mistress– '

'All will be well, child. Ask no questions and do as I say. Now, a contact of mine awaits you at the inn by the market place. You know it? Good. He will approach you and you are simply to follow him. You will be taken to meet Marsallas. Then you will give him the scroll. He will give you something in return.'

Freia pursed her lips. This was worrying.

Bernicca went on: 'My contact will ensure that the exchange is successful. Then you are to hurry back immediately. Is that clear?'

'But mistress, why do you ask me?' Freia was unable to hold herself back. Surely this crossed the boundaries of duty? And furthermore she had a bad feeling about the contents of the scroll. Freia recalled the conversation she had witnessed between Marsallas and Drufidius. And what about the secretive expression she had seen on Bernicca's face? Freia was certain that no good could come of Bernicca's actions but what could she do?

'I've told you, Freia, I can trust you. You will be safe – don't look so worried, child.' Bernicca smiled reassuringly and stroked Freia's cheek. 'Such a pretty one,' she murmured, 'No wonder the boys find you irresistible.' She grasped Freia's hand. 'Perhaps we can arrange a little treat for you tomorrow? Just do this for me and you will be well rewarded.'

Freia forced a smile. 'Thank you mistress.' She took the scroll from Bernicca's pudgy hand, tucked it into her tunic and left the chamber as quickly as she could before Bernicca could ask her anything else.

Freia moved furtively through the darkened streets of Calleva, clutching the papyrus as if her life depended on it. Her hood covered her face and her eyes flicked this way and that as she checked each passing shadow for danger. She was rarely out after dark and despite the groups of patrolling soldiers she felt vulnerable and conspicuous. It started to rain so she drew her cloak around her and pressed the document to her body, fearful that it would be damaged and made unreadable. She tried not to speculate on its contents and pushed aside any thoughts of disobedience. It was not her place to judge the actions of her owners, nor to reflect on their outcome. But the nagging thoughts persisted and Freia's natural curiosity would not be suppressed. She stepped into the shelter of a doorway lit by a single burning torch and reached under her cloak. Her fingers were cold and she fumbled with the vellum, unrolling the document until the first column of script was revealed. Thanks to Drufidius' insistence that all slaves in his house should learn to read and write she had sufficient grasp of the language to figure out that the contents was not, as she had hoped, just another of Bernicca's love interest rebuttals, but a structured list of military supply references and dates. She bit her lip as she scanned the facts and figures, names and annotations that meant nothing to her, but which no doubt held great significance for the people involved. The rain worsened, turning from fine droplets to sodden sheets that gusted into her refuge and threatened to put out the torch. Freia quickly tucked the document away and hurried along the street, head bent against the downpour.

By the time she reached the inn, her clothes were sodden and her face was numb with cold. The door opened and two soldiers staggered out, stumbling as their hobnailed sandals slipped on the wet paving stones. One of them belched and raised a drunken hand towards her but his friend muttered something and dragged him down the street. Smoke billowed out of the open door along with the smell of roast meat and human sweat. She took a deep breath and entered.

Within the lamplit interior a number of tables were arranged about the central fireplace, above which hung a selection of skewered meats and fish. To the right of the fire a serving table was manned by two women busy doling out spiced and honeyed wine to a group of soldiers. Other citizens, predominantly male, sat eating and drinking around the tables. The noise and smoke contributed to Freia's anxiety as she peered into the room wondering how she was supposed to recognize her rendezvous. She squeezed past the first table and moved closer to the fire.

'Bad night out there.' The comment came from the nearest table where several troopers reclined, cups in hand. A soldier next to the one who had spoken belched loudly. The first, a young dark-haired recruit, addressed her again: 'Forgive my uncivilized colleagues,' he said. 'Allow me to introduce myself, Gaius Rufrius Pavo at your service.' His friends responded with catcalls and shoves that Pavo resisted by squaring his shoulders and aiming a deft kick at the hecklers. Freia gave him a slight bow in response. She felt exposed and uncomfortable. Steam began to rise from her damp cloak. Pavo persisted, 'You're wet,' he took her arm, 'and very pretty. Sit down and dry yourself. Here now, let me buy you a drink.'

'Thank you, but I am on an errand.' Freia pulled her arm free.

'Come on,' Pavo was unperturbed, 'just one. Won't do you any harm.'

Freia hesitated, searching for a reply that would cause the least offence

'Problem?' The landlord had heard the exchange and had sidled over to investigate. He was a huge man, a full head and shoulders taller than Pavo whom he eyed with friendly yet firm intent.

Pavo grinned. 'None at all, Plautius. Just offering assistance to the young lady.'

'You lads have been warned before. No trouble on my premises, right? Now the young lady has some business with me, if you don't mind.'

Pavo half saluted and rejoined his companions. 'Carry on, Plautius. No offence.'

Relieved, Freia followed the innkeeper across the rush-matted floor, feeling the eyes of the tavern upon her. The innkeeper led her through the back door to a ramshackle outhouse. Two men were seated around an upturned box in the centre of the building. The first, an old man with a fringe of grey hair encircling his bald scalp, was inspecting something by holding it up to a flickering taper. The other, a younger man in tunic and cloak rose to greet them as they entered, pushing the hood back from his face and extending a hand in welcome. 'Ah, the prettiest courier in Calleva,' he beckoned with his finger. Plautius delved into the corner of the room and produced a wooden stool which he dusted quickly with the broad palm of his hand. 'Here you are, missy. Don't worry, you won't catch anything.'

Freia gingerly sat, arms hugging the scroll beneath her cloak. She inspected the stranger's face. Some features were similar to the Marsallas she had served at the house, but something was different. As if reading her thoughts, the man spoke. 'It's me, my lovely, don't be worried about that.' Freia squinted and tried to imagine him in the borrowed toga once again. Marsallas was clearly a master of disguise. The old man interrupted her inspection. 'Very fine. Very fine indeed,' he wheezed in a cracked and bronchial voice. 'You have yourself a fine fortune here, young man.'

Marsallas nodded and smiled inclusively at Freia. 'Indeed I have. And that, I believe, is the confirmation we were after.'

Freia looked at the innkeeper, Plautius. She wondered what part he had in this. Bernicca was obviously a well-connected woman – from *vicarius* to innkeeper, they all seemed to dance to her tune. Plautius gestured to the old man who passed him the stone for examination. Marsallas observed with a cynical glint in his eye. 'What does an ex-soldier like you know about precious stones, eh Plautius? You wouldn't know a real 'un from a piece of bottle glass!'

Plautius grunted and returned the stone. 'It's up to Bursa here to give us the nod.' He looked at the old man who responded with a toothless grin and an affirmative shake of the head.

Marsallas clapped his hands, making Freia jump. 'There you are. All genuine, as I told you. And now my dear, if you will. . . '

Biting her lip, Freia reached under her cloak and reluctantly felt for the scroll. She wanted to make a break for it, get away from these men. She felt a terrible dread, as if she were handing over the key to Hades itself. The door rattled in the wind, carrying the hubbub of the inn across the yard. A burst of song, a swell of laughter. Marsallas eyes' brightened in anticipation. 'Come my dear, don't be shy. Let's see what you have brought us.'

Freia counted the seconds as she hurried home, gathering her skirts from the deep puddles that had formed in the cobbled streets. As she rounded the next corner she almost collided with a group of uniforms coming the opposite way. She muttered an apology, and then stopped as one of the soldiers spoke out. 'Aha. The blondie again. And where are you off to in such a hurry, eh? Give me a cuddle before you go.'

'Get lost, she's mine, Pavo,' said another, the cheek flap on his helmet flapping as he wagged his head knowingly, 'you've had your chance. It's me the young lady really wants.' He reached out unsteadily and grabbed Freia roughly around the waist. She stumbled and pulled away, dropping the precious pouch onto the cobbles. 'Oh ho, what's this then?' Pavo scooped it up, fumbled with the drawstring and fished out a large opal. He whistled softly. 'So, you've been earning a good rate tonight my love, have you? Old Plautius have his wicked way with you, did he?'

'He doesn't have that sort of buying power,' offered Pavo's rival, 'so what's the likes of her doing with it? I could afford a country estate with that.'

'I think you'd better come with me, young lady. You've got some explaining to do. Who's your master?' Pavo held her arm in a strong grip, pulling her to him. Freia almost gagged at the stink of the soldier's alcohol-laden breath. Something snapped inside her. Her scrabbling fingers found the edge of his shield, gripped the edge and swung it at Pavo's unhelmeted head. Pavo grunted in surprise and reeled back. He swore and lurched forward but Freia slid from his grasp. She heard one of the soldiers shout, 'Get the bag!' And then she saw the pouch, lying where Pavo had dropped it. In a moment she had scooped it up and was running blindly into the darkness.

Chapter 7

Marius led his horse into the courtyard and returned Pelio's greeting. The cobbles were still shining from the heavy rain but the sky promised a fair day in return. The sun was low but bright and Marius shielded his eyes with a free hand as he made his preparations to depart. As he saddled his belongings and checked that the girth was secure he wondered again what had happened to Freia. Drufidius had sent out a search party at first light but there had been no sign of the girl. Marius couldn't stop thinking about her. What had happened? Had she run away? Where would she go? She wouldn't get far on her own, not without a horse, and even if she had managed to slip past the sentries unchallenged it would only be a matter of hours before she was picked up by an army patrol. And then she would be in serious trouble: a runaway slave faced probable execution. Marius couldn't bear the thought; he wanted to search the town until he found her. More than that: he wanted to protect her. But there was nothing he could do now because he had to escort Fraomar to Corinium. He consoled himself with the thought that, once he had carried out Lucius' order, he would be free to return. But by then it might be too late . . .

'Councillor?'

Marius started. 'Sorry, Pelio. I was miles away.' He clapped Pelio on the shoulder and pressed a coin into his hand. 'Until next time, old friend. Remember to send word if there's any news.'

'On my oath, councillor.' Pelio gave Marius' horse an affectionate slap on the rump. 'You'll be the first to hear.'

The horse knelt obligingly at Pelio's command, allowing Marius to settle comfortably into the cushioned frame. Soon he was guiding the horse through the Callevan streets to meet the Corinium entourage at the west gate.

'*Salve* Marius! You're riding with us today?' A young centurion hailed him as he picked his way between the confusion of slaves, horses, carriages and items of baggage arranged haphazardly by the gate.

'*Salve* Portius.' Marius tapped his horse gently on the head and the animal set him down. 'I am indeed – I've a gladiator to deliver to the Corinium games.'

'Wish I could join you,' Portius said. 'I'd like to see this Fraomar in action. Doesn't give much away, does he?' Portius pointed to a group of four auxiliaries waiting for the command to depart. In their midst stood Fraomar, glaring coldly at the bustling preparations.

Marius shook his head. 'No, he doesn't. I'd better have a little chat with him. Talk to you later, Portius.'

'Have fun,' Portius said with a grin. 'And good luck . . . I reckon you'll need it.'

Marius squared his shoulders and walked purposefully to where the auxiliaries were keeping a close watch on the Alamanni warrior. He passed a covered wagon and caught a glimpse of a woman and child within. The woman was pretty and her daughter was chattering to her in excitement. Marius was surprised at her accent; the girl sounded cultured and well spoken yet was dressed in peasant clothing. Marius hesitated, his curiosity almost getting the better of him. But the gates were opening and the convoy was being ushered through. He needed to establish contact with the gladiator. Marius hurried on and greeted Fraomar's minders, then addressed the Alamann directly.

'We'll be on our way to Corinium shortly,' Marius told him. 'You will be barracked comfortably until it is time for the games.' Marius hesitated. Should he mention Lucius' intentions? He saw no harm in sharing the information – whether the news was good or ill for Fraomar he had no way of knowing. 'I have to tell you that there is a strong likelihood you will be leaving Britannia for Trier shortly afterwards. The emperor has expressed great interest in meeting you.'

Fraomar raised his eyebrows and growled something in his native tongue.

Marius stepped back with a curse as a covered wagon clattered round the corner, narrowly missing him. He recognized the driver as the Christian official whose church he had sheepishly entered some days before. No sooner had the wagon passed by than it was halted for inspection by two of Portius' men. The soldiers quickly removed the covers but as soon as they caught sight of the contents they moved away, one of them making a superstitious sign. Marius could see why; in the centre of the wagon was a solitary coffin, decorated with a simple wreath of flowers.

'My name is Barnabas,' the wagon owner told them. 'Bishop of Corinium. I am returning the body of my niece to her parents.'

The soldiers conferred, then waved him on. The bishop eased his wagon forward. Marius left Fraomar to his escort and brought his mount alongside. 'May I join you?'

Barnabas quietened his horse and turned. 'Your face is familiar. Ah, of course,' the bishop smoothed a hand over his bald scalp, 'you were in my church the other day. Am I correct?'

'You are,' Marius admitted, feeling as if he had been caught doing something illegal.

'It will be an honour to ride with you, councillor.' Barnabas smiled. 'Perhaps you can be persuaded to tell me what piqued your curiosity.'

They made camp at dusk. Enclosed within the circle of carriages, wagons and horses Marius sat by the fire, watching the soldiers gaming and drinking. He finished his meal of salted tuna and washed it down with the raisin wine supplied by Drufidius' cook. He grimaced at the tartness of the wine and wiped a hand across his mouth. Barnabas was attending to his wagon, although in what capacity Marius couldn't imagine – his freight was surely beyond any need of earthly assistance. When the bishop eventually joined him at the fireside, Marius' curiosity got the better of him. 'I don't mean to pry, but I overheard your conversation with the gate sentries. About your niece.'

Barnabas chewed his bread thoughtfully. 'Some duties are forced upon us. May I?' He touched the flagon of raisin wine.

'Help yourself,' Marius offered, 'but it's a little course.'

'I am no expert,' said Barnabas. 'Enough that it washes the food down.'

As the bishop poured a measure Marius noticed that his hands were covered in a white powdery substance, like chalk. It was common enough practice to occasionally whiten one's toga by such means, but the bishop wore only black.

'Room enough for another at the fireside?'

Marius and Barnabas looked up to see Nennius, the *lanista*, the overseer of the gladiators, in search of food and company. Marius nodded. 'Join us, Nennius. Are your charges fed and watered?'

'As best as I can offer 'em. I'll be 'appier when they're safe and sound behind four walls again.'

'You enjoy your work, Nennius?' Barnabas asked.

'Been doin' this so long, can't imagine anything else,' Nennius said thoughtfully. 'May I?'

'Help yourself,' Marius said and the *lanista* filled his cup.

'Ah. That's better. Lubricates the throat a treat.' He drank deeply.

'I imagine you could tell us some stories,' Barnabas said, exchanging a conspiratorial look with Marius.

Nennius laughed. 'Not to a man of your holy persuasions, bishop; some of 'em'd make yer blood run cold.'

'I've not always been of this 'persuasion',' Barnabas said with a shrug. 'I shan't take offence.'

Nennius evidently needed little encouragement to begin a story. 'I had a swordsman once, long ago. Picked him up in Africa.' Nennius stared reflectively into his cup. 'Black as coal 'e was. And never spoke a word. But in the arena – ' Nennius paused for effect. 'He was a devil.'

'Go on,' Marius said.

'It's a strange place, Africa. Hot as Hades. And the people there – the tribes of the deserts. Their gods are close to them. This one, he had the look of Egypt about him, but there was something in his eyes. Something dark. When he fought he knew no fear. He'd take risks the like of which I never knew any man to take. But he always came out on top. And I couldn't say how.' Nennius shivered and edged closer to the fire. 'Because he never seemed to be that much of an expert – not like Fraomar. Anyway, one night I was doing the rounds and there he was. Stark naked, with his carved statues placed all around him. No one else in sight – the others avoided him like the plague. And as I watched, I saw the statues rise up in the air – I swear I hadn't had a drop that night. And he turned and saw me.' Nennius moistened his lips. 'And they just floated, turning round and round. And his eyes, they were like a snake's.'

'I've heard of powers within the dark continent,' Barnabas said. 'I believe they are as real as the God I worship, but perhaps not gods themselves.'

'Then what?' Marius asked. 'Spirits of the dead?'

'No,' Nennius said shaking his head, 'something older. Something evil. I felt it in this slave.'

'The fallen ones,' Barnabas said, 'those who were cast from the presence of God for their rebellion. They made their home in this world. And perhaps they are more active in the unconquered, uncivilized regions where they can exert influence on – and sometimes even possess – a man or woman who so desires.'

'Maybe, maybe. I could believe that,' Nennius said, 'whichever gods you worship there's powers we can't understand. And shouldn't mess with.'

'What became of this slave?' Marius asked.

'I sold him,' Nennius winked, 'then I could sleep again at night.'

The entourage set off at first light and the morning passed without incident. No matter how hard he tried, Marius' thoughts continually returned to the mystery of Freia's disappearance. He could see her clearly in his mind's eye, pretty as a sunrise, the light dusting of freckles on her cute little nose, the way she had looked at him when he told her that Fraomar was safe. *Come, Marius, pull yourself together. She's a slave, that's all. Just a slave . . .*

As the road wended into a narrow cutting, the woodland gave way to grassy embankments that rose steeply to the right and left. A shout went up from the front of the column. They exchanged curious glances. Two soldiers rode back towards them on either side. 'Stand fast. Enemy skirmishers spotted in the woods to the north.'

'You're joking– ' Marius was incredulous, but the soldiers had already moved on to ensure that the message was relayed to all.

Barnabas pulled over, jumped down and rummaged in the back of the wagon. He produced a belt, scabbard and short sword. 'Have you a weapon?' he asked Marius.

'A dagger.' Marius' heart was hammering in his chest. Since he was a boy he had looked forward to the day he would fight in a real battle. He had always imagined some far flung barbarian country; never in his wildest imagination had he considered the possibility of fighting to the death on his own doorstep. Barbarians? *Here?*

Nennius was unfettering the gladiators, who began stretching and rubbing their ankles and wrists where the metal had chafed the skin. Portius could be heard issuing orders: 'All of you, move into one group. *One* group, by Mars!' he pushed and bullied. 'Steady behind the shields.' His men moved among them, cajoling and shoving the medley of travellers into line and forming a protective circle around them.

Silhouettes appeared on the ridge. Ahead, beyond the cutting where the land stretched towards the woods, Marius saw riders forming a ragged line. *Barbarians*. One came forward, a tall, heavily built man whose thick beard was drawn into a long, knotted plait, trailing down his stomach like a wolf's tail. He wielded a two-handed sword which he planted in the ground with a flourish. Resting his hands loosely on the hilt he eyed the Roman troops insolently. The giant yelled something in an unrecognizable tongue.

'They're *Scotti* – Irish warriors,' Portius said, 'cheeky devils have probably come up the channel. But how did they get so far inland?'

'They'll not charge the shield wall with horses,' Barnabas said in Marius' ear, 'they'll come on foot, and the mounted men will wait to see the result. We have a chance.'

'Hold your positions,' Portius encouraged his men, 'the line must hold. What did he say? Anyone speak the language?'

'A little,' one of the soldiers offered, 'something about fighting women.'

Marius laughed grimly. It was a reference to the knee-length leather aprons of the Roman auxiliaries.

The barbarians raised their weapons and filled the air with a sonorous chanting. It was a weird, unsettling noise. As it ululated around the cutting the soldiers began to mutter amongst themselves.

'Stand your ground.' Portius told them. 'They're trying to get you rattled.'

The chanting stopped abruptly at the spokesman's signal. Without further warning the barbarians charged down the ridge. The auxiliaries' spearheads met the first arrivals at the road and Marius was amazed at the recklessness with which the Scots threw themselves at the line of bristling *pilae*. It was almost as if those in the vanguard were deliberately flinging themselves onto the sharpened points to render the weapons ineffective and protect those who followed. So far the wall of shields had held, but even as the thought flashed through his mind Marius had to defend himself as a Scot came crashing past the soldier in front of him. He heard Portius shouting to close the gap, but the breach had been made and the barbarian Marius downed with a stabbing dagger thrust was replaced instantly by another. There was no time to dwell on his first kill. He retrieved the barbarian's weapon and hefted it. All around men were falling. Half their number had been wiped out and the horsemen were waiting patiently to finish off any stragglers tempted to make a run for it. The air was filled with curses and the sound of clashing metal.

Marius found himself fighting back to back with Barnabas, parrying spear and axe thrusts as their numbers were slowly eroded. Then he caught sight of Fraomar, released from his bonds and fighting like a man possessed.

Marius knew they had but one chance: 'Barnabas – the horses!'

'I'll go for the wagon,' Barnabas shouted. 'If we can make it to the woods we might get away,' he pointed with the bloody tip of his sword.

'Watch out!' Marius saw a barbarian preparing to strike Barnabas down, but before he could help was forced to defend himself against another assailant. This time he was knocked off his feet by the power of the attack and found himself staring into the crazed face of an Irish warrior. The man's eyes glazed over and he slumped to one side with Fraomar's sword in his back.

The fight became a blur: Portius, dead beneath a pile of bodies, face bloodied. Wagons overturned, a severed head in the mud. Blood on the road, white spume on the flanks of Fraomar's horse as the gladiator hacked his way through the melee, reached out a muscular arm and hauled Marius up behind him. Marius hung on grimly as arrows whirred past his head. *Why is he helping me?* he thought wildly. Then they were in the open and riding full tilt towards the woods, Barnabas, half-on, half-off his mount, thundering alongside. Marius stole a glance behind and his body stiffened with shock. Could it be? Were his eyes deceiving him? No, it was her for sure. Beside Barnabas' overturned wagon, surrounded by a semicircle of barbarians, was the slave girl, Freia.

Chapter 8

'Have we lost them?' Barnabas called. 'Wait!'

They reined in their horses and listened for pursuing hoof beats. The woods were silent.

'They will find our trail soon,' Fraomar said. 'We must ride on.'

Barnabas brought his horse alongside. 'Are you wounded?' he asked, scanning Marius and Fraomar for injuries.

Marius conducted a cursory inspection of his body. A few cuts and his shoulder felt bruised, but otherwise there seemed to be no damage; the bloodstains on his clothing belonged to others, but his heart was still battering against his ribs.

'Very well,' Barnabas said tersely. 'Let's keep moving.'

As they broke cover Marius caught sight of a pall of smoke curling lazily skywards on the horizon. With a shock he recognized the tree line, recognized the road that lay at the foot of the gentle slope ahead and his heart sank. He knew it well. It was the road that led to his home, his murdered parents' villa. Now he feared for Lactantius and Saturnus. He thumped Fraomar's shoulder to get the Alamann's attention and shared his anxiety. Barnabas led the way down to the road, keeping a watchful eye for pursuers. Marius' stomach was a hard knot as they approached the gate because, in his heart, he knew what he would find.

Barnabas and Fraomar stood respectfully aside as Marius fixed his eyes on the desolation that had been his home. The east walls were intact, the remainder was still burning and the roof had gone. In its place was a gaping chasm from which belched thick tendrils of eye-stinging smoke.

Barnabas said, 'Marius, we haven't much time. They are not far behind.'

'I have to know the worst,' Marius replied, staring into the flames. Surely nothing could have lived through this? He selected a hefty piece of deadwood to use as a makeshift weapon and crept around the outer walls, but found no sign of life. The heat from the burned out villa prohibited a closer inspection. But where was Lactantius? – he had to find him. The earth began to tremble and vibrate. Fraomar came running, signalling to the woodland perimeter. Marius ran to his horse and followed the gladiator into the shadows, reaching the trees as the first riders thundered into the clearing.

The Irish horsemen were a daunting sight with their rounded iron helmets and flowing, unkempt manes of hair. The leader dismounted and scanned the clearing, his eyes boring into the darkness of their hiding place. Barnabas' hand was on his arm. He whispered urgently:

'They will search – we cannot stay here.'

Marius thought quickly. 'Follow me,' he turned and led them down a convoluted path that seemed at first to lead in a circuitous route back to the villa but turned away sharply along a narrow lane that ran parallel to a thick growth of quick thorn. A field opened up to their left and they led the horses into the grassy space, leaving the animals to feed and rest. A hundred paces on they came to a seemingly impenetrable wall of bramble. An ancient oak sprouted from the mulchy carpet of yellow and brown leaves, its branches reaching upwards and outwards like blackened fingers. Marius squeezed between tree and bramble and Fraomar followed, his shrewd eyes narrowing in suspicion. Hidden in the foliage was a squat, square temple, set deep in shadow, with a deep growth of ivy and bindweed clinging to its walls. As they set foot on the portico Barnabas stumbled on a warped section of flooring, drawing a warning grunt from Fraomar. The temple smelled musty and disused, deserted it seemed even by the *genius locii* to whom it was dedicated. Marius had not set foot inside since his parents' murder and here he was once more, he thought bitterly, hiding from those who would kill him. He pushed the thought aside. He must be practical and decisive, hold his nerve . . .

Marius was thrown to one side as a figure launched itself from the shadows and fell upon him with a cry. Hands were around his neck, squeezing the life out of him. He struggled and managed to grapple one of his assailant's hands away from his windpipe. Then the pressure was released. He heard the swish of a withdrawn sword, a snarl from Fraomar. He rolled over and saw the gladiator's arm raised for the killing blow. A young man was crouched before him, arms raised in a futile attempt to protect himself. Then with horror, Marius recognized him. 'Fraomar! No!'

The Alamann hesitated long enough for Marius' attacker to roll away from the death blow. But as he tried to regain his feet, he gave a cry of pain and sank to the floor.

'Stop!' Marius threw himself between the prostrate man and Fraomar's lunging sword. 'It's all right. I know him!'

Fraomar's sword bit into the temple floor with a hard *thunk*.

'Saturnus!' Marius caught the man by his shoulders. 'It's all right. It's me, Marius.'

'Master!' Saturnus groaned. 'Thank the *Lares*. They have protected me.'

'You're hurt.' Marius took in the spreading stain on Saturnus' tunic. 'What happened?'

'A spear,' Saturnus gasped. 'I was outside, tending the garden. They came, so suddenly. I ran, but they threw their missiles...am I going to die?'

'Not if I can help it,' Marius said through gritted teeth. 'We need some light. Barnabas, quickly, hold this cloth to the wound.'

Marius found a box of flints and tallow, untouched since his boyhood. The first refused to cooperate but the second filled the temple with a dim yellow light. Between them they staunched the blood and bound Saturnus' wounds as best they could. The slave sank into a fitful sleep while Marius watched him anxiously. 'He is my good friend,' Marius said. 'And a fine swordsman.'

'We've done all we can for the moment, Marius,' Barnabas said. 'We must make sure of our own safety first - then we can get him the medical attention he needs. We must hope that the wound does not fester.'

'I will keep watch,' Fraomar said, and made as if to step outside.

Barnabas caught his arm. 'Wait,' the bishop said firmly, 'there is something you should know.' His expression foretold bad news.

Marius guessed what was coming and braced himself for Fraomar's reaction.

'You must know; I was not travelling alone,' Barnabas said quietly.

Fraomar snorted dismissively and shrugged the bishop off. 'What is that to me?'

Barnabas went on. 'I was travelling with a girl– '

'I know,' Marius interrupted, 'I saw her. It was Drufidius' slave, Freia.'

'You saw her? I told her to stay in the wagon–'

Fraomar seized the bishop by the shoulders. 'What are you saying? What was she doing with you?'

Barnabas pulled away from the gladiator's grip, displaying remarkable strength. He held up his hands, palms outward, to try to calm the Alamann. 'If you will allow me to explain– '

Fraomar glared at the bishop, clenching and unclenching his fists.

Barnabas let his hands drop to his side. 'She is known to me through the church. Her mistress sent her on an errand – she was to deliver and collect something from the inn at Calleva. She ran into trouble with the military – a group of soldiers returning to barracks after a night out. You know how they are…' the bishop shrugged and Fraomar's expression blazed anger. 'In any event,' Barnabas continued, 'there was a scuffle. It appears that Freia got the better of her assailant, but left him with a deep wound to the head.'

Fraomar was shaking his head in disbelief.

Marius wiped a hand across his cheek, feeling the stubble rough against his palm. 'An assault by a slave on a Roman soldier is a serious offence, and so she came to you. That explains it.'

'Yes,' Barnabas nodded, 'but there is more. She was in possession of a small fortune in precious stones.'

'But how– ?' Marius frowned. This was a bizarre twist. Where on earth had they come from? Then he remembered Marsallas, the opals . . .

Barnabas shrugged. 'I don't know. She wouldn't tell me. But she was afraid to return home because the soldiers would find her. And the stones – well, they are a further complication. Perhaps she feared that her owners would be compromised in some way.'

'And so you agreed to smuggle her out of Calleva – a runaway slave?' Marius could hardly believe what he was hearing.

'Let me finish. First she went to a friend. One Domitius,' Barnabas went on, 'he is a slave in a neighbouring household. On his advice she came to me for help. What do you think would have happened if she had returned to her master and mistress?'

'It would have been her word against the military's,' Marius replied.

'Exactly.' The bishop placed a hand on Fraomar's shoulder. 'My friend, I acted in her best interest.'

The gladiator was silent but Marius could sense his rage. 'So she was in the coffin all along,' Marius added quickly. 'and that chalky substance on your hands …came from her face; to mimic death's pallor for anyone suspicious enough to pry– '

Barnabas inclined his head in affirmation. 'A little potion I concocted.'

'I am going back to the road.' Fraomar announced flatly.

'You'll never get past the villa,' Marius protested. 'We must stay put until they move on. If Freia is alive they will lead us to her.' Marius watched for Fraomar's reaction. *Don't look away*, he told himself. *Don't show any weakness. . .*

After a moment's consideration, Fraomar gave the briefest nod. 'You are right,' he said. 'We will wait.'

Marius was woken in the night by a sharp prod in the ribs. His hand went immediately for his sword but was halted by an urgent whisper: 'It's all right. Take this bag and keep it safe. I have a feeling it may come in useful.'

Marius exhaled with relief as he recognized Barnabas' voice. He felt the weight of the bag and knew its contents. He nodded his acquiescence, tucked the bag under his blanket and held it close, thinking of Freia.

The grey dawn woke Marius from a fitful sleep. They had taken turns to keep an eye on the barbarians who had set up a makeshift camp by the remains of the villa and although a search of the grounds had been made the invaders had failed to discover the hidden route to the temple. Saturnus slept on, his breathing even, his face at peace. Marius began to dare to hope that he would survive. But he was in no fit state to travel with them. Somehow they would have to get him to Corinium.

Fraomar appeared at the door, blocking out the early morning light. 'They are moving,' he said. Barnabas stirred, moaning and massaging his neck as he coaxed his body to wakefulness.

'I need to search the villa,' Marius said. 'I have to know what happened to my uncle. Saturnus will be safe here for the moment.'

They picked their way along the narrow route from the temple grove to the villa. Mist clung to the tree roots and a rabbit scuttled across the path, causing Fraomar to draw his sword in a blindingly quick reflex action, reminding Marius of the gladiator's recent victory in Calleva's arena.

Marius picked his way through the blackened roof timbers which, along with ash and smoke-damaged debris, covered the mosaic floor. A soot-covered statuette of Orpheus gazed at them sightlessly, even now surrounded by his menagerie of charmed beasts. A bronze cast of Ceres, somehow undamaged, stood on its marbled pedestal in the corner. He found his way into what was left of his bedchamber. The room had been ransacked before the fire began but he discovered the oak chest containing his clothing relatively undamaged. He opened the charred lid of the chest and extracted several tunics along with two warm cloaks and a pair of heavy-duty sandals.

Barnabas shouted, bringing Marius and Fraomar at a run. A body lay huddled in a corner of the hall, contorted and broken. The arms were held up as if to ward off the flames but the savage wounds on shoulder and neck told the true story of his death. 'Lactantius,' Marius said quietly. 'My uncle.'

They buried Lactantius beside the scented lime tree where he had often sat, Fraomar pacing impatiently to and fro while Marius stood with bowed head. Barnabas laid a hand gently on his shoulder, 'Marius, we must make haste. The trail will grow cold.'

Marius turned to the bishop, 'Can your god account for these days, Barnabas? Has he an answer for the murder of a good man?' Marius stooped and laid his palms flat on the earth covering his uncle's body. When he lifted his head he felt the tears hot on his cheeks and wiped them away angrily.

'I am sorry, Marius,' the bishop spoke softly, 'God has many answers. When you are ready to hear them we shall talk. But now I must make haste to Corinium with your slave. I will ensure that he gets the attention he needs. You and the Alamann must follow the Irish.'

'But how do you know Corinium is safe?' Marius frowned. For all they knew it could have been overrun already by the barbarians.

'I don't,' Barnabas replied. 'But where else are we to find adequate treatment for Saturnus?'

Fraomar jutted his bearded face into the bishop's. 'You wish to leave?' He shook his head. 'No. You will stay.' The Alamann drew his sword and blocked Barnabas' way.

Barnabas folded his arms and stood his ground. 'I have done everything in my power to protect your sister, gladiator, I swear it. Saturnus needs our help; if we leave him here he will die. I will rejoin you as soon as I am able. Remember, Freia is my responsibility as well as yours.'

'Let him go, Fraomar. His intentions are merciful.' Marius stood between the two men.

'How will you find us?' Fraomar hefted his sword from hand to hand.

Barnabas said: 'The roads are good and I usually find what I am looking for. It is reasonable to anticipate that the Irish are heading northwest, towards the coast. Besides, you will be travelling a great deal slower than I.'

Marius gave the bishop a puzzled frown. 'Why do you think that?'

'Because Marius, the Irish progress will be hampered by prisoners, stolen cattle – by sheer weight of numbers.'

'Very well,' Marius said. 'We shall look forward to your return.' The bishop's mind was obviously made up, and it made sense for him to have charge of Saturnus. But something about Barnabas' manner made Marius ask a further question.

'Was there something else, Barnabas? What is troubling you?'

Barnabas hesitated. 'You are very perceptive. Only that I have arranged to meet with my novice, Romanus, and he will be concerned as to my safety. And there are now other – rather delicate – matters requiring my attention which I regret I am not in a position to disclose. But one thing is for certain: I am in dire need of your help, and for this reason I swear on oath that I shall return.'

Marius shrugged. 'Then be assured; I will help you in whatever way I can.' He could see there was little point in pressing Barnabas for more information; whatever Barnabas' business might be, it was for him to decide when and with whom to discuss it. Moreover, he felt confident that Barnabas could be relied upon, a view which Fraomar seemed not to share.

'If you do not come back,' Fraomar said gruffly, sheathing his sword, 'I will find you, bishop. Be sure that I will.'

They found the horses undiscovered by the barbarians, grazing contentedly in the field. Marius returned to the temple to collect Saturnus. He found him sitting up and, while obviously in pain, the slave seemed alert and fever-free. He half-walked, half-carried his friend to the field and helped him onto Barnabas' horse.

The slave smiled weakly, holding the saddle horns tightly. 'Master, I thank you and wish you the gods' blessing.'

'I'll see you in Corinium, old friend,' Marius said with affection. 'Barnabas will look after you.'

The bishop raised a hand in farewell and led the horse across the bridge. Marius muttered a prayer of protection as they disappeared from sight. There was nothing more he could do and he could not have wished for Saturnus to be in better hands.

'And you, boy. What will you do now?' Fraomar had mounted his mare and guided the horse in a wide circle around Marius.

'You and I are going to stick together,' Marius replied. He knew he had to assert his authority, had been expecting Fraomar to challenge him.

'And why should I agree?' Fraomar began to close the circle, passing closer to Marius each time.

Marius stood his ground. 'Because without me you will be picked up by the first army patrol that spots you, that's why. I can give you safe passage.'

'Has it come to this, then?' Fraomar said, half to himself. 'That you must rely on a *boy*, Fraomar of the Alamanni?' Now he was almost on top of Marius, the mare's hooves passing within a pace of Marius' feet.

Marius drew his sword. 'You are my prisoner, Fraomar. I will kill you if I have to.'

Fraomar brought the mare to an abrupt halt. She whinnied and shook her mane. 'Ha!' Fraomar laughed aloud and jumped down. 'You would be dead if I hadn't picked you out of that fight like a wilting sheaf of corn!'

'That's a lie. I held my own.' Marius retorted. He remembered the noise, the clamour of bodies, the blood. And his fear.

'Your head was this far away from being sliced clean off,' Fraomar said, holding up finger and thumb.

'What of it?' Marius was furious now. 'Well then; let's see if you can finish the job.'

Fraomar's horse stamped and snorted impatiently. Fraomar slapped her flank and grinned. 'Like this one, lad, you have spirit, I'll give you that.' He came towards Marius in a low crouch.

Marius stuck his chin out. He was scared but he couldn't let Fraomar see that. He gripped the *spatha* firmly, concentrated on the gladiator's body language…

Fraomar drew his sword and, quicker than Marius could follow, had its edge at his neck. Fraomar's voice hissed in his ear. 'Boy, I could slit your throat and bury you with your uncle. But for one thing – that you speak kindly of Freia.' Marius felt the blade's pressure on his windpipe. His arm had been pinioned by some immovable object. Then, suddenly, he was free. A second later he was flipped onto his back and the wind was knocked out of him. Marius writhed on the grass, fighting for breath. After a few seconds he succeeded in getting some air back into his lungs. It began to rain, cold droplets wetting his face. Fraomar bent over him, hands on hips, grinning from ear to ear. A brawny arm hauled him to his feet. 'Come, lad. We've no time to waste.'

Marius brushed himself down. His pride was hurt but better that than a cut throat. Surely there was no shame in being bested by a man of Fraomar's skill and experience? At least the gladiator had agreed – so it seemed – to ride with him. He nodded curtly. 'What are we waiting for?' He took to his saddle and wheeled the horse, trotting briskly across the bridge to the road.

He turned in his saddle and gave the villa a long, lingering look. Such memories. Happy, and sad. Doubly sad now that Lactantius had followed his parents to the afterlife. Marius shivered. Perhaps it would not be long before he joined them.

Chapter 9

When Freia heard the alarm raised she quickly considered her options. She could stay where she was and be killed or captured; she could climb out of her premature coffin and call on the troops to protect her. But then she would expose herself to arrest, should there be any soldiers left to arrest her. The only thing to do was to sit tight and pray. She clapped her hands to her ears as the noise escalated and the wagon rocked perilously from side to side, pulled this way and that by the frightened horses. After a while, fear of the unknown overcame the fear of exposure and she gingerly pulled the wagon cover aside. In the din of clashing metal she could see that the tide was against them. A knot of auxiliaries were fighting back to back against the barbarians' wild assault. Her heart missed a beat as she recognized her brother in their midst. Surely they would be overrun at any time? But several figures broke from the edge of the fight and pelted for the horses. She gasped. It was Barnabas and the Corinium councillor. They would never make it. Then Fraomar burst from the press and overran the pursuing Irish, cutting them down in mid stride. She cried out, but her voice was lost in the racket of battle. Fraomar caught up with the bishop and, mounting a horse in a single leap, heaved Marius up behind him in one practised motion. With her heart in her mouth she watched as Barnabas first failed then succeeded in securing his mount. He wheeled the animal and looked over, his expression anguished. She waved him away, shaking her head emphatically. It would be futile to try to help her. And then a loud cry rose from the centre of the road where the fight had been at its most intense; the barbarians raised their swords to the sky in victory, chanting in their weird foreign tongue. Freia's heart thumped with the slow rhythm of fear and she withdrew behind the wagon covers to await death, her one consolation being her brother's escape.

As she prayed and the sounds beyond the wagon changed from victory elation to methodical searching and looting, an idea came to her. She climbed into the coffin and folded her arms about her chest in an attitude of death. Presently the wagon cover was torn aside and she heard hands scrabbling against the wood. Freia shut her eyes tightly. Eventually he lid was raised. A grunt was followed by a prod in the ribs to which she made no response. The voices appeared to disagree on the next course of action. Freia took a mental deep breath; it was time to take the initiative. She opened her eyes and sat bolt upright in the coffin, letting out a strangled cry. The effect was instantaneous. The two warriors fell back with a gasp of horror. Freia turned her head this way and that, as if assessing the circumstances of her rude awakening from the sleep of death. She gave a low moan and climbed stiffly out of the coffin, her shroud billowing around her. Freia stepped forward, raised her arms to the heavens and shrieked as loudly as she could. As one man the Irish stepped back, muttering and averting their eyes. Freia's heart was pounding as she wondered what to do next. The charade was working better than she had dared hope, but what now? Her only option, since her audience seemed unwilling to come within ten paces of her, was to keep walking until challenged. The throng of Irish parted like a wave as she made her way towards the road with as much supernatural dignity as she could muster. She reached the road and stopped dead as she saw the extent of the blood letting. The bodies of horses, soldiers and barbarians lay amongst the steaming debris of battle; swords, spears, shields and, to her horror, human limbs told their own story of the desperate fight for survival that had taken place.

She willed herself to walk on but her path was suddenly blocked by the largest man she had ever seen. At his side hung a battleaxe and his hair hung loose and unbraided over his massive shoulders. His face was covered with course red hair, the overall effect reminding Freia of a large wild boar. The voice, when it came, was deep and guttural, and although the language was unknown to Freia, the tone carried a clear challenge. Freia swallowed hard then saw that a smaller, impish figure was examining her closely from his vantage point behind the warrior. The creature took a hesitant step forward and waved two wands of bone in the air. From the first hung a shrunken head; from the second a small, crafted talisman of bronze. Slowly, the little man circled around her, shaking his arms gently then more vigorously as he completed each circuit. The tall warrior looked on in silence while the ritual was performed. Eventually the shamen stepped back, apparently satisfied. He spoke rapidly to the warrior and concluded with a strange rattling movement of the wands. Freia flinched slightly and prayed for a favourable verdict. She became aware that the entire raiding party had assembled in silence behind her; she had transformed the Irish mood from battle elation to a kind of superstitious inertia. At last the big man grunted, lowered his head and sank slowly to his knees. Up to this point he had shown no fear but whatever warnings his magician had imparted to him he evidently took very seriously.

Freia folded her arms on her chest and let out a soft, mournful sigh, followed by a lilting tuneless chant which she hoped would put the Irish in mind of the afterlife. The warriors followed their captain's example and dropped to their knees, bowing their heads and muttering whatever incantations were a comfort to them. Presently, the chieftain rose to his feet and motioned for his magus to come forward. The little man put out a wavering hand and touched Freia's robe softly, as if expecting his hand to pass straight through. He looked directly into her eyes and spoke several words that Freia judged to be a question. She shook her head and said in colloquial Latin: 'Why have you disturbed me? You have wakened me from the deepest sleep of all.' She knew immediately by his expression that the man had understood. He replied in the same tongue which, although heavily accented, was clear except for the last word which she did not recognize: 'Are you spirit or *Buitseach?*'

What should she say? The magus reached out his bony arm a second time and squeezed her exposed shoulder, squinting at the resultant mark left on her pale skin. Freia felt relief wash through her. It seemed that he was going to answer the question himself. After a moment he turned to the warrior and excitedly relayed his conclusions. A name was repeated several times, which she judged to be the name of the boar-man chieftain: '*Faelan*'. The magician turned to the assembled war band and with much pointing and shaking of wands, shared his findings. The warriors exchanged glances and several made elaborate signs in the air; perhaps, Freia wondered, they were signs of supplication to their gods for protection against the spirits of Britannia, one of whom seemed to have blessed them with a personal visitation.

Faelan shouted a command and the men disbanded, each returning to his allotted task. Freia was left standing before the leader and his earthbound familiar. Faelan looked her up and down, turned on his heel and left her in the care of the wand-man. He made a sign that she should follow and as they moved amongst the warriors she noticed the reactions; the surreptitious glance, the shrinking away from their passing. A shout went up from the roadside and she realized with a shock that some of the Callevan entourage had survived. Three, no four, of the Roman escort stood dejectedly as their captors removed their armour and stripped them of their clothing. The Irish began to push the soldiers from one warrior to another, sending them spinning with blows to the head or body. One attempted to fight back. He swung his tied hands and knocked a warrior to the ground. The Roman stood proudly and caught Freia's eye. It was Gaius Rufrius Pavo, the man who had caused her flight from Calleva. The Irish warrior approached Pavo, teeth bared, axe held loosely in his hand. He swung the weapon, gradually building momentum until the axe became a blur. Pavo closed his eyes. Freia held her arms aloft and screamed. The effect was dramatic. All eyes turned to her, Pavo's included. His mouth fell open as he recognized the source of the distraction and his attacker sank his axe into the mud, making the same sign of protection she had seen before. Freia conveyed her displeasure with exaggerated, sweeping negative movements of her arms and much tossing of her hair. She strode past them like a queen, head aloft, leaving the Irish magus to follow in her wake.

The war band were preparing to move, shouldering the spoils and dispatching any lingering casualties with careless spear thrusts. Freia wondered when the Irish horsemen would return and if they would bring any evidence of her brother's fate. Faelan strode by, giving her just a cursory glance as he encouraged his men to make haste. Freia was puzzled at the Irish confidence; they were behaving as if they expected little retaliation from the provincial army. She felt a bony hand on her arm. The wand-man spoke again, jabbing a thin finger into his chest: '*Iuillath*. Walk with me.'

Pavo and the other survivors were being driven from the road towards the woods and Iuillath beckoned Freia to follow. She fell into step alongside the magus, her mind racing, wondering fretfully whether she would have an opportunity to make a break for it. But for now she had little choice but to obey. As she followed the witch-doctor into the trees she prayed that the war band's superstitions would be enough to protect her from whatever trials lay ahead. The poplars skirting the copse were thick with rooks and their harsh, impatient cries followed the line of warriors and prisoners as they faded into the woods. Immediately the cawing ceased and an eerie silence descended. Freia shuddered. It didn't take much imagination to understand why – the rooks would not go hungry today.

Chapter 10

Calleva was sealed following news of the Irish raiders and, although the garrisoned troops had made forays into the surrounding countryside, they had not found a single war band. It seemed that the barbarian effort had been concentrated in the west and Calleva, by virtue of its central location, had so far escaped the attention of the invaders. This did not mean, however, that all was well. Supplies into the town were not guaranteed because traders had to travel through largely unpoliced country and by all accounts it was an unsafe passage for most. Rumour had it that a recent patrol had discovered the remains of a rich merchant of wine and his retinue who had chosen the wrong time to travel south from York to the Londinium estuary. He had met his doom only an hour from the safety of Calleva. The wine was missing along with the heads of the victims. Stories like this made Drufidius nervous. No, this was not a full scale invasion but the effects were far-reaching. His imagination was further stimulated by the fact that communications were at a virtual standstill; there had been no imperial post messenger since the news of the raiders had first arrived and as a consequence Drufidius, along with the rest of Calleva, could observe the effects purely at a local level. But the great thing was, he mused as he headed for his pre-bath toilet appointment, that he was safe in Calleva, surrounded by its strong walls and the comforting presence of its regular patrolling squaddies.

Drufidius entered the latrine and was pleasantly surprised to find that he was its sole occupant. With a sigh of pleasant anticipation he eased himself onto the warm wooden bench. Having the place to himself was a rare luxury. The room was humid but less odorous than usual – probably, Drufidius conjectured, because the facilities benefitted from a higher standard of hygiene than the Forum toilets where he was habitually obliged to attend the daily call of nature.

But the peaceful silence was shattered by the sound of gruff voices and a moment later Lucius Septimius barged into the room. The Praeses hurried to the opposite bench, hoisted his toga to the waist and emptied his bowels with a deep sigh of satisfaction. Drufidius wrinkled his nose and contented himself with a half-hearted evacuation. Was there nowhere he could escape Lucius' attention? He squatted by the water channel and irritably fished a sponge from the basket.

'And where have you been?' Lucius glowered, trumpeting another burst of wind into the thunder box. 'Didn't you get my message?'

Drufidius replaced the sponge in the communal pot. 'No. W–What message?'

'That we have a visitor.'

'A v–visitor?'

Lucius finished his business, wrung out his sponge and glanced around to make sure they were still alone.

'Yes. Nipius Quintilius. From Gaul – Trier, actually. Nasty piece of work. He wants to question us on the whereabouts of your friend, Fraomar. We need a plan,' Lucius beckoned, 'so come along, we can continue this conversation in the baths.'

Drufidius, full of foreboding, followed the Praeses to the changing rooms where the two men stripped and placed their clothes in adjacent stone niches. Drufidius examined the worn soles of his sandals, making a mental note to ask his wife to send for a new pair. '*My* friend, Fraomar?' Drufidius muttered, 'well, w–we can't be sure *where* he is at present.'

'No, we can't. But that may not go down too well.' Lucius scratched his armpit and flexed his shoulders. 'By the gods, I need a massage. I'm stiff as a board.'

'What are you going to tell them?'

Lucius placed both hands on Drufidius' narrow shoulders. '*We* are going to tell them the truth. That we have placed him in a colleague's safekeeping pending the Corinium games where he is due to perform a demonstration to the *Praefectus*.'

'But we know he hasn't arrived at Corin– '

Lucius waved away the objection. '*I* know *we* know that. But I'm not going to let on to Nipius Quintilius. It looks bad.'

'Of course,' Drufidius muttered unhappily. The two men proceeded to the hot room where they baked their flesh until driven to the cold plunge. Lucius was first in and when he emerged, dripping from the freezing water, he gave Drufidius a playful shove, sending him unprepared into the chill depths. The shock of the temperature change knocked the breath from his lungs and as he sank deeper, the weightlessness, darkness and sheer, numbing cold panicked him and he pushed urgently for the surface, half expecting a hand to reach down and hold him under. Heart pounding, he heaved himself out of the pool to find the Praeses heading back to the hot room. Drufidius followed and they stretched out on the smooth wooden benches.

'He's a powerful man, this Nipius,' Lucius continued. 'I'm not going to risk upsetting him. What do you imagine the emperor's brief to be, eh? He'll have Nipius' crown jewels impaled on his tent pole given an unsatisfactory outcome. And what d'you think will happen to the likes of us then? So. We sent Fraomar to Corinium with a full escort, did we not? And what happened after that, is neither here nor there. That's up to Nipius to find out. We acted in good faith. And so, we shall entertain the emperor's man and his colleagues as best we can and send them on their way.'

The door of the *tepidarium* opened and Drufidius jumped in alarm. A dark-skinned slave entered carrying a jar of oil and set it down beside Lucius. He poured a quantity into his cupped hands and began to massage Lucius' broad back. Drufidius lay on his stomach, eyes firmly shut, feeling the heat bore into his muscles.

When the slave had left, Lucius sat up and ran his hands through his thick curly hair. He adjusted the position of his towel and settled his backside onto its soft and accommodating folds. 'We have to be seen to be compliant. After all, we've done nothing wrong.'

Ten minutes later Lucius left to pay a last visit to the cold room. Drufidius remained where he was, glad of his own company. The only sounds were the odd clatter of a slave's pail or mop as he moved about his routine cleaning tasks. A door slammed and once he heard voices outside but no new customers entered to disturb his peace. The heat of the room lulled him gently into an uneasy sleep where strange shapes lurked in the shadows of the darkened Callevan streets, beckoning and beguiling, ultimately tempting him away from the safety of the crowds into their own twilight world.

Drufidius tried to compose himself as he paced up and down in Lucius' cramped quarters; the Calleva inn was not renowned for its sophistication and décor. Which was why Lucius spent most of his time at Drufidius' house. More's the pity, Drufidius thought to himself, unhappily. His heart gave a skip as he heard footsteps approaching.

Lucius strode in, preceded by a ferret-like man in military uniform with the wearied look of imperial service about him. He didn't look like someone given to pussyfooting about. A results man, Drufidius concluded miserably. Lucius performed the introductions and Drufidius detected an edgy quality in Lucius' voice.

'Wine?' Lucius inquired.

'Thank you.' Nipius removed his helmet and smoothed his hair.

There was a short silence as wine was brought and set down. 'So. How was your journey?' Drufidius asked.

Nipius appeared to consider the question. He ran a finger around the rim of his goblet and repositioned it on his courtesy table. There was an awkward silence. Nipius steepled his fingers and put them to his lips, leaving the wine untasted. 'It was most – instructive,' he said finally. 'The fact of the matter is that we're lucky to be alive, let alone supping wine in Calleva. Doubtless you have heard the news from the Saxon shore?'

Drufidius cocked his head to one side. 'N–News?'

Nipius paused, toying with his cup. 'Evidently not,' he said at last. 'Well then, I have to tell you that Count Nectarides is dead and that the channel is awash with Saxon warships. The east coast of this island is overrun and whatever field army Nectarides had under his command has ceased to exist.'

There was a longer silence while this information was digested. Eventually Lucius said: 'Then it's worse than we thought. We are undefended from the east, by all accounts also from the west and who knows what is taking place in the borderlands of the north. Has Valentinian heard about this?'

'He is aware. But he has other fish to fry in Germania. And they are proving most troublesome,' Nipius nodded, pondering his assessment. 'It is a less than…happy situation.' The visitor drank at last and set his cup down with a flourish. 'So, how do you imagine all these things have come about?'

Drufidius spoke up. 'Through the depletion of the provinces' manpower. If troops are needed in Gaul, or anywhere in the east for that matter, they are requisitioned from B–Britannia. This island is always the first to compensate for any military shortcomings in the rest of the Empire. Grunts and grain. That's all we're good for.'

Nipius scratched a chin still covered by three days growth of stubble. 'True. But I was hoping for a more specific reason.'

Drufidius looked blankly at Lucius but the Praeses returned an empty gesture.

Nipius sighed. 'Very well. Let me provide the specifics. Have you heard of a Gallio Velius Marsallas?'

Drufidius' heart missed a beat.

'Well?'

Lucius shook his head and shrugged. Nipius fixed his eyes on Drufidius and raised an eyebrow.

'I, I – that is to say, I may have heard– '

'Yes, councillor?' Nipius leaned forward. 'You *may* have come across him? Well, let me refresh your memory. He is purportedly one of the *Areani* based on the Welsh borders. But it seems he was not content with his career and has taken an alternative mission. Basically, to line his pockets at the Empire's expense. Anyway, Marsallas is playing a double game. We were fortunate enough to run into him – literally – as we left Gaul. And you'll like this bit, councillor.' Nipius smiled thinly at Drufidius who looked in turn to Lucius for support, but the Praeses was standing with his arms behind his back, facing the window overlooking the courtyard.

'Marsallas was captured whilst attempting a Gallic landing in a *Saxon* vessel.' Nipius settled back into his chair, awaiting a reaction. When none came, he prompted: 'A curious form of transport for one of the Empire's finest, wouldn't you say?'

Drufidius glanced at Lucius but once again found only the Governor's uniformed back and posterior. 'Very curious indeed,' he managed.

'Happily our coastal units were more alert than their opposite numbers in Britannia. The vessel was impounded, the Saxons despatched, and lo and behold there was Marsallas. And wasn't he a slippery one? But he was eventually . . .' Nipius searched the air for an appropriate word, '. . . restrained, and no doubt we'll be hearing more in due course, because he was in possession of a *most* interesting document. I've sent him to Valentinian for a little debriefing.'

Drufidius felt sweat trickle from beneath his armpits. A terrible possibility had dawned on him. But Nipius had moved on.

'Now, about this *Alamanni* fellow. He's been moved to Corinium I understand?'

Lucius swivelled and nodded vigorously. 'Yes, that's right. I always feel it's important to keep up morale in my province, so he was to be the special feature of the games – as a non-combatant of course. But you'll be aware how much the *Praefectus* enjoys a good demonstration.'

'Of course. Well let's hope we find everything in good order. I suppose I shall just have to risk the journey. But there is one problem.'

'If there is anything f–further we can do–' Drufidius began.

'Do?' Nipius replied. 'Why, yes.' He affected a look of surprise. 'You could begin by preparing for an early departure. We leave at dawn.'

Drufidius looked at the Praeses who pointedly failed to make eye contact. 'We?' Drufidius struggled to make sense of Nipius' words.

Nipius drained his goblet. 'Of course. That's our problem. How are we to recognise this man if you do not accompany us? I can't afford any identification problems.'

Drufidius panic was rising to epic proportions. 'And what of my d–duties here, my responsibilities?'

Lucius waved his objection aside, an action Drufidius witnessed with horror. 'We shall provide adequate cover for you, my dear fellow. Do not fear.'

Drufidius slumped in his chair. Of course, Lucius had intended this, probably suggested it.

Nipius was at the door. 'Tomorrow; an hour before *hora prima*. West gate. We'll be waiting.'

After Nipius' departure there was a pregnant silence. Lucius was the first to speak:

'Well, that could have been worse. Less of the long face, man; I'm sure you'll make an excellent guide.'

Drufidius was stunned. He found no adequate response. His tongue was glued to the roof of his mouth.

Lucius went on, conversationally. 'Now then, what of the runaway? Any news? Your wife must be anxious.'

Drufidius shook his head. Up until this morning Freia's disappearance had been his primary problem. Now Bernicca had questions to answer. He took his leave of the Praeses and set off to find his scheming wife.

Bernicca looked up in surprise. 'Ah, I was expecting you earlier, but I see– '

'Quiet, woman. Get P–Pelio to prepare a horse. I'll need provisions and clothing, and– '

'Whatever for?' Bernicca interrupted, 'it's not safe. Haven't you heard– '

'Of course I've heard,' Drufidius replied testily, 'and you should know, shouldn't you?' He squared up to Bernicca, fixing his eyes on hers. The blue-tinted brows stared back.

'Do you think I am a complete f–fool?' Drufidius paced the room, glancing nervously out to the corridor. 'This is your doing. I can f–f–feel it.'

'Well. What of it? You wouldn't listen.'

'*What of it?* We have a slave m–missing under suspicious circumstances. And then I am commanded to travel through hostile c–countryside in the company of a professional homicidal maniac, looking for an equally murderous and desperate enemy of the state – '

'I swear to you. I don't know what happened to Freia.'

'You sent her somewhere, didn't you? This has something to do with M–Marsallas, yes? Am I getting warm?'

'I didn't expect this to happen.'

112

Drufidius rubbed the heel of his hands over his eyes and sank wearily onto the couch. 'You'd better tell me everything. I'll find out anyway.'

Bernicca fell silent. 'All right,' she said at last. 'I obtained what Marsallas wanted. Freia delivered it to him. And that's the last I saw of her.'

'You released classified information – but where– ?' Drufidius stopped in mid flow as his mind gathered the pieces and slotted them into place. He shook his head in disbelief. 'It was you. In Londinium. The missing scroll.' He held his head in his hands. 'And we were g–guests of the *Praefectus*.'

'Listen, you weak fool. It was a fortune. And we can still have it. And what's more, I have another idea.'

'Oh gods, spare my grey head,' Drufidius said, his voice reduced to a whisper.

'Don't tell me you wouldn't like to get back at Lucius.'

'What do you mean?'

'He's played you like an idiot, as usual. He wants you to do all his dirty work while he lives it up at our expense.'

Drufidius went to the door and yelled down the corridor. 'G–Get me some wine. Now!' The request was met with a patter of feet and slamming of doors. Returning to the couch, he looked miserably at Bernicca. 'You're right.'

'Of course I'm right. Now listen. I have the original Londinium scroll – and some influence over Lucius. Do you see? We can shift the blame and get him off your back once and for all. This is what we have to do…'

Chapter 11

Marius stoked the fire with his sword and huddled closer, trying to warm his bones. Nearby, Fraomar slept soundly. Since the villa the two had ridden far with little conversation, each lost in his own thoughts. He wondered if Barnabas and Saturnus had found Corinium intact and well-defended, and particularly whether Saturnus had survived the journey. He also wondered about Barnabas' appointment with his understudy. The bishop seemed determined that the Irish encounter should not hinder his mission to Wales, and such was his desire to spread the Christian gospel that he was prepared to risk danger not only from the invaders but also the Welsh tribes, many of whom were openly hostile to Christianity. But the bishop had more than mission on his mind, Marius was convinced; Barnabas' cryptic comment about 'other matters' had been playing on his mind ever since they had parted company. Still, it was no use speculating. Barnabas would no doubt share his thoughts when he was ready. If they ever saw him again . . .

Marius sheathed his sword and blew into his hands. He heard some waterfowl cry out with a harsh *craik* but otherwise the night was still. He reflected on the past twenty-four hours; He had to admit that Fraomar had proved an excellent tracker. They had followed the war party northwards along the meandering river travelling from daybreak till dusk, shunning the main roads and instead finding their way through light spruce woodland or, when they were forced away from the river by its degeneration into marshy swamps, along the higher, secretive paths of sombre ancient forest where the spirits of an older Britannia could be felt flitting shadowlike amongst the oaks and ashes.

Keeping the Irish in sight yet remaining unseen was proving a strain but Marius was sure that, sooner or later, the barbarians would make camp in a location suited to some kind of rescue attempt. He felt not only responsible for Freia's safety but was also aware of some deeper emotion he didn't care to examine too closely. He recalled her expression of relief when he had given her the news that her brother was safe. He remembered her eyes, her corn-blonde braided hair, the graceful movement of her young body. Marius drove his sword into the earth. *Enough*. He had to think like a general, not a lover, to have any hope of success. True, he had Fraomar, but the Alamann was but one man against many. The most worrying thing of all was the absence of provincial military support. It was an ill omen indeed when an enemy force could move unchallenged through the heartlands of the Brittanic provinces. Marius reasoned that reinforcements must be on the way, but unless these were well organized there was no guarantee of success against the roaming war bands. And moreover, Freia's chances of survival were probably higher whilst she remained in captivity. If the barbarians were challenged the prisoners would be the first to die.

Fraomar stirred and turned in his sleep. The moon was full, the stars sparkling in the heavens. Marius stood and stretched. Perhaps a brisk walk would warm him better than the dying embers of the fire. He made his way towards the sounds of flowing water. A penetrating dampness pervaded the air, creeping into his clothing and making him shiver. The river, lying below like a silver sword in the moonlight, churned by indifferently, swollen by the recent bouts of heavy rain. Marius could scarcely believe the events of the last thirty-six hours, and still less the reality of his gutted villa and murdered uncle. These last few years he had been lulled into the routine of study for his impending council duty, sometimes almost forgetting his history of loss and persecution. But now here was proof of the fragility of his humdrum existence. Marius drew his cloak tighter around him. He had lost his parents; and now his faithful carer, dear Lactantius. A name kept repeating itself in his mind. 'Paulus'. *'Catena.'* A name he had not heard in years, a name he had repressed until the spy had attempted his bribe: *'He is not dead. He sends his greetings...'*

'You cannot sleep?' A deep voice spoke behind him. Marius whirled to see Fraomar standing by a clump of osier, arms casually folded. Marius relaxed his grip on his sword.

'I did not mean to startle you. Come. The fire is a warmer companion than the river at this hour.'

Marius followed the Alamann to their makeshift camp. The fire had dwindled to a red glow. Marius piled on wood, watching the sparks spiral skywards.

'My parents and brother died during the battle of Strasbourg in my homeland,' Fraomar said, unprompted. 'My father was forced to surrender and died in captivity. My mother followed; the plague. My brother was killed in the fighting.' The German paused. 'I understand how you feel.'

'Do you?'

'To have lost those you love. It is hard to live with the memory.'

'I don't want to live with memory. I want to avenge them.' Marius gripped his sword hilt, feeling the familiar bitterness wash over him. 'Don't you hate Rome? Don't you want revenge for your dead?'

Fraomar shook his head. 'I do not fight for revenge – it is a canker that eats the soul. I fight to defend my people, the living. My people ask only to live and trade in their homeland as they have done for generations. They would live peacefully, given the chance, but your Roman Empire will not be satisfied until it has sucked the lifeblood from all freeborn tribes and forced them to embrace Roman ways, to live under the yoke of the empire.'

'*My* Roman Empire?' Marius replied bitterly. 'My family were killed at the hands of an emperor's servant. I wanted no part in such an empire, an empire which hunts down its loyal supporters and condemns them for their adherence to the gods that made Rome great in the first place. Were it not for the change of *Augustus* I would have renounced my citizenship when I came of age.'

'So, you are an enemy of Rome as well as I.'

Marius shook his head. 'Not any more. I am an enemy of persecution, of injustice. Of man's inhumanity to man. I respect the Emperor Valentinian; he has done much to redress his predecessor's failings. And the empire brings obvious benefits. Look at this country,' Marius replied, stirred by Fraomar's questioning.

'Yes, look at it,' Fraomar said quietly. 'Overrun, pillaged and raped because it has overreached itself. It cannot defend what it has conquered and, like an animal that does not know it is mortally wounded, staggers on regardless.'

'Wounded, perhaps. Mortally, I doubt it.'

The firelight danced in Fraomar's eyes, challenging Marius to disagree. 'Can't you see it? That the heart of Rome is poisoned? And now its limbs, the provinces, are rotting. The heart will wither and die, and then what will become of Britannia?'

Marius knew the Alamann was right. Their present situation proved the point. He held Fraomar's gaze, not wishing to make any concession, to give any ground. 'You are very opinionated for a gladiator and a slave,' he said, watching Fraomar carefully. 'But you have not spoken of your sister.'

Fraomar stiffened. 'What of her?'

'She was the last person you expected to run in to, wasn't she?' Marius probed. He wanted to talk about Freia, find out everything about her . . .

Fraomar nodded slowly. 'The very last. I only hoped that she was safe. And now...'

'Barnabas did the right thing – at great personal risk,' Marius said. 'She would be awaiting execution had she remained in Calleva.'

Fraomar growled. 'That mad holy man. I should have killed him for what he did.' He spat into the fire. 'What hope has she? He may as well have cut her throat himself.'

'She is still alive. I feel it.'

Fraomar studied Marius carefully. 'You speak with fondness – has she stolen your heart already?' He laughed sadly. 'Everyone loses their heart to Freia.'

'Tell me about her.'

The gladiator was silent for a few moments. When he spoke it was in a low, hushed voice. 'What can I tell you? That she is full of life, clever, caring. Faithful. Beautiful.' Fraomar paused. 'But you know that already, Roman, don't you?'

Marius said nothing. Were his feelings that obvious?

'*I* will find her, and *I* will save her from the western tribes and from her Roman master's condemnation.' The fire was back in the Alamann's eyes. 'With or without your help, boy.'

'I am a man, not a boy,' Marius replied, offended. He was twenty one years of age. He had sat on his first council meeting. He could use a sword. Was he not a man? Marius tried to keep the irritation out of his voice. 'Do not patronize me, Alamann. You need me more than I need you. Besides, we don't know the full story, yet. As a Roman citizen I can speak up for your sister's life. I know Drufidius; he respected my father. I will see that justice is done.'

Fraomar laughed dismissively and spat again. 'Hah. Roman justice. I have seen that in action before.'

Once more there was silence as the fire crackled between the two, as if marking the division of culture and circumstance which Marius hoped could, in time, be broken down. There was something about the gladiator he liked despite the aloofness and the terse manner. He detected a warmth, perhaps buried by the past tragedy he had described, which in time could be revived. If they were to survive the days to come they had to trust each other. With that thought Marius spread his cloak on the damp earth and rested his head on his mare's saddle. A long time later he fell into a fitful sleep.

They broke camp at dawn, giving the Irish a measured start. Passing through a peasant village they were able to barter for food and dry clothing while Fraomar's horse had a shoe replaced in the smithy where a group of vacant-looking locals watched the two men with studied idleness. The villagers had little news worth reporting and when the horses had been fed and rested they moved on.

The light was failing as they found the river and rode cautiously through the water meadow. The river wound onwards, keeping them company with its throaty rush as it tumbled towards the western sea. Marius was lulled by this watery accompaniment to the familiar rhythm of his horse and was unprepared for the sight that met them as their path led into a gentle bend. Fraomar pulled his horse up violently and caught hold of Marius' halter, so that both beasts reared and all but lost their footing save for the expert handling of the Alamann. Fraomar pulled his horses' neck firmly but gently so that the animal fell compliantly onto its side – Marius followed suit. They flattened themselves beside their mounts' prone bodies. Marius' heart thumped as he spied the barbarian encampment across the river. There were knots of prisoners – women and children – along with a herd of stolen cattle grazing in the lush pastures of the riverbank. Marius said tersely: 'Were we seen?'

The Alamann shook his head. 'I think not. But we will soon know.'

They were a hundred paces from the nearest cover but with the river dividing them there was no immediate danger. Marius strained to see Freia in the huddle of captives. There were a number of older women preparing food by the water's edge, but they were too far away to make any positive identification.

'Quickly,' Fraomar said. Casting an appraising look across the river he remounted, using the animal's strength to pull him into the saddle as it righted itself. In seconds he was under the shelter of the chestnut trees. Marius joined him, trying to control his impatience. 'How deep is the river here?'

'Too deep to cross safely,' said the Alamann thoughtfully. 'It runs fast. And there is little cover by the water.'

Marius pondered briefly. 'We can wait until nightfall.'

Fraomar nodded. 'And then?'

'They don't seem organized,' Marius ignored the cynical glint in the Alamann's eye. 'They'll have sentries posted, but only a handful, I'll wager. Does it look as if they're expecting opposition?'

Fraomar picked up a chestnut, rolling it with his fingers, testing its ripeness. 'No, it does not. But we would be spotted crossing at this point, even in the dark. It is too exposed.' He indicated the pall of smoke rising from the camp. 'The Irish are roasting meat and they will drink tonight. Eventually they will sleep.' He pointed to the north. 'In the meantime we must find an easier crossing and somewhere we can hide the horses, then we can enter the camp under cover of darkness.'

Marius conceded with a brief nod. 'Very well.' There was nothing to be gained by giving in to his impatience, he told himself, but everything to lose. The Alamann was an experienced warrior and he would be a fool not to give heed to Fraomar's advice.

There was a roll of thunder to the west, prompting Fraomar to test the wind with his braceleted hand held high. Fat, black clouds were blowing in their direction, gathering shape above the tree line beyond the river. 'Good.' The gladiator clapped Marius on the shoulder. 'Then let us be on our way before the weather turns against us.'

But the weather quickly deteriorated and by the time night fell the rain was drumming heavily through the treetops.

'We must use this to our advantage,' Fraomar said. 'Make sure our horses are secure. Without them we are lost.'

Swallowing his irritation at Fraomar's use of the imperative, Marius turned to check that their mounts were securely tethered. Of course the Alamann was right. If they managed to rescue Freia and perhaps one or two others they would soon be caught by the fleet-footed barbarians if they attempted to escape on foot. But as Marius patted his mare's flank and made sure of her ties he felt a heavy blow on his head and fell senseless to the ground.

Marius' head was throbbing as he gingerly opened his eyes and tried to fight through the muzziness to full consciousness. He was wet and cold, despite the two woollen blankets covering him. Somewhere nearby a wolf howled plaintively. What had happened? Then it all came back. *Fraomar*. The Alamann had decided to go it alone, as he had threatened. Now Marius's pain was replaced by a hot anger. How dare a slave treat him like this! He sat up and the rain gusted horizontally, plastering his hair to his forehead. Marius got groggily to his feet and stumbled along the riverbank to find the crossing they had selected earlier. When he found Fraomar he would show him who was in charge. With this and other vitriolic thoughts firing through his mind like ballista missiles, Marius alternately waded and hopped across the shallows until his feet stood on the opposite bank. He began to pick his way through the darkness but was soon soaked to the skin, his teeth chattering as the wind numbed his cheeks and slowed his progress to a stumble. He peered through the gloom. With a shock he realized that he was standing on the very edge of the camp. The fires had been extinguished, either by the rain or deliberately he could not tell, but he could see figures moving purposefully in the blackness. In these conditions he was virtually anonymous; prisoner or captor would be hard to tell apart and with this in mind he moved further into the encampment, head bent against the fury of the storm.

Shapes appeared out of the murk, one clutching the hand of a smaller figure. Marius put out his arm and grabbed the leader's cloak. Wild, frightened eyes stared back at him. He shouted over the threnody of the wind: 'Have you seen a girl, blonde hair–?' The man shook his head and pulled the child to him. The hood fell back and revealed the white, scared face of a boy of ten or eleven. The man shouted: 'His name is Cassius. He has no family. Let us pass.' Marius watched them recede into the darkness. He turned into the torrential rain. He had little chance of finding anyone in this chaos. A knot of four or five mounted men were attempting to shepherd stragglers into the scant cover afforded by the riverside trees, but the horses were clearly terrified and becoming unmanageable. As Marius watched, a rider was thrown and the horse bolted in panic towards the river. A jagged rip of lightning caught the treetops and clove the largest down the centre, illuminating the scene. From the corner of his eye, Marius glimpsed figures fleeing towards the blurred shape of a distant copse. Could one be Freia? He hoped the barbarians were too preoccupied controlling their horses and stolen cattle to worry about a few missing prisoners. Marius broke into a run, expecting to feel an arrow or spearhead in his exposed back at any moment. He plunged into the copse and the wind dropped. But where was Fraomar? Marius hesitated. What should he do? He was shaking with cold but his mind was clear. He could not spare precious time to look for the Alamann, for if he did so he would lose the opportunity of questioning the escapees. He turned and felt his way through the undergrowth while the storm raged on, the wind whistling and bumping against the trunks and branches high above.

Part Two

The Shadow in the West

Chapter 12

The Rhine Frontier

'Now lad,' the emperor said, 'you'd better come along and see what needs to be done here. It's no use hiding these things from you – you'll have to deal with them yourself sooner or later.'

'Shall I finish my reading first, father?'

Valentinian smiled at his son. 'Gratian, for a boy your age you have an interest in books I find quite extraordinary. But life, with all its variety, cannot be tackled just by immersing oneself in literature and the arts.'

'Well, you have your sculpture, father.'

'I do,' laughed the emperor, 'but I see myself more as a sculptor of men. And we have some earthy business to attend to. Come.' Valentinian beckoned his son with a long forefinger. The emperor's men on either side of the tent entrance saluted smartly at their exit.

They walked together through the camp, Valentinian casting a critical eye at the grey clouds and muttering a curse under his breath. Would the weather ever lift? It did his mood no favours and by the time they reached the stockade at the edge of the camp the emperor's mouth was set in a grim line.

'So, how is our guest?' Valentinian addressed the supervising *ordinarius*.

The commander saluted. 'Still alive, *Caesar*. I think he'll talk.' The man pointed to where a man was lashed to a framework of wood. His head was bowed and it appeared that he was not supporting his weight, but rather hanging from the cords that bound him. His clothing was torn in several places, revealing crimson stains beneath.

'Good. Then let us converse. Come Gratian, come.' Valentinian gestured to the boy who followed reluctantly, glancing nervously at the grim-faced soldiers standing to attention as they approached. The emperor got hold of the man's hair and pulled until his face was revealed. The eyes opened and flashed hatred. 'Treating you well, Marsallas?' Valentinian asked in an even voice.

Marsallas glared back. His voice was barely audible. 'As you can see.'

'Splendid. Now then, let's get this over with. In the past you've proved a useful fellow. No sense in prolonging the pain.' Valentinian forced Marsallas' chin up to face him squarely. 'So, tell me all about your friends from the ship. And how my *comes,* Nectarides, came to grief. It appears that you were in possession of all the necessary details.' Valentinian paused and smiled encouragingly at his son, who was watching the scene with trepidation. The emperor went on: 'Let's see. Numbers, supplies, locations, rotas. You had it all. Very impressive. I'm sure your Saxon friends were delighted.'

Marsallas laughed harshly. 'They're not my friends.' He shook his head until Valentinian reasserted his grip.

'Well, who *are* your friends then – and where did you obtain this information?' The grip tightened.

Marsallas closed his eyes. Valentinian moved his grip to Marsallas' throat and squeezed until the eyes reopened.

'I'll kill you,' Marsallas spat. 'With my bare hands.'

The emperor wiped his face. 'Don't make me lose my temper, Marsallas. *Ordinarius?*' The commander stepped forward. 'Your sword please– '

Valentinian put out his hand, ' – thank you. Now then.' He turned back to Marsallas, pleased to note that fear had at last crept into the man's eyes. 'I'm a simple soldier, Marsallas. Doubtless you are aware that I have to march against the *Alamanni*, and soon, before the weather deteriorates. My men are wet, cold, and bored. They need me here and they need organizing. Right now, Britannia and its problems I can well do without. So be a good fellow and tell me firstly who gave you this information and secondly whatever else I need to know to put a stop to this business across the channel.'

Marsallas twisted his mouth into a grin. 'I'll let you kill me happily, *Caesar*, if I go to my grave knowing I've told you nothing.' Marsallas broke off in a fit of coughing.

'You flatter yourself Marsallas,' Valentinian prodded his cheek with the tip of the sword. 'A grave's too good for you. The latrines will have to be filled in before we move on.'

Marsallas grimaced and shook his head, muttering an expletive. Rain ran down his bloodstained face in rivulets.

'Come, Marsallas. Now you're repeating yourself.' Valentinian pressed the blade home and a spurt of red issued from Marsallas' cheek. Marsallas howled and spat blood. Gratian stepped back and covered his mouth, but Valentinian caught him by the arm and turned him around. 'Take a good look, my boy. So that you can recognize a filthy, self-serving traitor when you see one.' He pressed the sword to Marsallas' throat. 'Latrine pit or talk. You have a count of five. No, I'm feeling generous. Ten.'

Valentinian began to count off the numbers. This creature would talk, he was sure of it. Marsallas was far too fond of his own skin to let it go without some attempt at bargaining. Valentinian had come across his type before. It was a question of approach. On the count of five he heard Gratian retching behind him, the *ordinarius* muttering a few barrack room words of comfort. On the count of nine, Marsallas looked up and hissed: 'All right. I'll tell you. I'll tell you and you can do what you will. It's too late to stop it now.'

Valentinian grunted and lowered the sword.

Marsallas lifted his head again with difficulty. 'Get me off this,' he gasped, 'and give me something to drink. Then I'll tell you.'

'More comfortable, Marsallas?' Valentinian enquired. 'A refill, perhaps?'

They had reconvened the interrogation in the emperor's tent. Marsallas had been given a change of clothing and some food. The colour was slowly returning to his face and he was beginning to exhibit some of his usual charm. The emperor spread his hands. 'So, begin.'

Marsallas fingered his cheek and winced. 'I need a cloth for this,' he said, wiping away a droplet of blood.

'Of course.' Valentinian clicked his fingers and an attending medic stepped forward to stem the flow.

Marsallas licked his lips and drank more wine. 'What guarantee can you give me that I will be spared?'

Valentinian shrugged. 'I'm a fair man, Marsallas.' He smiled benevolently at Gratian who was reclining on a nearby couch, glancing wistfully at his pile of reading material. 'And I wouldn't want to subject the boy– ' here he nodded to Gratian '– to any unnecessary unpleasantness.'

Marsallas appeared to relax slightly. 'Britannia has been targeted,' he said, 'because it is weak. For months now, the island has been subject to close scrutiny. Your border troops, the *limitanei,* have become disheartened. Their numbers are greatly reduced because of your wars here. This fact has not gone unnoticed.'

Valentinian toyed with his cup, running his finger around the beveled edge and tracing the convex patterns that swirled about its elaborate stem 'And so? The barbarians are still subject to our generous treaties – certainly in the north.'

'They have been persuaded that the emperor's generosity leaves something to be desired. Mindful of the prosperity of the southern provinces, the northern tribes have had their eyes opened.'

'By whom?' The emperor frowned and narrowed his eyes.

Marsallas raised his eyebrows. 'With your advanced intelligence network, I'm surprised you do not know.'

'Try me.'

'Paulus *'Catena'.*

'Constantius' notary? The Christian zealot?'

'He has rejected Christianity for something a little more – *exotic.*' Marsallas seemed to shrink in his chair.

Valentinian raised an eyebrow. 'I thought he was executed in Africa? Years ago.'

'He was sentenced and burned, yes.' Marsallas shuddered. 'He went to the flames, but then– ' Marsallas fortified himself with another gulp of wine, 'the execution squad reported that he simply disappeared. I knew the officiating centurion – Publius his name was. Experienced soldier; level-headed. He walked into the fire - *voluntarily*, I'm told. The rest of the squad died three days later. Lost their minds, all of them. . . '

Valentinian snorted. 'And this – *resurrected* man is poised to become the scourge of Britannia?'

Marsallas nodded. 'Even as we speak, it has begun.'

'And you have played your part.' Valentinian stroked his jaw thoughtfully. 'Tell me, Marsallas, do you fear this man more than you fear me?'

Marsallas' eyes flicked from the emperor to the impassive *seniores* officers, Valentinian's personal bodyguard. He took a deep breath. 'He is a devil. They no longer call him Catena; they call him *Serpens*. When he looks at you...'

The emperor held up his hand impatiently. 'Enough superstition. The Welsh mists have evidently got to your brain. Now, if you will, the details, please.' Valentinian unobtrusively signalled to the duty guard, who received the cue and silently left the tent.

'He is based at Mona. From there he is coordinating the invasion. He has many men from the *limitanei* allied to him; along with Crimthann from Ireland and the *Attacotti* chieftains in the north. He is planning an alliance.'

'Don't tell me. Between Ireland and *Scotia*?'

'Between Ireland and the Saxons. Crimthann is to wed the Lady Lawenya.'

Valentinian whistled softly under his breath. 'That's something I'd like to avoid. Go on. You haven't told me where you obtained your information regarding the Saxon shore.'

Marsallas licked his lips again. 'Indirectly – from the *Praefectus* in Londinium.'

'What?' Valentinian turned a shade of puce. He felt his heart hammering in his chest. He knew he should never have trusted that oily diplomat.

'Through a woman,' Marsallas added quickly. 'She is known for her dalliances with those in authority. The more senior the better, actually.'

'That idiot *Praefectus*. I'll have his guts. Right. Name.'

'The wife of one Drufidius of Calleva.'

'Thank you.' The tent flap parted and the officers returned, taking up position behind and on either side of Marsallas.

'Right. Anything else?' Valentinian leaned forward in his chair and rubbed his back with a grimace.

Marsallas shook his head and risked a smile. 'Am I to be guaranteed a safe passage?'

The emperor smiled back. 'You're fond of wine, Marsallas?'

'I am indeed.'

'Good.' Valentinian said. 'I'm feeling generous today.' He nodded to the officers who seized Marsallas by the shoulders and dragged him, protesting, out of the tent. Valentinian got up with difficulty, stretching his spine and groaning with the effort. He'd have to see the medics again. Just what he didn't need. 'Come, Gratian. You can go back to your reading after this.'

The boy followed his father out of the tent and was surprised to see the wooden frame on which Marsallas had previously been hung repositioned nearby so that it spanned a large barrel of liquid. Soldiers were beginning to gather in a circle around the contraption, laughing and passing comments to each other. A few were making bets. Marsallas was struggling violently but the grip of the *seniores* officers was unrelenting. His feet and hands were tied and Gratian watched as he was swung up and hung upside down above the barrel.

'Good quality vintage this, Marsallas. You'll enjoy it!' Valentinian said to the struggling figure. The watching troops roared. They loved a good execution and Valentinian was renowned for his innovation.

Marsallas was gradually lowered towards the barrel until his head could only be prevented from entering the wine by stretching his neck up at an acute angle. Even then his mouth was only just above the surface. After a few seconds the soldiers began chanting: *'Lower, lower, lower.'*

As his head disappeared beneath the surface, Marsallas began to drink. The absurd thought occurred to him that if he could drink it all, he would live. But he knew it was hopeless and when he could no longer hold his breath he cried out in frustration. The onlookers watched the bubbles rising to the surface and when at last the wine was still the crowd dispersed and returned to its business of preparing for war.

Valentinian went with Gratian to find his own notary, patting the boy affectionately on the shoulder as they squelched through the endless puddles which were beginning to join together, turning the camp into a quagmire. All about them soldiers hurried this way and that, saluting as they passed on their errands. A camp in transit had a thousand components to get moving. Arms, supplies, paperwork. Gods, the paperwork. Valentinian exhaled vociferously at the thought of it all. At length they reached a smaller tent and ducked under the flap to find a small man seated at a makeshift desk, writing tablets piled up on either side of him like some wavering, ancient siege engine.

Valentinian wiped the rain from his forehead. '*Salve* Orthrus.' The notary stood up to attention amidst a clatter of tablets. 'Sit down Orthrus, for Jupiter's sake. It's too cold and wet to stand on ceremony.'

The notary bowed and reseated himself, picking up the fallen artifacts from the muddy floor of the tent. 'What can I do for you, Caesar?'

'I need you to send word to Britannia.'

Orthrus bowed. 'To whom are we to deliver the message?'

'To Barnabas. He'll be in Corinium by now. At least he'd better be. And find Jovinus for me. We have to send a task force to Britannia, and quickly.'

The notary moistened his lips. 'The Lady Justina– '

'Yes,' Valentinian's face was dark, pinched with anxiety. 'She is taking Antonia to Corinium for the games. They are travelling anonymously, to show Antonia something of normal life in the provinces.'

'I recall the arrangement,' Orthrus said diplomatically. 'Caesar was keen to complete his daughter's education in this most practical way. And the Lady Justina was also very much in favour of– '

'So she was,' Valentinian nodded. 'So she was.' Sending his wife and daughter to Britannia for leisure and education had seemed a good idea at the time. The emperor bowed his head.

But have I sent them instead to their deaths?

Chapter 13

Freia marched on, shadowed by Iuillath, the Irish chieftain's magus. She was tired, close to exhaustion, but as one apparently vested with supernatural powers she could not afford to show any worldly vulnerability. The detachment of horsemen who had set off in pursuit of her brother had rejoined them briefly, but to Freia's dismay the riders bore no evidence to suggest what had become of the three fugitives. The riders had departed again after a brief consultation with Faelan, no doubt intending to plunder further towns and farms as they chanced upon them. Freia and the remnants of the Corinium entourage had tramped through the deep woodland for several days, with barely a few hours rest at a time and the speed of the Irish progress was such that some prisoners were simply falling to the ground as they walked. When this happened they would be kicked and struck with the butt end of a spear until they struggled to their feet. Freia estimated that, in total, the number of captives in the marching line must be around the hundred mark, a mixture of civilians – mainly poor, country folk – and the defeated military escort.

The chieftain, Faelan, regularly paced the line, back and forth, back and forth; with each pass he looked carefully at Freia as if to satisfy himself of her authenticity. She marched on, head erect, face impassive and as haughty as she could make it until his great lumbering figure receded back or forward up the line. Of all the prisoners the Roman soldiers fared the worst, and of all the soldiers Pavo seemed to be the one constantly under the scrutiny of his captors. At every opportunity he was singled out and beaten, either for marching too slowly, or for a mere glance at an Irish warrior. Freia wondered at his endurance; during one of the brief marching respites she saw the full extent of his injuries: his face was purple with bruising and one of his arms appeared to be broken. Freia had little medical knowledge but was able to use her status to move between the prisoners, placing a cool hand on a forehead here or binding a wound there. Iuillath followed her progress with interest, evidently hoping to learn something from his new, phantasmal charge. When she reached Pavo, she motioned for Iuillath to leave them. When he shook his head, she asked him plainly: 'I must have this one to myself,' and with his limited Latin he muttered a word of acquiescence and hobbled off to find other opportunities to dispense his magic.

Pavo squinted at her through half-closed eyes, puffy and swollen. 'Why are you helping me?' he managed, grimacing at the effort of speech. 'And what have you done to yourself? You look like death warmed up.' He attempted a smile and sank back onto the forest floor with a groan. Freia stole a look over her shoulder. 'That's exactly what the Irish believe,' she whispered, 'and it's saved my life. It might save yours too, if you let me see your arm.'

Pavo groaned again and let Freia clean his injuries as best she could. His elbow was clearly fractured, the bone swollen beneath the stretched skin. 'You'll need a surgeon,' she said, 'a trained medic. I can't do any more.' Pavo signalled with his eyes. She looked round to see

Iuillath returning, limping along with his carved pole. How he kept up with the battle-trained warriors was a mystery, yet he seemed to possess qualities of tenacity and doggedness in equal measure.

'Why am I helping you?' Freia shrugged. 'Because you're going to tell the truth if we ever get back to Calleva, that's why. And where is the Roman army when you need them?' she whispered hoarsely, before moving on to the next casualty where she made a show of gestures for Iuillath's benefit. She came presently to a small group of civilians. A small boy was being comforted by a woman, obviously of some status judging by her manner, and a girl Freia estimated to be twelve or thirteen years of age. They glanced up as she drew near and squatted beside them. The group eyed her with suspicion, no doubt believing her Irish due to her position in the marching column and the continual presence of Iuillath at her side. Freia smiled at the little boy. 'His name is Cassius,' the woman said. 'He's lost both parents.'

'We take it in turns to look after him,' the girl added. Her face was grimed with dirt but she sounded bright enough given the circumstances. 'He's sad but I've been cheering him up,' she grinned. 'What's your name – and why is your face so pale?'

'That's enough,' the woman said. Turning to Freia, she said in a hostile tone: 'Your accent is good for an Irish.'

Freia shook her head, nervously watching the Irish warriors getting up and stretching their limbs. Faelan strode amongst them, eager to be on the move. Every few paces he stopped and exchanged sharp words with any of his men he judged to be slow off the mark.

'I'm not Irish,' Freia whispered quickly. 'I am *Alamanni*; a slave in Calleva. But I appeared to them as if I had returned from the dead. They have not harmed me. If I can help you, I will.' She squeezed the woman's arm and was rewarded with a wan smile. 'Thank you,' the woman said. 'I will remember your kindness.'

The weather grew colder and wetter. Grey clouds scudded across the sky as they emerged from the forest into the open, lower lands of a river basin. The change of perspective went some way to reviving Freia's spirits as they entered the meadow with its proliferation of rye grass and meadow foxtail, but her main preoccupation was hunger. Never had she longed for Trophimus' kitchen as much as she did now. She would have gladly eaten the dogs' scraps rather than endure another day with so little food or water and when Faelan finally called a halt her stomach was a dull knot of hunger.

She watched as the Irish slaughtered a cow and began preparing a large fire on which to roast the meat. The captives could expect little but bones and fat to be thrown their way but she would eat what she was given; there was no guarantee when or if she would be fed tomorrow. Faelan had provided the odd piece of bread and once had fed her with part of a chicken he had found in a derelict farm. The bird had been pecking around the burned out buildings, foraging for whatever scraps were left after the buildings had been gutted in some earlier incident. The bird had met the same fate as its owners and Faelan watched with great interest as Freia twirled the remains of the chicken around her head then voraciously ate. Whatever his expectations he did not appear surprised that she still had need for earthly sustenance and she reasoned that she may as well make a show of it for the chieftain's benefit. Freia was blessed with a keen sense of direction and was confident that they had been travelling north west for several days. Now it seemed that they were following the river due north. She could only speculate as to their ultimate destination. Pragmatically, she admitted to herself that it was most likely to be Ireland, but she would board no Irish vessel. She would drown herself rather than let that happen. Freia looked up and smiled as Cassius ran up and dropped down beside her dejectedly. His face was dirt-encrusted and tear-stained. She greeted him sympathetically and he snuggled up to her, resting his head on her shoulder. She wondered what she could say to him today, what words of comfort she could impart. But the little boy was not in a talkative mood and she felt his head grow heavy as he fell into a deep sleep. It was better for him – sleep at least offered some promise of healing. She put her arm around him protectively and watched the smoke from the fire rise and drift above the oaks and alders at the edge of the meadow. From where she sat she could make out the opposite bank where the rushes and osier grew thick in the marshy environs of the churning water. Once she thought she saw movement; probably a heron or a fox, picking its way through the reeds. She was grateful for such distractions. It took her mind off the endless trudging that would come with the morning. Cassius shuddered in his sleep and she held him closer, drawing comfort from the warmth of his body. The wind began to blow and the sound of thunder rolled into the river valley from the north. The rain soon followed, heavy driving rain that brought a premature darkness to the water meadow and anxious frowns to the faces of the Irish.

Freia cradled the boy in her arms and hurried off to find his carers.

The Irish were marshalling the prisoners beneath the trees at the meadow's fringe but were hampered in their efforts by the power of the storm. Iuillath appeared at her side and beckoned, smiling as the lightning lit up the evening sky; he evidently enjoyed displays of power from the gods. Iuillath was tugging her sleeve and she had to bend her head close to his to hear what he was saying. He pointed to where, at the very edge of the group of prisoners, three shapes were edging towards the largest of the oaks, taking advantage of their guardian's lapsed attention. Iuillath hurried towards them, staff aloft. Freia followed, her thoughts tumbling over themselves as she wondered what to do. Reaching the oak before Iuillath she recognized the woman she had spoken to earlier, also her daughter and another man she didn't recognize. The woman screamed as she caught sight of Iuillath, grabbed her daughter's hand and ran towards the thick copse at the crest of the knoll. Iuillath screeched and lifted his staff to draw the attention of the warriors. One gave a cry of acknowledgement and broke into a sprint towards them, the others following close behind. Freia found her arms around the magus' neck, who began thrashing and pulling to escape. She caught hold of his staff and twisted; Iuillath screeched again and clawed at her face. Freia raised the staff and brought it down hard but Iuillath was stronger than she had anticipated. He parried the blow, which glanced off his shoulder and struck the trunk of an oak. At once, a huge flash lit up the area and Freia was thrown to the ground, releasing the staff to break her fall. Iuillath scrabbled for the totem as it rolled to the base of the oak and came to a standstill. There came another tremendous crash and Iuillath howled as a second lightning strike found its way to earth through his body.

Freia lay stunned for a moment then shakily got to her feet, amazed that she had survived. Iuillath's blackened body lay at the foot of the great tree, which had been cloven almost in two by the power of the thunderbolt. The pursuing Irish warriors had come to a standstill, muttering amongst themselves and pointing at Iuillath's remains. All eyes focused on Freia as, with a presence of mind she would marvel at later, she retrieved the smoking staff from the ground, raised it high and shrieked a cry of supremacy to the heavens. As one man, the Irish bowed their heads in wonder at the white-haired girl who could call down fire from the heavens to do her bidding.

Chapter 14

Marius' steps were leaden as he broke cover and found himself by a main road. He had trekked through the woods all night and was weary beyond belief. He had found no trace of the escapees from the riverside camp, nor any sign of Fraomar. For all he knew the Alamann had rescued Freia and made off with her to an unknown destination. He felt dispirited, cold, hungry and sick. He tramped onto the road, taking comfort in its solidity, and tried to clear his mind. He walked automatically, in a daze, his weakened condition numbing him to the dangers of solitary travel.

After what seemed an eternity a gift from the gods appeared in the form a roadside inn. Marius willed himself on, his muscles refuelled by the promise of rest, shelter, and perhaps even food. There was no sign of life. He paused at the gate and entered the courtyard. No one came to greet him; no one challenged him for his permit. He called out and his voice echoed eerily around the portico. In the centre of the building an arched wooden door stood ajar. Several *amphorae* were propped against the wall and a pile of logs lay stacked up beside them. The place appeared deserted.

Inside, Marius found a table and chairs. There was bread on the table and a pewter jug. He crammed bread into his mouth, washing it down with the contents of the jug. It was wine, flat but drinkable. He was overcome with fatigue. He climbed the wooden staircase to the upper rooms. The first contained a bed and another small table. He pulled off his sodden clothes, fell onto the bed and into a dream-haunted sleep. As he slumbered, fever slipped its tenuous fingers around him.

Day turned to night and night to day. Marius slept on, tossing and turning, tortured by vivid, fever-induced images. He was in a thick wood. Hooves thundered and a spectral horse galloped towards him. The rider's cloak swirled as he raised his spear and launched it at him. The weapon turned and spun, closing the distance, seeking his heart. Marius groaned and cried out. The phantom landscape faded to be replaced by Drufidius' dining room on the night of his encounter with Fraomar. Lucius Septimius stood in the centre of the room, sword drawn. Blood flowed from its tip, forming a pool on the mosaic. Now he was on the road to Corinium. Portius' face loomed close, pale and blood-flecked. 'I am dead Marius, but you must live,' the spectre nodded. 'You must live.'

All the while Marius felt that something was watching him from afar, something of indescribable malevolence. Marius twisted and turned, searching for his tormentor but it was hopeless; the evil was hidden. During brief spells of consciousness he felt he was not alone; sometimes he imagined water moistening his lips, but the dreams took him again and he could no longer distinguish reality from the fantasies of his sickness.

He woke with a start. The room was empty. Weak sunlight filtered through the window. A basin and jug stood on the bedside table. Marius sat up but his head began to spin and he sank back into the mattress. A heavy tread creaked on the staircase. Marius was so drained he could only lie helplessly and wait.

'So. You are back with us.' Fraomar came in carrying a loaf of bread and a pitcher of wine.

'*You!* I should kill you where you stand, you–' Marius felt a jolt of pain and slumped back onto the straw bolster. Mixed feelings raged inside him. On one hand he was relieved that his throat wasn't going to be slit by some outlaw, on the other he wanted to tear Fraomar limb from limb, however impossible that might be. 'How did you find me?' he croaked through a parched throat.

'It wasn't difficult. You Romans like your comfort,' the Alamann said.

'You left me for dead.'

'I did not,' Fraomar retorted. 'I intended to return for you, but when I did you had gone.' The gladiator shrugged.

'So, do I command such little trust?' Marius glared, 'that you have to render me unconscious rather than use my skills?'

'I told you that Freia's wellbeing is my business, not yours, Roman,' Fraomar snapped.

'Well then,' Marius challenged, 'did you succeed in your solo attempt?' He'd guessed the answer would be a negative and so he injected as much sarcasm into his voice as he could muster.

Fraomar turned away. 'No, I did not. It was an impossible task; the barbarians were too many and the storm only served to make the Irish more alert. But with you in the way, it would have been doubly impossible.'

'I do not think so,' Marius said disagreeably. 'Why do you treat me as an encumbrance?'

'Because you have little experience,' Fraomar said. 'Look at your hands.' He grabbed Marius by the wrist and turned his hand palm upwards. Marius tried to pull away but the grip was one of iron. 'See,' Fraomar said. 'Unmarked, uncalloused. A nobleman's hand.'

Marius snatched his hand away. 'I will prove you wrong, gladiator,' he said under his breath. 'And you will have cause to thank me.'

'We shall see.' Fraomar's expression was, as always, unreadable.

Marius looked away, irritated beyond measure. 'How long have I been asleep?'

'Four days in all.'

'Four days? But the Irish– ' Marius sat up with a jerk and wished he hadn't. His head felt as if it had been split with an axe. He groaned and collapsed again onto the bed.

'The Irish are still heading north – and we will catch them, do not fear. They have cattle and slaves. The bishop was right about that at least. Now, you must eat and drink.'

Marius found that his appetite was voracious. All traces of the fever had gone. He ate and then slept, this time without dreams of any kind, good or ill.

Two days later Marius stepped into the courtyard. It was late afternoon and the ground was dry – good riding weather. He was tugging the bridles to test them for wear and tear when he felt the vibration of a body of men on the march. He hurried to the gates. A troop of foot soldiers was approaching from the north. To his relief, they carried a Roman standard. Fraomar joined him and grunted when he saw the soldiers.

'This could be awkward,' Marius told the gladiator. I have no authority over the military. As far as they are concerned you're my prisoner and I'm returning you to the nearest town until you can be brought to trial.' He pointed to the stables. 'Fetch some rope – we'll bind your hands for their benefit.' To Marius' surprise, Fraomar complied without question. But the soldiers were already at the gate. He turned to welcome them.

As the soldiers entered the courtyard Marius could see that they were tired, battle-weary men. Their uniforms were stained and their beards unshaven. He could smell them too, a pungent blend of sweat and leather. Marius called a greeting as their commanding officer approached. He was unhelmeted and sweating profusely. A scar ran diagonally down the side of his cheek where it fused asymmetrically with the downward curve of his mouth. The overall effect was disturbingly maniacal. Marius could smell wine on the man's breath. He was big, almost Fraomar's height, but heavier.

'Who's this, then?' The soldier pointed to Fraomar whose head was bowed in feigned subjugation. 'These facilities aren't for the likes of him. What's your business?'

'I might ask you the same.' Marius spoke with as much authority as he could muster.

'We're on leave. Our business is to get a bath, a change of clothing and food in our stomachs,' the big man said.

'On *leave?*' Marius frowned. Unusual. Unlikely, even.

The soldier laughed. 'We've earned it, boy. Now what's your business with him? We don't trust longhairs, not after what we've seen.'

'He is a German, of the *Alamanni* tribe. I am escorting him to Corinium.'

'Bit out of your way, eh lad? Anyway, he'll be safe enough where I'm going to put him.' The soldier drew his sword. 'Stand aside.'

Marius was unprepared for the swiftness of the verdict. 'I will not. He is my responsibility.'

'Then I'll kill you too. Draw your weapon.'

Marius held up his hand. 'This is a not a military issue. As a member of the Corinium *Curia* you have no authority over me.'

'I don't care if you're a member of the King of Persia's harem – and *this* is my authority,' the soldier brandished his sword. 'Now stand aside.'

'I'll offer a wager.'

The troopers murmured their approval. One called out, 'Two *denarii* on Scapulus.' There was a ripple of laughter.

Marius thought quickly. 'No. If I win, we leave unmolested. If you win...' He shrugged. 'Then it's up to you.'

Scapulus' battered face split wider in a grin of anticipation. 'Agreed.' The centurion called for his helmet and began to make preparations for combat.

Marius caught Fraomar's expression as he led him to the portico. He pressed the handle of his dagger into Fraomar's bound fists. 'If I die,' Marius whispered, 'then take your chance. Find your sister and remember me to her.'

'He's using a *gladius* – watch him; he'll thrust forward. Your weapon is longer – make use of the advantage. Also his helmet is fractured,' Fraomar said in a low voice. 'The cheek fastening is perished. Strike his head on the right and you may dislodge it.'

'I know what a *gladius* looks like,' Marius replied tersely.

'Why am I waiting?' Scapulus sang tunelessly, banging his *gladius* against his shield.

Marius walked to the centre of the courtyard where Scapulus stood, feinting with his short, stabbing sword in his right hand. The soldiers' barracking died away as the two men squared up to each other.

Marius focused his concentration on Scapulus' sword-bearing arm. He could pick out each pore on the man's grime-stained face. The *gladius* moved back and forth searching for a way past Marius' guard. Disconcertingly, he could see the notches on the blade where the weapon had previously found its mark. *What am I doing?* Marius thought, *this man is a seasoned veteran. . .a centurion, no less. Think,* he told himself, *think of your training with Saturnus...*He felt the slow thud of his heart, tightened his grip and struck out. Scapulus' blade deflected it effortlessly, but Marius knew where to strike and his next cut caught the soldier a ringing blow on the side of his helmet. The rivets holding the cheek guard shattered and Scapulus disdainfully shook the dangling metalwork away. Marius thrust again and Scapulus parried. They circled once, twice. The big centurion had the advantage of experience and weight but these alone were no guarantee of victory, Marius knew. But he could feel himself tiring, the effort of sustained sword strokes beginning to sap what little energy he had. And then, without warning his leg gave way and he fell awkwardly, cracking his knee. The soldier's face leered above him, a sheen of sweat coating the labouring muscles of his forearms. Scapulus pressed home his workmanlike assault and Marius felt the biceps in his sword arm turn to strands of pain. Now he was on both knees. A terrible fatigue was creeping through his limbs and he almost welcomed it. It would be easy to relax, to lie down, for everything to be over. The pain would be momentary, or perhaps it would linger; he found that he didn't care. Let it end here then, in a bloody, futile fight with a man paid to defend the provinces but who was in the process of killing one of its own. Marius almost laughed at the irony and let his arm fall to his side.

Chapter 15

If Drufidius had disliked Nipius at first acquaintance he liked him even less now. They had ridden north west from Corinium along the even Roman road whilst twenty foot soldiers front and back afforded them the protection their status demanded. Each hour brought fresh sights of destruction caused by the storm. Trees were broken and scattered like kindling and the buildings of several farms they passed had been all but swept away by the ferocious winds of the previous night. For the most part, Drufidius kept his thoughts to himself. He had been shocked at the burned remains of Marius' villa, their first point of reference, and affronted at the callousness with which Nipius and his second in command, Terricula, had treated the civilians they had come into contact with. At Corinium they had spoken to the acting officer in command of the local militia, one Plautius, and so had learned of the attack on the road and the death of Portius, a man known to Drufidius from his past associations with Corinium. Nipius had nodded impatiently, his expression only changing when Plautius had told of an eyewitness account reporting three escapees; a tall, Germanic-looking barbarian with a younger passenger and a bald man in the attire of a Christian holy man.

Nipius broke the silence as they rode. 'So, how do you imagine your young decurion is managing a barbarian gladiator? Is he up to the job, or is he an effeminate hen-pecked desk-squatter like yourself?'

Drufidius ignored the slight. 'He may be young but he shows promise.'

'Does he indeed?'

'I have no doubt that he will acquit himself well. The boy has integrity.'

'*Integrity?* – you are hardly in a position to talk about *integrity*, councillor.' Nipius narrowed his eyes. 'I conducted a little interrogation of my own before I passed Marsallas into Valentinian's care.'

'You did?' Drufidius swallowed hard.

'And surprise, surprise; whose name should crop up during our conversation?'

'I have n–no idea,' muttered Drufidius.

Nipius caught Drufidius' halter and stopped the horse in mid-stride. The animal tossed its head and almost unseated Drufidius.

'No?' Nipius hissed. 'I'll give you a clue. Begins with 'B'; female; rhymes with an infamous queen of the Iceni. Shall I go on–?'

'By the gods of my household,' Drufidius stammered. 'I tried to tell her. I– '

To Drufidius' amazement, Nipius began to laugh. When he had control of himself he looked Drufidius up and down with a mixture of contempt and amusement. 'You fool. You have no idea how useful your indiscreet wife could be.' Nipius leaned over and slapped Drufidius' horse smartly on the neck; the animal whinnied and pawed the ground before moving on at a brisk trot. 'Tell me,' Nipius asked, 'what do you know about me, councillor? What have you heard?'

'Only that you are acting on Valentinian's behalf– '

Nipius threw back his head and roared with laughter. 'On his behalf? That Jew-worshipping, clay-moulding waste of space?' Nipius wiped a tear away with a gloved hand. 'For the moment, perhaps. In the long-term I act only for myself. And you could be useful in that regard.' Nipius was about to continue when one of the foot soldiers raised his spear and cried out, pointing the shaft skywards.

Ahead, a tall plume of black smoke stained the evening sky. Terricula issued several sharp orders. They halted while the leading two foot soldiers ran ahead. The remainder split and turned to face left and right with shields and *pilae* raised defensively. Drufidius felt a sense of dread. Forty troops, however skilled, were not sufficient to protect them from a barbarian ambush. But maybe the reports he had received at Calleva were true – that the barbarians had no stomach for a real fight. They had targetted rich villas, plundering and taking captives, meeting little opposition from unprepared country folk and smallholding peasants. Where in the name of Mars was the army? His last sighting of the militia had been during the afternoon of the Calleva games, following which all this misery had begun. The cohorts had moved off towards Londinium and had not been seen since. His thoughts were interrupted by the return of the foot soldiers who gave the all clear. Terricula nodded and signalled the troops to stand easy. He brought his horse alongside.

'No problems. Farm outbuildings – mostly burned out.'

'Survivors?' Nipius enquired.

Terricula shook his helmeted head. His horse pawed the earth impatiently. 'Just corpses so far, but they haven't checked *all* the outbuildings.'

'Then let us find out for ourselves.'

'Wanton destruction,' Drufidius said aloud. 'How can these savages claim to be civilized?'

Terricula laughed. 'Civilized? You should hope that they're Irish, not *Atacotti*, if we run into them.'

'Why?' Drufidius replied fearfully.

'Because the *Atacotti* will carve you up and eat you, bones and all, that's why,' Terricula finished triumphantly. 'A Saxon or an Irish would kill you outright and leave you to rot. Now that's civilized.'

Drufidius swallowed hard. They passed several bodies stretched out on the mud. One had been cut almost in two. Terricula deployed the troops to search the remains. He cantered slowly between the smoking shells. The smell of burning peat hung in the air.

'In here!' A trooper emerged from a low barn that still boasted part of its roof intact. Nipius' eyes lit up. The man disappeared into the barn and re-emerged pulling a screaming woman. Terricula dismounted, took hold of the woman's hair and slapped her. She raised her arm but Terricula caught her by the wrist. 'Aha. I like a woman with spirit.'

The woman looked up defiantly. When she spoke her voice was cultured. Terricula stepped back, suddenly unsure.

'Yes. I am of high birth. Not some farm wench you can manhandle.'

Drufidius' mouth fell open. 'By all the gods, the Lady Justina?'

Chapter 16

Marius crouched, waiting for death. There was a bitter taste in his mouth and everything had slowed down. He braced himself for the moment Scapulus' sword would bite into his neck.

But it never came. He felt instead the firm clap of a brawny hand on his shoulder. Dazed, Marius looked up. Scapulus grinned and saluted. Getting shakily to his feet, he faced Scapulus and became aware that the soldiers were applauding the fight.

'Not bad for a youngster,' Scapulus said. 'What do you think, lads?' He appealed to the men who shouted their agreement. One of them called out – 'Nearly had you with that head stroke, though, didn't he?' to which Scapulus scowled and raised his sword as if to slice the jibe from the soldier's mouth.

'Did you think I'd kill you, eh?' Scapulus asked, sheathing his sword with a flourish.

'The thought crossed my mind,' Marius said, 'that the likes of you and your men are supposed to *protect* Roman citizens, not dispatch them to the afterlife.'

Scapulus flung his huge head back and guffawed with laughter. 'To tell the truth, councillor, I'm surprised to find any left to protect.'

'Well here are two for starters, centurion.' All heads turned to the gate, where two men stood, watching the scene. Marius shook his head in amazement as the man who had spoken approached with outstretched hand, which Marius shook warmly.

'Barnabas. Good to see you – and Saturnus– ?'

'Is making a good recovery,' Barnabas clapped him on the shoulder. 'And sends his greetings.'

'Thank the gods,' Marius said with relief. At last, some good news.

'Wait!' Scapulus strode towards them. 'Sorry to break up the reunion, but you're forgetting something.'

Marius turned to face him.

'Your fate is my decision; that was the agreement.' The big man nodded, waiting for a response.

'Then make your decision quickly, centurion.' Marius glanced uneasily at Fraomar whose expression was, as usual, totally unreadable under his thick blond moustache.

'My decision is– '

Scapulus was enjoying himself. A few soldiers called out suggestions but Scapulus waved them away dismissively 'Wait for it, lads, wait for it. My decision is. . . that nothing is ever agreed satisfactorily on an empty stomach, so we'll call the wager settled if you lead us to the food and drink.'

As they sat eating and drinking with Scapulus and his troops, Scapulus told of their skirmish with an Irish war party.

'You were with Fullofaudes further north?' Barnabas asked with interest, 'and the news there is as bad?'

The big man nodded. 'Worse. They were waiting for us. We had our backsides kicked into next week and no mistake. Never knew what hit us. They cut the *dux* into four pieces, apparently, and stuck them up on poles like the butchers they are. But I was out of it by then. Lucky to get out at all.' He looked at his men. 'We all were. Only thing for it was to head south – that's where we ran into the Irish.'

'But how were you caught napping?' Marius asked. 'The *dux* had experienced units under his command.'

'We reckon they had access to information about our comings and goings. They knew exactly where to wait and where our weaknesses lay.'

'The *Atacotti?*' Barnabas prompted.

Scapulus wiped his mouth with the back of his hand and nodded. 'Yes. The *Atacotti*. And let me tell you those barbarian bandits don't fight by any recognized rules of honour.' He glared at Fraomar. 'What makes you think you can trust him? I'd still put him to the sword. You'd sleep easier.'

'I have no reason to mistrust him,' Marius said. *Apart from when he knocked me out cold.* He didn't share this thought with Scapulus.

'Valentinian's giving his people a hard time on the Rhine frontier,' Scapulus retorted. 'What loyalty does he owe us? It'll be a knife in the ribs at the first opportunity.'

'I have promised him safe passage and that is what he shall have,' Marius spoke quietly but firmly. He knew he had to assert his authority or Scapulus and his men would take the law into their own hands. 'You would do well to respect him,' Marius went on. 'I have seen no better combatant in the arena.'

'He is a gladiator?' Scapulus' interest was aroused. 'Then he is a slave.'

'He is my companion. If peace returns then his status will be reevaluated. For now, it matters little.' Marius paused, wondering whether to suggest what was on his mind.

'I shall be honest with you,' he said eventually. 'The barbarians destroyed my house and killed my good friend, an old man who deserved a better death. I have no intention of returning Fraomar to whatever authorities may still exist at Corinium, or Calleva for that matter, but he is nevertheless my responsibility and mine alone.' Marius watched carefully for Scapulus' reaction. When he was satisfied he had the man's attention, he made his entreaty: 'Put aside your enmity towards Fraomar and help us. Then I can at least promise that you will have the opportunity to settle the score with the *Atacotti*.'

'I may have useful information in that regard, Marius,' Barnabas added. 'The Irish are heading for Mona.'

'Mona, eh? The isle of mystery.' Scapulus eyed Barnabas suspiciously. 'I know it. Flat as a board. A few farms, a few settlements. Nothing special. Miserable posting.'

'I have reason to believe the invasion forces will converge there,' the bishop said. 'They will use it as a stepping stone to Ireland. The island can be defended at the straits, and there are natural harbours at its western point.'

Scapulus said: 'Have you obtained this information via your spiritual connections, holy man?'

'I have a mission to the western provinces,' Barnabas said. 'With my understudy, Romanus.' The bishop pointed to the studious young man sitting in a corner, apparently lost in thought. 'And you're right. My agenda is not altogether worldly but I keep my ear to the ground; old connections are apt to link together.' The bishop looked at each of them in turn. 'My sources spring from a reliable authority. And I have been asked to give you as much help as I can.'

There was a pause while they digested Barnabas' words.

'Thank you, Barnabas,' Marius said finally. 'Mona is a logical destination for the Irish. But who is behind all this? Who has brought these warring tribes together?'

Barnabas hesitated. 'I think you know the answer to that already, Marius.'

'Paulus. *Catena.*' Marius felt his fists clench and his blood rise with a fierce joy.

Barnabas nodded. 'He is in command of the fortress at Cunedum, the north western tip of Mona. There he is gathering strength along with booty from his Irish alliance. Slaves, gold, silver.'

Scapulus' expression registered his interest. 'A traitor, eh? Well, our wages are long overdue,' he said, scraping a hole in the earth beneath a cracked floorboard with the tip of his spearhead. After a moment he looked up and smiled the smile that was almost a grimace. 'Well, why not? I'll put it to the lads. A day to rest up and recoup their strength and they'll be after something to keep them occupied. They'll not take much persuading if what I'm hearing is true.'

'You invited them to ride with us?' Fraomar's displeasure was apparent. 'Why do we need them? They are deserters, *mercenaries.*'

'They're all we've got – and they are loyal to the emperor,' Marius retorted, 'or they would have killed us both out of hand.'

'Loyal? They're freebooters – if the holy man hadn't mentioned the spoils they'd have killed us as soon as our backs were turned,' Fraomar said.

'Strange. That's what Scapulus said about you.'

Fraomar swung himself into his saddle without another word and trotted out of the courtyard. Marius shook his head in exasperation and followed the Alamann to the head of Scapulus' ordered column. The centurion gave the signal to depart and, with a final trumpet blast, they left the posting inn behind.

A frost had coated the earth during the early hours and the ground was hardened into a comfortless bed. Marius dreamed he was entombed, lying as if paralyzed on a stone dais. The cold intensified and blackness closed around him. He could make out a shape in the darkness, human yet distorted, as if bent in the agony of some tortuous death. The light grew brighter, picking out the contours of the writhing silhouette. Marius lay still, sweat drying cold on his forehead. The figure curled in upon itself forming a ball of flame, then spread into a chain of fire. Marius felt its heat and his mouth opened in a silent scream. A face took shape in the fire, eyes first, then a mouth; then lips curled in a thin, malicious smile.

'In the name of the gods of the eternal city, be still!' A voice hissed in his ear and a firm hand covered his mouth. Marius struggled to free himself. 'Be *still!*' the voice came again. 'You'll wake the whole camp and advertise our presence to every bandit within earshot!'

Marius relaxed as he recognized Scapulus' voice. The dream had been so real he could remember every detail. Shuddering, he muttered a vague apology and sat up. 'What time is it?'

'Time to be moving on,' Scapulus replied. 'Here, try some soldier's wine.' He handed Marius an evil smelling cup. 'Thanks.' Marius drank and almost gagged at the bitter taste.

'Thought that'd do the trick,' Scapulus growled.

Marius groaned and massaged his limbs. After a frugal breakfast the party was back in the saddle. The dawn sun cast red and orange rays across the bleak landscape, warming the exposed boulders and rocks that seemed to erupt from the rough ground. The spine of mountains that ran down the centre of the land of the *Ordovices* rose to one side like an axe head, as if embedded there by some ancient race of giants. The shafts of light picked out the drops of moisture that clung to the scrub of the valley floor and dazzled Scapulus' men who had hurriedly broken camp after Fraomar's dawn reconnaissance. Delicate web traceries covered the tough grass like curtains of vapour spun from the breath of some mountain deity. High above a solitary kite circled, drifting on the currents of air as it scanned the ground for carrion. Marius shivered and drew his cloak about him to maximize the effect of the warm air rising from his horse's body. Fraomar rode alongside while Scapulus had taken up position a length ahead, his helmet turning from side to side as he watched for signs of ambush. Marius felt the weight of the leather bag in his tunic and wondered again about Barnabas; for a holy man he seemed to know a great deal about the barbarian conspiracy.

Chapter 17

A sudden jolt brought Freia back to the present. In her half-awake state her mind had wandered back to the darkened Callevan streets and she was searching, searching for something…her hand involuntarily felt for the bag. The jewels, her mistress …

'Buitseach!' Faelan drew alongside her and pointed. She saw a fortress in the distance, shrouded in sea-mist. This, then was their objective. Freia's tongue clove to the roof of her mouth. She was thirsty and hungry but she was still alive – and after the events at the river encampment this was not something she took for granted. Her lips moved in prayer as Faelan strode to the head of the column. Whatever lay ahead was beyond her power to control. She felt as if her destiny were somehow caught up in the fogbound landscape and damp air of this island. She knew its name: The Isle of Mona. It was a bleak place, a place of secrets and sorcery. Her brother had told her a story once of the Romans long ago who crossed the waters to fight the priests of the old religion. Mona had been their haven but they had fallen nevertheless to the power of the Roman sword, turning the waters of the straits red with the blood of their sacrifice. And what secrets had perished with them? Did these yet lurk amongst the rocks and tombs, or had they vanished into the sea, never to return? There was a palpable fear amongst the Irish, as if they too felt the weight of the island's bloody past.

Freia felt a small hand in hers and looked down at the girl, whose wide eyes seemed to echo her own thoughts. The girl with no name. Again Freia wondered at the girl's reluctance to disclose her identity. All she could get out of her was that her mother had told her not to tell, and the girl was sticking to that command come what may. Freia's heart went out to her; she and her mother had fled the night of the storm only to become separated in the confusion and she had been recaptured by the nimble Irish scouts. Freia could only imagine the mother's anguish and had half expected the woman to return to the camp but she was apparently made of sterner stuff and had probably reasoned that such an action would have been suicidal. She had been right. Recriminations had been swift and merciless. Of the eleven prisoners who had escaped, seven had been recaptured and executed and two had been tortured in front of the remaining captives. Freia's status, however, had been elevated by the incident of Iuillath's death. Many had seen what had occurred and the eyewitnesses Freia had spoken to amongst the prisoners were clear in their testimony. As Freia had wielded the magus' staff, fire had descended from the heavens and burned him up. This apparent miracle had granted her immunity from the warriors' attention; only Faelan continued to have social interaction with her, communicating with grunts and sign language now that his interpreter was dead. What his intentions were for her future she did not know, but it appeared that whatever role Iuillath had played it now fell to her to divine the intentions of the gods, with no blame attached to her for the death of the Irish occultist. Freia had used her status sparingly, not wishing to draw suspicion but had nevertheless been successful in keeping several prisoners alive. Pavo was one of her beneficiaries and although his wounds were serious, he was able to continue to march. Those of his colleagues who had proved less able had been decapitated and left behind where they fell. No doubt this spurred the soldier on, but Freia had slim confidence in his ability to keep up the punishing Irish regime. The girl squeezed her hand and she looked up. Her heart leapt. Roman troops were approaching on the double. But there was something wrong: the warriors did not seem to regard the newcomers as a threat. Faelan strode to meet them, planting his axe in the ground and splaying his feet. The Roman commander approached and the two men signalled in some pre-determined sign language. Freia caught Pavo's eye and guessed at the murderous thoughts running through his mind as he took in the scene and realized that the troops were in alliance with the Irish. Faelan stood back and the Romans were suddenly among them, herding the prisoners towards a stockade to the east of the fortress. A rough hand fell on her shoulder but Faelan was at her side, threatening the soldier with a shake of his axe. The soldier shrugged and, plucking the girl from Freia's hand, dragged her off to the stockade. Freia dug her fingernails into her hands. She raised her hand and called a word of comfort, doubting in her heart that she would see her young charge again.

'You!'

Freia turned to see the commander of the Roman troop staring at her.

'Yes, you, Blondie. You spoke Latin, so don't pretend you don't understand. Tell this hairy oaf that Paulus wants to see him,' he pointed to Faelan, 'I can't get the message into his thick skull. I don't care how you tell him, just tell him.'

Freia had no idea who the commander was referring to but she could smell his fear. She attracted Faelan's attention and pointed to the fortress. The commander stamped his feet impatiently. Freia could see movement on the battlements, soldiers peering down at the new arrivals. Freia shivered as Faelan grunted something in his native tongue and gesticulated with the axe. The Roman commander led the way to the fortress gates. Freia followed, having performed a series of threshold feints and passes with her hands to satisfy Faelan's need for his gods' approbation. Watched curiously by both Roman and Irish warriors, they passed through the gates and disappeared into the fort.

Freia could hear the slap of the sea against the keep walls and caught a glimpse of grey waves through a slit window as they followed the commander up a winding stone staircase. The commander rapped sharply on an arched door and stood aside to let them enter. Faelan barged in and stopped abruptly. She saw at once the reason for the barbarian's hesitation: a man was sitting in the centre of the room, but such a man as Freia had never seen before. His head was bald and his ears glinted with circlets of gold. His eyes, deep shadowed sockets, seemed to suck her in. She couldn't tear herself from that gaze, which felt as if they reached into her very soul, searching and probing. When at last the figure spoke the voice was soft and even, but laced with an almost physical menace.

'Step forward, Caelius,' the figure said, 'and make your report.'

'You wished to see the Irish chieftain,' the Roman commander said. 'Name of Faelan. Speaks no Latin.'

'And this is his – interpreter?' Paulus enquired.

'She belongs to him. Some kind of religious function, I believe.'

'Is that so? But you do speak the emperor's tongue? You do understand me?' Paulus looked Freia up and down.

'Yes, *dominus*,' Freia replied. Whoever this was he was evidently used to being obeyed without question.

'Good. Then tell the barbarian this: we have extra space because Crimthann has provided additional ships. He is to return to the mainland and return with a further batch of slaves and as much booty as he and his men can manage. Which will be considerable – or he will answer to me.'

Freia conveyed the message in the sign language she had developed. At the mention of the name Crimthann, Faelan shook his head emphatically and slammed his axe on the floor.

'Problem, Caelius?' Paulus asked, softly.

Faelan stepped forward. He raised the axe and blocked Caelius' attempt to come between him and Paulus. Paulus remained seated, and simply raised his hand. Faelan was immediately pushed back as if by some invisible hand. The axe fell from his grip and the barbarian was pinned against the door, his muscular arms flattened against the wood.

'I won't tolerate unreasonable behaviour,' Paulus told the struggling chieftain. He let his arm fall and Faelan staggered forward, almost losing his balance. The barbarian retrieved his axe, turned on his heels and was gone.

'Keep an eye on him, Caelius,' Paulus said.

The Roman commander saluted. Freia made as if to follow but to her horror the soft voice called her back. Caelius hesitated but Paulus waved him away. 'I'll look after this one.'

'Faelan needs her. I would advise– '

'When I require advice, Caelius, I will ask for it.' The eyes narrowed. Caelius saluted, the door closed and Freia was alone with Paulus.

Paulus rose from his chair and paced the room. 'Something of a healer, I understand?'

'I have a little ability.' Freia tried to master the fear that gripped her. There was something about this man that iced the blood in her veins.

'Good. Then you will be of infinitely more use here than in the field of battle.' Paulus stopped by the narrow slit recess. A shaft of light flicked across his face and he moved aside as if stung. 'Sick prisoners are no good to anyone,' he said, 'so you may go about your business in the stockade.'

Freia bowed, awash with relief. She made as if to leave but Paulus called her back a second time.

'First,' Paulus settled into his chair and steepled his fingers beneath his chin, 'tell me about yourself. You're not Irish, that's clear. More Saxon, by your look.'

'I am of the *Alamanni*,' Freia said.

'Ah. Of course. German. Experts in forest lore. Herbal remedies and so on.'

'I have some knowledge, yes.'

'Don't be coy – you're a clever one, I can tell.' Paulus smiled. 'You're a survivor, as am I. And you've impressed that barbarian buffoon. Pulled the wool over his eyes. I wonder how you did that?' He laughed, a low chuckle. 'I like your spirit.' He beckoned. 'Come here.'

Freia made her legs move until she was standing beside him. Her flesh crawled.

Paulus placed a hand on her cheek and she stifled the urge to scream. His hand was as cold as the stones beneath her feet and his eyes were the deepest green, their pupils, she thought with a shudder, slitted like a snake's.

He tilted her chin. 'Do you know who I am?'

'No, my lord,' Freia replied honestly. She wanted to look away but the eyes forbade it. They were pools of emerald, deep as the ocean, holding her fast.

'No,' he murmured. 'Of course you don't.'

Paulus moved away, hands clasped behind his back and Freia let out her breath, which she realized she had been holding.

'I was a man of the empire,' Paulus said. 'An imperial notary of high repute. Sadly, those days are over,' the smile returned, revealing a row of small white teeth. 'Sadly for the emperor, I mean, not myself.'

Paulus was talking, Freia realized, not to her but to himself.

Suddenly he spun and faced her. 'Tell me, have you ever been falsely accused?'

Freia nodded. *Oh yes*, she thought, *oh yes*.

'As was I, as was I,' Paulus said. 'They dogged my steps to Africa. And condemned me to be burned.' Paulus leaned on the chair's backrest. 'The fools,' he muttered, 'they had no idea what they were dealing with. You see, by then I had acquired a deep knowledge of Africa. Such knowledge, my young diviner, as you can scarcely imagine.'

'Yes, my lord.'

Paulus clapped his hands. 'Yes my lord! No, my lord!' He chuckled. 'You are a very accommodating young lady, are you not? I could put you to much better use than that barbarian clod.' He drummed his fingers on the backrest for a moment, then appeared to arrive at a decision 'Come with me, witch, and let's see what you make of my new friends. They should be here anytime.'

A westerly wind was blowing inland from the Irish Sea, filling the sails of the long ships in the final stages of their journey. Gulls, corpulent and colour-matched with the grey sky, clustered around the masts, wheeling and diving as the Irish vessels drew closer to the harbour.

Freia stood next to Paulus and watched Caelius organize his men on the quayside. Paulus then addressed the troops. As he spoke the Irish sails gusted in the bay, providing a spectacular backdrop for Paulus' rhetoric which, to Freia's ear, seemed designed to cement the loyalty of his supporters. As he concluded his speech the soldiers cheered and clashed their shields. Paulus gestured to the ships. 'Our allies! Let us welcome them!' The troops cheered with renewed vigour as the first cast anchor and lowered its sails. Paulus went along the quay to meet the Irish king, Crimthann, an unmistakeable figure with braided hair and an intricately embroidered cloak of green and gold. His chin was shaven, but in the Irish style his upper lip was resplendent with luxuriant moustaches. He wore a gleaming helmet of bronze inlaid with swirling patterns and at his side hung a sword, sheathed in silver and gold. There was a moment of silence, the air hanging heavy with anticipation until Paulus advanced and clasped Crimthann's hands in his own. A cheer echoed across the bay, startling the gulls into panic-driven flight. Freia swallowed as she saw the king's gaze flicker past Paulus to rest upon her. She murmured a prayer under her breath. The Son of God had protected her this far, now let Him show her the way forward. 'Deliver us from evil,' she muttered under her breath: '*Sed libera nos a malo.*'

Freia winced as a roar rent the smoke-filled banqueting hall. Crimthann's retinue and Caelius' men seemed to be enjoying themselves and the bonds being forged evidently pleased Paulus and the Irish king. Even the cautious Caelius seemed more relaxed.

'Friendly lot, aren't they?' Paulus observed, fingering the handle of his knife, 'good to see them getting on well, isn't it Caelius?'

Caelius forced a smile and helped himself to a draught of wine from the communal pitcher. He tasted it and grimaced. Freia noticed the Irish king's gaze resting on him with amusement. Crimthann fingered his long moustaches thoughtfully, his keen eyes piercing the gloom of the lamplit hall. 'It is not to your taste, Roman? Well, there will be better to come.' He gestured to the open hall. 'Tonight the men are relaxing but they are keen to explore your plentiful land.' His voice was sonorous, commanding respect, his movements relaxed. He reminded Freia of a wild cat, composed and confident, yet ready to spring into action at the slightest provocation.

'And you, my lord,' Paulus said, 'will be busy with your nuptials. The lady will be joining us shortly.'

Crimthann's eyes creased in response. 'They have arrived?'

'As I promised.'

Freia stepped back from the table, hoping to slip away but Paulus turned his head. 'Stay close, my young healer. I may need your advice. And– ' he reached out and clasped her arm. 'this is not the place to be wandering alone – even for someone with your knack of survival.'

'The Saxons have proved their worth?' Crimthann asked.

'They have achieved great success in the north and east. That pompous ass Nectarides will give us no further trouble. The coast is clear, and a cordon has been placed around the shores of Gaul to inhibit any interference from his imperial majesty. Not that he is in any position to retaliate. Sadly, he is kept busy by the Germans and is unable to join our party.'

Crimthann and his Irish lords roared with laughter.

Paulus continued as the laughter died down. 'The Lady Lawenya's beauty has won her many suitors,' Paulus said. 'I am sure she will please you.'

'Has she not chosen well?' An Irish lord spread his hands to the gathering for their communal assent.

'My good lord,' Paulus feigned mock astonishment. 'Had the choice been truly hers, could she have chosen a Saxon over a Scot and still have been blessed by the gods?'

'Which gods?' Crimthann asked. 'The gods of Rome? I imagine your allegiance to them is long past.'

'I am owned by no god,' Paulus replied. He addressed the company. 'I have yet to find one worthy of my attention.'

The Irish lords muttered to themselves and Crimthann shook his head ruefully. 'We ignore the gods at our peril, Paulus. It is a brave or foolish man who would seek to do otherwise.'

Freia watched for Paulus' reaction. When it came it was diplomatic and chilling in equal measure. 'My lord is entitled to his opinion,' Paulus said, 'but there are stranger things than the gods on this earth to reckon with.'

Crimthann grunted and refilled his cup. At that moment, an announcement caused all heads to turn to the hall portal. 'My lords, the Saxons.'

Into the hall strode four Saxon warriors but it was the lady in their midst who drew the attention of the revellers. For the first time Freia forgot her situation and gasped at the splendour of the woman's clothing. She was dressed in a flowing multicoloured gown that reached down to her ankles. Her head was adorned with a golden torc, her fair hair interwoven with tiny precious stones which glinted in the torchlight. Her white arms were graduated by glittering bracelets and her eyes were clear and pure. An amber necklace lay against the fair flesh of her neck. She was tall, and very young. 'The Lady Lawenya,' Paulus said softly, 'our star of the north. And the beginning of the end for Rome's rule over Britannia.'

Chapter 18

Scapulus withdrew his sword and pointed. Across the water lay Mona. It was raining, a fine spray that mingled with the salt of the sea to create a maudlin atmosphere, as if the spirits of the isle remembered the dark days of slaughter. Marius pointed out a few rickety coracles and a larger vessel which lay abandoned, no doubt the property of local fishermen careless that any should take an interest in their craft.

Scapulus made a quick assessment. 'Should get us across – who'll be the ferryman? How are your water skills, barbarian? I'll give you a coin to Hades!' He cocked his head at Fraomar who was standing with his back to the water, facing the lowlands over which they had ridden. The gladiator gave no sign that he had heard the question. Suddenly one of the centurion's men cried out. Marius followed the soldier's pointing finger. Silhouetted against the grey sky he saw what Fraomar had already spotted: two crosses set back from the straits on a small hummock. The circling birds told them all they needed to know about the two unfortunates nailed to the wooden beams.

'That's a sight I've not seen for many a long year,' Scapulus murmured quietly.

'It is an outlawed practice,' Marius grimaced. Who would do this even to his worst enemy?'

Scapulus laughed harshly. 'Whoever's responsible for that is no respecter of the law.'

The presence of the hanging bodies affected the optimistic mood of the party, and Barnabas insisted on taking them down and giving them a proper burial. 'Whoever they were, they didn't deserve a death like that,' the bishop muttered grimly.

'Didn't your god die on a cross like this, bishop?' Scapulus asked with his twisted grin.

'In a manner of speaking, yes,' Barnabas said, 'but there was a great deal more to it than you suppose.'

They watched Scapulus' soldiers filling in the shallow graves. The bodies were naked and unidentifiable. 'Pull the crosses down as well,' Scapulus instructed them, 'no sense in upsetting the locals more than they have been already.'

'Agreed,' Marius accompanied Scapulus to the water's edge. 'We should make camp here. I don't think a night crossing is a good idea. There's no telling what's waiting on the other side.'

'Makes sense,' Scapulus agreed. 'this whole business is risky enough already without splashing around in the dark.'

'Rest,' Barnabas said, 'you'll need your wits about you tomorrow.' It was the beginning of the second watch and Fraomar had relieved Marius at the camp's perimeter. Scapulus and his men sat a few paces away, quietly talking and drinking. There was an occasional burst of raucous laughter as the soldiers showed their appreciation of a punch-line or scrap of army gossip.

'I have dreams,' Marius said distractedly, 'and sleep no longer refreshes me,' he stared into the fire. 'I see him in the flames. Waiting. And when I close my eyes, he is there.'

'Paulus?'

Marius nodded.

Barnabas spoke again. 'He is powerful. But Marius–' the bishop paused, as if considering whether it was right to continue. 'There is one more powerful, if you would trust Him.'

Marius made a dismissive gesture. 'Your crucified god?'

'Let me tell you more,' the bishop offered. As if drawn by the exchange Romanus, Barnabas' protégé, came and sat alongside. He glanced nervously at Marius and extended his hands to the warmth of the fire.

Barnabas began.'I will tell you the story, but thank God, it is more than a story – it is the truth of our condition. And more importantly, the remedy to it.'

Marius was tired but felt drawn by a curiosity more powerful than his weariness. 'Very well, apothecary of souls, I'll listen to you,' he grinned in resignation, 'tell me your story.'

'In the beginning,' Barnabas said, 'when the world was new, the Father of all created man from the dust and set him in a garden. A paradise called Eden. The man was given charge of the world, the animals and plants and all things that grew. He was given a helper, when the Father saw that he had need, and the Father made the woman. The man and the woman knew God, and God walked with them in the garden. It was a perfect world, free from evil. The Father gave the man and woman all things; mastery of the natural world and the animals. But there was one condition. He told them that they must not eat of the forbidden fruit of one tree in the garden.' Barnabas paused and firelight flickered in his keen eyes.

'Time passed and the man and woman were happy, but a great evil lay in wait. Satan, the father of lies, took the guise of a serpent, and when the woman was alone he asked her: 'Did the Father *really* say you were not to eat of the fruit? For if you do, you will become like Him, and know all there is to know.' Barnabas paused. The camp was silent now, but for the occasional soldier's snore or the quiet passing of a sentry.

The bishop went on: 'The woman listened to the serpent; she took the fruit, ate it and gave some to the man. And at that moment of disobedience, mankind was lost, cut off from the creator.' Barnabas bowed his head. 'The whole of creation was rent from top to bottom, from the stars in the sky to the very earth on which the man and the woman stood in the garden. Then God came looking for them.'

'What did they do?' Marius was intrigued.

'They hid. What else could they do? The Father, who had given them everything they needed, who had been their friend, could now no longer walk with them, nor even look upon them. They had sinned. The curse was given. Death entered the world.'

'But it was a trivial thing surely, to eat the fruit. Surely they could have been forgiven, given another chance?'

Barnabas paused, considering his reply. 'You are making the same mistake others have made before, are making still and will make again.' He leaned in close, linking his hands together to illustrate his point. 'Listen Marius, the Father is perfect, He is holy, set apart. He dwells in purity and light. He cannot look upon anything that is tainted. But – and this is a significant but – He is also loving and just.'

'Well, if he is loving and just then he should also forgive.'

Barnabas clapped his hands. 'Yes, exactly! And He does. But, here is the puzzle: how does He forgive and satisfy His perfect justice at the same time? How can He punish the crime and lovingly forgive? It's a dilemma. A divine dilemma.'

'He *did* punish the man and the woman,' Marius frowned. 'He banned them from the garden, is it not so? And they died estranged from their paradise?'

'They died. And death has been a part of life from their time onwards. It is sin's curse. But not just physical death – spiritual death. Such a death is a direct result of sin; it must be so.'

Marius spread his hands. 'Then where is the forgiveness, the fairness?'

Barnabas smiled. 'The scriptures are clear. Even as the Father cursed the human race, he promised a Saviour. A Redeemer. Someone to pay the price of sin. And Satan, the father of lies, was also cursed,' Barnabas went on, 'he fled trembling, knowing his doom had been sealed. 'You will strike His heel', said the Father to Satan, 'but He will crush your head.' It is a reference to Christ on the cross, where the hosts of Satan's army flung their venom at the Saviour. This was God's justice; He cursed his own Son.'

'And this Son, this Saviour was *Yeshua* the Jewish rabbi?'

'It was He. The Jewish scriptures foretold His birth. The signs were unmistakeable to those who would give them heed. Sadly his own race, for the most part, did not, even if the accounts of His life here on earth leave little room for doubt that he was of divine origin.'

Marius' brow furrowed. 'But how does his death affect us. It *cannot* affect us, surely?'

'Yeshua knew that He was born to die, to bear the consequences of man's sin. Mine, yours, all men's, past and future.' The bishop noted the incredulity on Marius' face. 'Yes, it is amazing. God's justice was satisfied in His

Son's punishment; this same Son revealed The Father's spotless love and character by living a perfect life – the life you and I could never live, even if we tried for a thousand years. An exchange was therefore made possible by His death. A great exchange.'

'Exchange?'

Barnabas paused again to emphasize his words 'Yes. Our sin for His perfection.'

'But how– '

'By trusting Him, by believing in what He achieved. This forgiveness is for all who accept Him, for all who simply take Him at his word and trust Him. There is nothing else to be done. He has done it all.' Barnabas leaned over and gripped Marius' shoulder. 'This is the gospel, Marius. There will be many seeking to distort its truth, to add to it, to take away from it, even to ridicule it. Priests, bishops, emperors. All may profess unity with Christ, but in their hearts, perhaps– '

'They have not accepted Him, and are yet uncleansed?' Marius frowned, turning the idea over in his mind.

'Just so. It is into your heart that He will look when you are called to stand before Him. Not at your outward professions, or your good deeds. If you truly trust in Yeshua, the Christ, it will be His righteousness that protects you as you stand before the Father, not your own soiled life. If there was another way to the Father, would He not in His wisdom have told us? He did not spare his own Son, so that we could be freed from an eternal death.'

'It's astonishing,' Marius said, 'the most unlikely thing I've ever heard.'

'But does it not have the ring of truth about it?' Romanus piped up. 'I have read the Jewish scriptures and they all point to the One who was to be born into the world.'

'Do you imagine that our race could invent such – to quote your own words – an astonishing solution?' Barnabas said.

'No,' Marius said thoughtfully, 'I don't imagine we could.'

'And as the scriptures say,' Romanus chipped in, 'if *He* is with you, then who can stand against you?'

They fell into a contemplative silence and eventually Marius drifted into a deep sleep, for once untroubled by the visions that had haunted his nights and troubled his days since the name *Catena* had re-entered his life.

Fraomar shook Marius awake. 'We have company.' Marius felt the slow thud of his heart in his chest as he searched in the early light. Somewhere between the silhouetted mountains to the south and the paler hue of the heath land, he was able to make out a slight flux which quickly swam into focus as a company of soldiers, moving at speed.

Scapulus had swiftly organized his men into battle readiness. They advanced at Scapulus' command, fixed their shields and raised their lances.

Fraomar stood his ground, disdainful of Scapulus' shield wall.

Marius could pick out the helmets of the approaching troops clearly. How many? Thirty? Forty?

Two horsemen preceded the soldiers, another pair bringing up the rear. The first rider approached Fraomar. He was helmet less and his iron-grey hair was clipped short. Behind, his men waited in silence. Marius noticed with dismay that these included a company of archers whose bows were clearly visible amongst the bristling spearheads. Fraomar stood his ground. He had not drawn his sword, nor had he raised the borrowed shield at his feet but instead stood confidently, legs apart and arms folded.

The rider looked Fraomar up and down. 'You look the part,' he said, 'I would guess you to be our man.' He turned and signalled. Another rider moved forward to join him. From his gait on the horse, he was clearly less than an expert. Marius peered into the gloom. There was something familiar. . . surely not. *Drufidius?* The first rider spoke again.

'This is the man?'

Drufidius nodded in affirmation.

'Then I have to inform you,' the rider said to Fraomar, 'that the emperor has requested your presence at his winter quarters. You are to be of some use, I understand.' He turned his attention to Marius. '*Salve*. I am Nipius Quintilius, former *magister equitum* and Valentinian's envoy. Are you in charge of this slave?' Nipius dismounted. 'You are aware that he is a wanted man?'

Marius joined Fraomar outside the shield wall, an action that drew a sharp warning from Scapulus. He kept his hands at his side. 'Your authority over me is questionable, Nipius. Fraomar of the *Alamanni* is officially in my charge, and will remain as such.'

Behind him, Marius heard Barnabas' sharp intake of breath. The bishop's voice whispered in his ear. 'The *woman*, Marius, look at the woman!'

'Ah!' Nipius smiled. 'You have spied our noble lady. She has been, what shall we say, a less than model travelling companion.'

'By the gods, you shall pay for your insolence!' A chestnut mare broke free from Nipius' troop and trotted forward. The rider was female, her hair dark and braided and Marius could see that, although her clothing was dowdy she was a woman of high breeding.

A soldier ran forward and caught her halter. He leered through broken teeth and ran a hand down the woman's leg, the other firmly gripping the horse's bridle. The woman stretched away in distaste. 'Do not touch me with your stinking hands, Terricula!'

'You see?' Nipius opened his hands wide and shrugged. 'Hard work.'

Barnabas stepped forward. 'Take care, Nipius. You are foolish indeed if you think the emperor will overlook the mistreatment of his wife.'

Marius' mouth fell open. 'The Empress Justina?'

'I am she,' the woman replied. 'And you shall answer to Valentinian for your misdeeds, Nipius Quintilius.'

'I have little time for this,' Nipius replied dismissively. 'Fraomar will provide me with exactly the leverage I need to put a little pressure on our fractious emperor. The Alamann is to ride with us. Now.'

'Blackmail,' Marius heard Scapulus growl. 'Another would-be tin god.'

'Look,' Marius appealed, 'we have business on the island. And we could do with your help. Let us work together – I can guarantee the emperor's favour if we succeed.'

Nipius laughed. 'Posthumous favour is no good to me.' He leaned forward in his saddle. 'I know what's going on over there,' he pointed to the dark shape of Mona with the tip of his sword. '*Catena* has at least a cohort at Cunedum – and another five hundred barbarian allies. Do you think I'd be stupid enough to take them on with twenty-five foot-soldiers and a few archers?'

Scapulus raised his voice. 'Doesn't loyalty mean anything to you, you double-dealing slice of offal?'

'Bravery behind a shield wall counts for nothing,' Nipius called back. 'Come out little man, and let me see your valour.'

Scapulus burst through the wall, his face burning. 'Anytime, Quintilius. *Gladius* or *pilum*, your choice.'

Marius caught Scapulus' arm. 'This isn't getting us anywhere, Scapulus. If he won't march with us at least he can give us a little time.' Marius turned back to Nipius.

'The Alamann stays with me – for two days. We will return from the island and meet you here. Take this as insurance.' He found the leather bag and held it out. The soldier Terricula snagged it with his sword, flicked it up and caught it deftly in a gloved hand. 'What's this, bribery?' He opened the bag and murmured his appreciation, passing it to Nipius for inspection. 'Very nice,' Nipius retied the bag and returned it to Terricula. 'But how do I know you *will* return? I think additional insurance is required.' He nodded to Terricula who grinned and placed a proprietary hand on Justina's halter. 'My finest acquisition,' Nipius smirked. 'How much d'you think Valentinian will pay for her safe passage?'

Marius stiffened and reached for his sword. He heard a flickering of bowstrings as Nipius' archers flexed their weapons. Marius found Barnabas' hand on the hilt of his sword. 'Let it be so, Marius. I will go with them to ensure the lady's safety.' He lowered his voice. 'It is best – trust me, Marius, I know this man and what he is capable of.'

Justina spoke up, her voice carrying just a hint of a tremor. 'My daughter is still a captive.' She wrenched herself free from Terricula's grip and pointed to the island. 'I know she is over there, somewhere.' She appealed to Nipius directly: 'I am asking you for safe passage to go with these men. For my child's sake.'

Nipius' mouth compressed into a hard line. 'Not a chance. You stay with us, my *Lady*.'

The tension was palpable. Marius opened his mouth to protest but Barnabas silenced him with a look. He reluctantly relaxed his sword arm and heard the answering shiver of loosened bowstrings. Justina, to her credit, said no more, her calm expression belying the turmoil that must be raging inside her.

'So. Two days, then,' Nipius agreed. 'Any longer, and we'll be waiting. By then your holy friend will be dead, and as for her– ' Nipius wheeled his mount, 'I think you get the picture.'

Barnabas beckoned Romanus to accompany him and raised a hand in farewell. Marius watched them go with a heavy heart. He had come to rely on the bishop's company and sound judgement. He hoped that Barnabas was right this time, for all their sakes.

Chapter 19

Mona was, as Scapulus had correctly remembered, mostly flat and featureless. Peasant homesteads were scattered here and there and the occasional hunched figure could be seen tilling the soil. The column moved westwards unchallenged along the well-worn coastal paths. Eventually Scapulus moved the column inland and called a halt. 'This'll do for now,' the big man ordered. 'Down tools. Rest up and share out the food.' Marius watched him approach. He was feeling the strain of the arduous foot slogging, having left the horses on the mainland. 'How's the feet?' Scapulus enquired, observing Marius' efforts to rebind his blistered soles. 'Piss in your boots. It's the only way.'

'Very helpful,' Marius said, wincing as leather met raw skin, 'but I'd prefer a horse.'

'You've gone soft, boy.' Scapulus grinned his lopsided grin and got down on his haunches. 'The bishop told me you're after a commission? I had you down as a scroll shuffler.'

'Appearances can be deceptive.'

Scapulus laughed. 'As you say. You fight well for a lad. And you're a natural leader too. If you survive this party I imagine Valentinian will grant your request.'

Marius fixed the strap of his boot and stood, testing his makeshift first aid. 'You think so? But for now I only wish to avenge my parents and my uncle.' He declined to mention Freia. It would only encourage more ribald remarks.

Scapulus nodded. 'I feel the same about the *dux*,' he said, then shook his head fiercely. 'There was nothing I could have done. None of us could.'

'You will avenge him, and soon. But we must have a strategy. Call your ten best men together. We need to know the lie of the land before we make any decisions. We should send one or two of your men to scout ahead. I expect Fraomar will want to accompany them.'

Scapulus scowled but didn't contest the suggestion. Marius had correctly assessed that the professional in Scapulus would overcome any prejudice when the die were cast, especially if the stakes were high enough.

Fraomar returned at dusk with one of the scouts. The scout was limping badly, the cause evident: an arrow was embedded firmly in his shoulder. The man was bleeding and white as a bleached toga.

Scapulus raced to the spot, calling his men. 'Quickly, bring cloth and water. What happened?'

'We were attacked,' Fraomar said simply. There were but a few – near the watchtower. They didn't stay to fight.'

'Did you see them?'

'They were Roman auxiliaries, I am sure of that.'

'Were you followed?' Scapulus asked, examining the wounded man's shoulder 'Hm, you're right – this is an army issue shaft.'

Fraomar removed his cloak and sat down heavily on the mossy floor of the grove. 'We were not followed, but we will most likely be hunted now they are aware of our presence.'

'And Fabius?'

'Fabius and two others have followed the auxiliaries and will confirm their destination. The harbour in the north west of the island is my guess. And it tallies with what Barnabas has told us.'

Scapulus looked the wounded man in the eye. 'This will hurt, but I must do it. You understand?'

The man grimaced and nodded. Scapulus made a quick incision, exposing the barb of the arrowhead. He worked quickly, easing the iron head free from the man's flesh.

Marius looked on, his expression grim as he watched the operation. The soldier gasped in pain. His head fell back.

'Fainted.' Marius' lips were set in a firm line.

'Good,' Scapulus said. 'Better for him. Ah. There.' He pulled the point free. 'Now bandage him up,' he told the assisting trooper, 'tightly, man. D'you want him to bleed to death?'

'Come. There are decisions to be made,' Fraomar said sharply. 'We must take action before we are hunted down.'

'Have you lost your wits completely?' Scapulus was staring incredulously at Marius. 'We might as well give ourselves up now.'

'No, he is right.' Fraomar insisted. 'We will not be seen as a threat. We are too few. We just need food, shelter– '

'And they could probably use a few bodies in return,' Fabius finished.

Scapulus looked over to his second who was carefully greasing his sword and testing the ease with which it could be withdrawn. He was a tough little man with a great hook of a nose and a missing finger on his right hand, a veteran in every sense of the word. 'What do you estimate their strength to be, Fabius?'

Fabius sheathed the long *spatha*, apparently satisfied. 'Difficult to say. In the fort, probably several hundred. In the camp outside, anything between three hundred to eight hundred Irish. And there are many prisoners.'

Scapulus nodded. 'All right. If this Paulus has bought army support he could probably use a small detachment of trained soldiers. He must feel *some* insecurity working with the Irish. I'd be uncomfortable mixing with those stinking barbarians. I know what I'd like to do to them, and by Mithras if I get the chance– '

'You'll have your chance,' Marius said, 'if we are willing to take a risk and get close to them.'

'But if Paulus doesn't buy it,' Scapulus said, 'then we're walking voluntarily to our deaths.'

'We've come this far,' Marius shrugged. 'And Fraomar's right. We're too small in number to take them on. How in the name of Jupiter do we fight our way in, kill Paulus, rescue the prisoners and fight our way out? It's ludicrous.'

'And I need time for a good look around,' Scapulus reminded them. 'My men aren't in this for fun.' There was a general chorus of assent from the troops.

'So, this is how it will be,' Fraomar concluded. 'Marius, Scapulus and twenty of his men march openly to the fortress. They present themselves as available mercenaries. Once admitted, it will be a matter of observation and opportunity. I will take the remainder and find a suitable spot nearby in case anything goes wrong. If it does, we will arrange a distraction that will give you a chance to save yourselves.'

Scapulus frowned. 'That's a plan?' He scowled at Fraomar.

'You have a better idea?' Marius challenged the centurion and was pleased to see a hint of respect in Fraomar's keen eyes.

'It's what's normally referred to as a high risk strategy,' Scapulus said with a wry grin, 'but then, everything we've done in the last six weeks has been high risk. I'm in.' He drew his sword and planted it firmly in the ground. 'Who's with me?'

Chapter 20

Freia picked her way through the huddled bodies in the stockade. It was bitterly cold and the only shelter was against the fort walls where at least there was some relief from the biting wind and stinging rain. She found Pavo lying beneath his cloak and, cold and shivering though he was, the soldier managed a smile of recognition. 'I need to speak to you,' he raised himself up on his good elbow and winced. 'I was beginning to think you weren't coming back.'

Freia reached under the folds of her cloak and produced a chunk of bread. 'Take this – and eat it quickly. If they see me feeding you, it'll be the end for both of us.' She eyed the patrolling Irishmen. None appeared to be looking in their direction. Pavo took the bread and buried it in his clothing. 'Listen, I – I never had the opportunity to apologize. My actions that night, I was drunk, I – '

Freia shook her head and held up a pale hand. 'That was then. I hold nothing against you. I am hardly blameless myself.'

Pavo frowned. 'Meaning?'

'Meaning I should have gone to the authorities that night, not the inn.' Freia paused, 'Or at least to my master.'

'It's to do with the stones, isn't it – what happened in Calleva? Where did they come from?'

She gave him a smile 'Another time. I must go. I will bring more food when I can.'

A bundle of fur lay beside her but the girl had made no use of it, judging by the coldness of her skin. Freia picked the wrap up and forced it around her shoulders. 'Why are you not using this? If you get any colder you'll sleep and never wake up. Is that what you want?'

The girl looked at her miserably. 'I don't care. And this was given to me by one of *them*,' she pointed to a group of Roman auxiliaries standing by the fort gate.

'Which one?' Freia asked.

'The one with the crested helmet.'

'Caelius? He brought you this?' So she had been right. She had detected something about the man that denied his rebel status. Under his armour there lay a kind heart. Perhaps that could be used to her advantage.

The girl shivered and Freia looked around for anything that would provide warmth. All the prisoners were cold and wet. At this rate there would be no survivors to ship to Ireland.

'You must fight. Use your will. Do you think your parents want you to give up? Your mother will be searching for you and she is a strong woman.' She took the girl's cold hand. 'Don't give up. Not now.'

'What's the use,' she said, 'we'll never get out of here. Look, there are more of them coming. I thought the army were on our side. I thought they were loyal to my father.' She sobbed and buried her head in her cloak.

Her father? Freia sat next to her. 'Is your father in the army? What is his name?'

'His name is Valentinian,' the girl said.

Freia heard a commotion and craned her neck to the approach road where a squad of perhaps twenty Roman auxiliaries were approaching the gates, drawing a great deal of interest from the Irish. Freia guessed from the warriors' behaviour that these reinforcements were unexpected.

'I'll be back soon,' Freia said, giving the girl a reassuring hug. She walked to the stockade fence to get a closer look at what was going on. Caelius was conversing with the leader of the new arrivals. Freia passed through the stockade gate, noticing with satisfaction that the Irishmen on either side averted their eyes as she passed and made the strange Irish sign to ward off evil. She took up an unobtrusive position within earshot.

Freia counted twenty-two men in total. Caelius was addressing their leader, a large centurion with a battered face: 'What gives you the confidence to approach, centurion?'

The big man grinned. An extraordinarily long scar ran from his mouth to the corner of his eye. 'The sight of Roman uniforms suggested we might be of some assistance to you. And we need food, a change of clothing, shelter, somewhere we can use a toilet without getting frostbite.'

'Where have you come from? There are no forces mobilized here, not for many miles. Not since Segontium was razed.'

The big centurion laughed. 'No. We've marched from the north. We're part of what's left of Fullofaudes' army.'

Freia thought she detected a flicker of unease on Caelius' face. 'I see,' Caelius said, 'but where is your loyalty now?'

'Where it is required and where it can be rewarded with the basics a man needs to live. We're tired of living like scavengers and there is no one left alive to pay our wages.'

The centurion's men murmured their assent and rapped their shields with their spear shafts. More Irish warriors were beginning to join the onlookers and Freia felt the hostility in the air as the Roman arrivals were surrounded on three sides.

Caelius said, 'My scouts report that they wounded one of your men. Why did you not come straight away instead of skulking in the bushes like bandits?'

'Don't tell me you wouldn't have checked the place out first,' the big man replied.

'Point taken,' Caelius replied, 'I suppose I'd have done the same.' The commander appeared satisfied. 'Very well. Come with me and I will explain our circumstances to you. Your men can join mine for food and drink. But a word of warning–' Caelius stopped their advance with a raised hand, 'I am not the overseer here. You will meet him, but listen well – he is not to be trifled with. He will know if you attempt anything contrary to his will.'

Freia continued to watch as the centurion led his men into the keep and the fort gates closed behind them. Some instinct made her glance up to the fortress battlements and she saw a tall figure framed for an instant against the tumbling skyline. Then it was gone.

Freia took every opportunity to explore the fortress. Paulus allowed her freedom of movement to attend sick prisoners, provided she reported to him before sunset. She dreaded these interviews but knew that, if Paulus wished, he could banish her to the stockade with the others. More ships had arrived that morning and she guessed that, with the wind in favour of the return voyage, prisoners would soon be taken onto the waiting vessels. As she made her way to the stockade she was greeted by the sight of a handful of captives being inspected by one of the Irish sea-captains. He was clearly in the process of selecting the fittest from their ranks. Pavo, she noticed immediately, was not among them, but the girl was. Her heart sank. There was nothing she could do but watch as the chosen were herded out of the stockade. Her only option was to find Caelius and trust her judgement. As she crossed the inner courtyard she felt a sharp pain in her head. The walls of the fortress became grey and indistinct. She fell to her knees and a wave of panic flushed over her; if she was ill she'd be thrown into the stockade for sure. The thought gave her the incentive to prop herself against the wall and she blinked hard to try to clear her spinning head. And then came the vision: a field of battle, rank after rank of yellow shields, the air darkened with arrows and spears, the sun blotted out. And the ground turned to red. She saw the open mouths of Irish and Roman warriors, heard the clash of axe on shield boss, felt the movement of the horsemen around her, the thudding cacophony of their hooves trampling dead and wounded alike into the mud and detritus of the battlefield. And then a face was looking into hers, a familiar face. But it couldn't be real. The battle was real. She saw men fall in rows, as if an unseen wind or flight of invisible arrows was blowing them over. The voice came again, and the face swam back into focus. And this time it spoke. 'By the gods, Freia, *Freia, Freia.*' Her name. She hadn't heard the sound of her name for so long. She tried to open her eyes but the images persisted and she saw the backdrop of the battle, the looming fortress at Cunedum within whose walls she now lay. A hand was gently shaking her shoulder. 'Can you hear me? *Freia?*' The voice was familiar but it was at the end of a long tunnel, receding and then coming close again. Suddenly the images disappeared, as if plucked away by some ghostly hand. 'Scapulus,' the voice said, 'pass me your water bottle.' She opened her eyes and looked into the face of Marius, the young councillor. His face was thinner and the beard longer, but it was definitely him. 'Shh. Not a word,' Marius whispered. 'Drink this.'

'Is she all right?' his companion asked, peering down at her. She recognized the twisted grin. It was the soldier who had led his men in earlier on.

'I think so,' Marius said, 'come on, a little more.'

She felt the cool liquid trickle down her throat and then remembered the girl, her promise to her mother. She pushed the bottle aside and tried to get up. 'The stockade,' she said, 'they're taking them to the boats. The girl– she–'

'All right,' Marius said, 'we know. You have a friend? In the stockade?'

Freia nodded. 'Many friends. But the girl – I promised her mother– '

'All right. Steady,' Marius said. He looked anxiously at Freia. Her body was so thin. He glanced around, conscious that they were beginning to draw too much attention.

'I must go – talk to Caelius. She's sick – shouldn't be moved.'

'Who is sick?' Marius asked.

Freia stood up shakily and Scapulus quickly reached out a steadying hand.

'I don't know – but her father is an army commander…his name is Valentinian.'

'By Mars,' Scapulus guffawed. 'He is no army commander. He is an emperor of Rome.'

Chapter 21

'Stay here? In this gods-forsaken place?' Drufidius turned to Terricula to confirm the decision. They had entered a shallow recess in the landscape, a quiet grove of trees within which rose a great barrow of earth surrounded by stones similar, Drufidius thought, to the megaliths he had seen in the south-west, although smaller in scale.

'What's up, councillor,' Terricula smirked. 'Not up to your usual standards?'

'It's a grave,' Drufidius said, 'a burial place.'

'Appropriate enough,' said Terricula.

'Terricula has a morbid sense of humour,' Justina said, 'I find it best to ignore him.'

Nipius dismounted and signalled to his entourage. 'We wait here.' He tied his mount to one of the nearby trunks. 'It's quiet, out of the way. There'll be traffic on the main thoroughfare to and from the island and I don't want any involvement with it.'

'Gives me the creeps,' a passing soldier observed, throwing his helmet onto the mossy ground and giving the standing stones a wide berth.

Barnabas took Justina's hand and helped her dismount. The bishop smiled. 'Whatever spirits lived amongst these trees are now long gone, lady. There is nothing to fear.'

'And you're the spirit expert, eh?' Terricula cleared his throat and spat on his hands. He rubbed them together and wiped them on his tunic. 'Keeps them supple,' he said to Justina, 'they get sore otherwise and then it's hard to handle a blade.'

'Give the lady peace, Terricula. As the emperor's wife, she is entitled to that at least.' Barnabas said firmly, guiding Justina past the pitted face of her tormentor.

Terricula spat again. 'Makes no odds to me, bishop,' he said removing his helmet and placing it on the ground beside him. 'Death is no respecter of status.'

Drufidius could hardly believe the fates had given him such ill luck. He consoled himself with thoughts of Lucius and the conversation he had had with Bernicca before their departure. Lucius had apparently received a report from the garrison commander concerning an assault on a soldier by a girl fitting Freia's description. This report had prompted the Praeses to begin a house-to-house search for the missing slave girl. Drufidius doubted he would find her. But Lucius' actions had angered Bernicca further, strengthening her resolve to frame the Praeses as she had suggested before. So, Drufidius thought, if he could get home in one piece all would be well. . . perhaps under the circumstances even a promotion... after all, it was his wife who had 'discovered' Lucius' treachery. Drufidius felt a pang of guilt which he quickly shook off. Because of Lucius, *he* was the one stuck in the middle of nowhere, taking all the risks. Still, he mused, in two days it would be over, whichever way events turned out. But what then? If Marius failed to return they would be forced to cross the straits to find Fraomar, and that was not a prospect he relished. Whatever danger he was in now Drufidius was sure there were worse things on the island. The question was, who could he trust? Not Terricula. Certainly not Nipius. But what about Barnabas? He was a strange one. Drufidius scanned the grove for the bishop and spied him and his apprentice in earnest conversation with Terricula. He wondered what they could be discussing. He saw Nipius approaching the group and noticed that the conversation abruptly ceased, the bishop and young Romanus moving off to busy themselves with other tasks.

Drufidius stretched his legs and sidled past the bustling groups of soldiers to the mound. It looked like an ancient burial place. Upright stones of uneven height, some crooked and out of alignment, surrounded the barrow. A narrow passageway was cut into the centre, the entrance to the tomb itself. He walked around the hillock and wondered what sort of people had built this monument to their dead. What significance did the stone circle have to this ancient race of men? Behind the mound stood a solitary stone, taller than the others that made up the circle, set firmly in the ground directly behind the passageway. Drufidius traced the spiral lines cut into the stone with his finger. The stone felt cool to the touch as he moved his finger across the strange patterns. He inhaled sharply and withdrew his finger. Was it his imagination or had he felt something? Gingerly he touched the stone again. Immediately he felt a sense of calm flow through him as he retraced the pattern. He found that he was humming softly to himself and the tension in his body had slipped away. He felt he had entered a dream in which he floated high above the island. He could see the surrounding water, the high ground at its western curve, the sails of ships clinging to the land, bobbing in the swell. He saw the countryside for miles around, the lines of trees delineating fields of crops, the circular thatched-roofed buildings of small homesteads. And more. There was an army, marching. He could see the yellow shields and the sunlight reflecting off the gleaming spearheads. If only he could get a little closer...

'Best not touch, Drufidius.'

Drufidius felt a hand on his shoulder and the vision dispersed. 'Barnabas,' he exhaled with relief.

'There are older influences in this world of which we know precious little,' the bishop said examining the patterns closely, 'the scriptures warn us against them. My advice is to leave well alone.'

'I felt something, I'm sure I– '

'Nevertheless. Shall we– ?' He steered Drufidius away with an arm over his tremulous shoulders.

'Gods. My heart is pounding – you could have sent me to an early g–grave, giving me a fright like that.'

The bishop laughed gently. 'You're made of stronger stuff than that, Drufidius. And I think you'll get to prove that over the next few days.'

'Few days? The future w–won't last that long, as I see it,' Drufidius said, examining his fingertips suspiciously.

'The future will be a good deal longer than that, I hope,' Barnabas said, 'but to ensure that it is so I need your help. There is something you need to know...'

Drufidius opened his eyes. It was dark, but the quality of the darkness indicated that dawn was not far away. His bowels grumbled and he cursed under his breath. After a while he could ignore their call no longer. Muttering to himself he threw off the cloak and blanket that had scarcely warmed him throughout the cold, hard night and crept off into the grove to find a suitable spot. As he moved through the trees he glanced fearfully at the silhouette of the barrow which loomed in the crepuscular light and prompted him to recite a series of short petitions to the gods. Fear increased the urgency of his mission and he squatted at the base of a tree a hundred paces into the grove, feeling the rough bark on his back as he leant on the trunk. As the steam from his waste rose about him he detected a rustle from the bushes several trees along. And then he saw a pair of eyes light upon him as a warrior emerged, pulling up his breeches. For a split second the two men looked at each other, then the warrior drew his sword and charged. Drufidius was frozen to the spot and only when the man had covered half the distance between them did he take action. He hauled down his tunic and with a shout of alarm fled towards the clearing. He heard the pounding of the warrior's tread behind and the sound lent wings to his feet. He half-turned and noted to his horror that there were more following; an arrow whistled past his head and embedded itself in an adjacent tree. Drufidius hollered and burst into the camp. All about him, men were tumbling from their sleep, grasping for their weapons. Nipius was on his feet, shouting orders. Drufidius almost collided with Barnabas who thrust a sword into his trembling hand. 'Get Justina,' the bishop said, 'and get her away. Quickly.'

Drufidius stood helplessly watching Nipius' archers pick off the warriors as they entered the clearing. Many got past the missiles and soon the grove was a confused welter of bodies, as each sought to gain the advantage over the other. Drufidius was faced with a large opponent who grinned before advancing with his two-handed blade. As the man hefted the weapon he was caught in the neck by a double salvo of arrows from two grove archers who had taken up a commanding position on top of the barrow. Drufidius watched the barbarian fall, hands scrabbling at the darts that were choking the life out of him. He turned and saw Terricula and Nipius locked together, Terricula clutching something in his left hand while his right forced a slim blade towards Nipius' throat. Where was Barnabas? And then he saw the bishop cutting his way towards them. His peripheral vision caught sight of Justina with her back to the barrow when he was knocked to the ground by a falling barbarian. The man landed on top of him and something wet and sticky covered his face With a cry of disgust Drufidius pushed him off and crawled away. He staggered to his feet and, bending low, made for the mound. Drufidius turned and peered into the grave mound's tunnel. He thought he detected a slight movement. 'Justina?' he called. There was no response. An arrow fizzed past his head and clattered through the leaves. That decided him. Gripping his sword tightly he crawled into the darkness of the tomb.

Drufidius lay still for a while and when the noise of conflict quietened, moved cautiously on his stomach to where a small crack in the stone filtered a brooch-pin sized shaft of light into his refuge. His field of vision was small but he could see no movement outside. Either everyone was dead or wounded or the conflict had moved on to a point beyond the grove. He flattened himself against the floor of the tomb and attempted to turn about to face the entrance, obscured from his present position by the turn of the mound at its half-way point.

He had just completed the manoeuvre when he felt a firm grip close around his ankle. He cried out and tried to pull his leg away from whatever had hold of it but the grip was strong. His panic gave him extra strength and he kicked out with his free leg, making contact with something soft and pliable. The grip relaxed and he was free, but a voice called out. 'Wait.' He recognized the voice. It belonged to Terricula. Drufidius turned about with some effort and whispered hoarsely into the gloom. 'What are you doing?' And then he felt the stickiness under his hands and heard the pain in the voice as Terricula crawled and collapsed onto his side in the dirt. 'I'm bleeding. I need something – ' he paused, coughed and spat blood, 'something to stop it.'

'Where is the wound?' Drufidius groped in the dark for the clasp that held his cloak in place and released it. He removed the garment and pressed it into Terricula's hands. 'Here. This will stop the flow – press hard.'

'Can't,' Terricula wheezed, 'arrow.'

Drufidius swallowed and felt for the shaft. It had entered just below Terricula's breast bone.

Terricula whispered, '. . . saw it coming. Couldn't get out of the way.'

'One of ours? Nipius' archers?'

Terricula grunted. 'He put them up to it. Was ready.'

'But you attacked Nipius. I know what I saw.'

'Valentinian's remit,' he laughed then groaned in pain. 'Thought Nipius suspected. He's a suspicious one–' Terricula took a series of short, harsh breaths. 'Didn't get these though, so not that clever.' He pressed a bag into Drufidius' hand.

'Ah.'

There was silence for a few moments broken only by Terricula's laboured breathing.

'And Nipius?'

'Don't know.' A pause. 'Won't stay around now.' Another pause. 'Knows Valentinian is after him.'

'Where will he go?'

'North. To Valentia. Has supporters there. He'll make trouble . . . '

'T–Trouble?' Drufidius shouted, then remembered where he was. In a lower voice he said, 'what in Hades is this if it's not trouble?'

Terricula attempted a laugh then broke off in a choking cough. He took another deep breath. 'Need to watch him. Dangerous.' And another breath. Then there was silence again.

'I need to get you into the open,' Drufidius said, 'I can't do anything if I can't see.'

'No,' Terricula said. His voice was weaker, 'forget it.'

'Look, I don't like you much, I'll be honest, but I can't let you d–die in here.'

'Why not? It's a tomb, isn't it?' Terricula coughed again.

Drufidius got hold of Terricula's shoulders and tried to pull him towards the entrance, but after a while he realized he was pulling a corpse. He let go of Terricula's scale-armoured jerkin and lay back, exhausted. When he had recovered his breath he wiped his hands on the powdery earth of the tomb's interior and wondered what to do next. He began a cautious crawl towards the light and then stopped, held his breath and listened. But the sound did not reoccur and he continued to emerge, blinking, into the light. The grove was still and silent. Bodies were scattered about the clearing, Irish and Roman. He walked carefully around the perimeter, mindful of the possibility of an Irish rearguard, with Barnabas' sword gripped in his hand. What had become of the bishop? As he approached each body he prodded gingerly with his toe. It seemed that his was the only preserved life in the grove. Even the horses had vanished, probably into Irish custody. Pausing to remove the armour from a dead member of Nipius' unit, Drufidius fastened it across his ample stomach and picked up the fallen man's helmet. Tugging it into place, he selected a smaller Irish shield and struck out into the trees.

Presently he found himself drawing close to a derelict settlement. Gritting his teeth at every snapping twig and flutter of bird he crept towards the nearest building. He saw that he had reached the edge of the sparse woodland surrounding the grove and that the old settlement faced open ground, commanding a good view of the countryside. He took a few deep breaths to steady his nerves, grateful to have put distance between himself and the grove of death. He was hungry and thirsty, and with no obvious prospect of refreshment was considering his options when he heard a muffled crunch, as if something heavy had been dropped. His heart recommenced its dance of doom and he ducked behind a crumbling wall, all his senses twitching. He listened. Nothing but the wind, soughing through the spaces between the ramshackle derelicts. He moved stealthily over a pile of fallen stones and cursed under his breath as he lost his footing and twisted his ankle on a loose pile of rubble. Massaging the damaged area with his left hand he limped forward to the next building. This was the only hut in the group that was left with its roof partially intact and it was in this that he found Justina, arms wrapped about her against the cold and a makeshift fire smouldering between the two large stone blocks she had moved together to shelter the flames from the wind.

'And Nipius?' Drufidius asked Justina. She shook her head. 'I don't know. I saw him in the trees. Then I slipped behind the mound and waited. When it was clear, I ran for my life.'

Drufidius shifted uncomfortably on the stone seat he had constructed from the ruins of the shack. 'And now what?'

'We are safe for the time being,' Justina said, 'but a few of Nipius' men must have survived. It would be best to look for them. Then we have a measure of protection at least.'

'A sound idea, my lady,' Drufidius agreed, 'but they will be more interested in their own survival now that their leader has fled. They may be heading east already. And then there are the barbarians . . . '

'I know,' Justina said quietly, 'I recognized their leader in the grove. And he saw me.'

'They are the same war party? You are sure?' Drufidius asked.

Justina drew her cloak around her. 'His name is Faelan. He is ruthless.'

They both sensed the vibrations underfoot at the same instant. Justina flung her cloak over the fire to smother it and pressed herself against the wall of the hut. Drufidius paced from one wall to the other in panicked indecision. A niche was set into the stone beside her and Justina looked fearfully through it into the enclosure formed by the settlement buildings. Drufidius stopped pacing and held his breath. He signalled a question to Justina and she returned the answer with a smile by holding up her hand with one finger extended. 'It's all right.' She climbed over the ruined wall and beckoned: 'Over here!'

Drufidius followed Justina and saw with relief that his fears had been unfounded. The bishop's protégé, Romanus, waved back with a grin and steered his horse down towards them, picking his way cautiously through the fallen rubble. His only other companion was Barnabas' horse, but the bishop himself was nowhere to be seen. 'Thank God,' Romanus shouted, 'I thought I was the only one left.'

Chapter 22

'The betrothal is today,' Freia said, 'so surely they will not sail until it is over?'

'That's a reasonable guess,' Marius said.

They had entered the main building, acting as an impromptu escort for Freia. The few Irish and fortress auxiliaries who had stopped to look them over had moved on, satisfied that nothing untoward had taken place.

'Something is going to happen here,' Freia said. 'I saw it.'

'Look, we can't be seen conversing,' Scapulus said. 'I don't care how many visions you've had. The only vision I've got is a spear up the backside.'

'Your strength is at a low ebb,' Marius said to Freia, 'and the mind does strange things *in extremis.*'

'I know what I saw,' Freia brushed her dishevelled hair from her eyes. 'We have to get away.'

Marius cupped her face in his hands. 'Listen, you're a brave girl. And we're going to get you out of here. Your brother is nearby and he'll be champing at the bit to rescue you, but we have to be cautious or all will be lost. The emperor's daughter must be saved – and as things stand you are her only hope. You know that, don't you? While you are in contact with her we have a chance. Thank the gods the barbarians do not know who she is. Can you find her warm clothing? Bread and wine to warm her?'

'We can forage something from the mess and pass it on,' Scapulus suggested.

'I'll try,' Freia said, 'but he watches me all the time.'

'Paulus?'

Freia nodded. 'And I don't know if the Irish will let me board the ship. If Paulus suspects–'

Scapulus hissed a warning. Caelius was walking briskly down the hall. Freia and Scapulus moved off in different directions as Caelius approached. 'Settling in?' he greeted Marius, 'there's plenty to do at the harbour if you're at a loose end.' The commander slapped his shoulder and passed on, his mind evidently on his current task.

Marius took stock. He guessed that Paulus had bought off the original coastal defense garrison troops with a promise of riches to come. The alternative had probably been unpleasant and he found it hard to blame them for their actions. But if and when order was restored in the provinces, he thought wryly, he would not like to be in their sandals when Valentinian's reprisals caught up with them, as they surely would. The emperor had a long arm and many had underestimated Valentinian to their cost. At that moment, a heavy wooden door to his right swung open and Marius was taken aback to see a young woman emerge, escorted by two warriors wearing the unmistakeable dress of the Saxon. The woman was redheaded, and beautiful. She wore a flowing gown of russet inlaid with delicate gold spiral patterns. Her hair was braided and she wore a golden torque around her slim, white neck. Her wrists were festooned with bracelets and her movements were graceful and authoritative. Without doubt she was of royal Saxon blood. The warriors fixed him with baleful stares as they passed.

Marius suddenly had a strong feeling that he was being watched. He looked up. A figure stood half in the shadows, silently looking down. He raised his hand in half salute, unsure of the man's identity. But the figure was descending the staircase.

'Ah. One of the newcomers. The mercenaries of the north, is that right?' The voice had a brittle, crystalline quality, like a blade being drawn across a wine jar. 'You have joined us at, how shall I put it, the *consummation* of our enterprise,' said the man, 'but perhaps that is all to your advantage. All this waiting is making the men restless. Or so my commander tells me. I trust he has made you welcome?'

Marius' heart hammered in his chest. A thousand emotions raged inside him. With a huge effort of will, he found his voice. 'Very. Thank you.'

'You're not averse to a little anti-empire activity I understand?'

'I have no reason to be loyal to the caesars,' Marius said with an effort. 'My parents died at an emperor's bidding.'

'I'm sorry to hear that,' Paulus said in a low voice. 'Most regrettable.'

Marius felt the eyes penetrating, searching. Surely Paulus *knew* . . .

'I noticed your admiration for the Lady Lawenya,' Paulus said. 'She is a rare beauty, ideal for a king, is she not?'

Marius felt the sweat trickle down his back. 'She is fair. I've heard that Crimthann is to take her as his queen. Such an alliance will have great potency.'

'Indeed. And with the emperor's precious provinces caught in the middle,' Paulus brought his hands together with a slap.

'– it will be the harder for Valentinian to defend the west,' Marius said.

'It will indeed. I almost feel sorry for him.' Paulus laughed then, apparently losing interest in the conversation, moved away down the length of the hall until the natural curve of the building hid him from sight. Marius stood in the same spot for several minutes, breathing slowly, before he felt able to continue his reconnaissance. He could not remember a time when one man had caused him to feel such terror. He shook himself angrily and gripped his sword. Flesh and blood, he said to himself. *Just flesh and blood.*

Marius found Scapulus at the harbour. There were three ships awaiting their human cargo and the quayside was busy with stevedore's stocking the holds with the spoils of the invasion.

'You all right?' the big man asked, 'your face is the colour of goat's milk. Seen a ghost or something?'

'Perhaps,' Marius said. 'Anyone boarded yet?'

'Not yet,' Scapulus said. 'Looks like they were selecting the fittest.'

'Freia's probably right. They'll wait until the ceremony's over. Then they'll load up and be off like a ballista shot. There's no point in even thinking about the stockade. It's guarded like the emperor's jewels.' He stole a sideways glance at Scapulus, 'Enough booty for you?'

Scapulus fired him a grin, 'It'll do.'

'Let's make ourselves useful, then, before Caelius smells a rat. I'm going to take a look inside one of the ships. When I make my move I need to know where I'm going.'

Scapulus pointed to the ships. 'That one over there and the one behind is reserved for livestock. The last one is the one I'm interested in,' Scapulus said with a wink, 'I'd better give them a hand with those sacks.'

Marius watched the centurion disappear into the hold of the nearest ship. He picked his way past the ropes that held the first ship to the harbourside and taking a quick look around, walked quickly up the gangplank.

Freia followed Paulus at what she judged to be a safe distance. She had seen him take this route before but a solo investigation had revealed only a blank wall. Paulus turned the corner and she stepped from behind the column and shadowed his tall figure. As she reached the intersection she hesitated, fearful that the notary had felt her presence and was waiting somewhere in the gloom for her to give herself away. She took a deep breath before going on and moments later was once again looking at an empty wall. She ran her fingers over its surface. Paulus had simply vanished. She began a fresh search and this time found a loose stone. Freia eased her finger into the gap and was rewarded with an audible click. She stood back in amazement as a section of wall swung inwards and a dark space opened in front of her. A sweet, cloying smell, some kind of incense, floated from the gap. She looked into the corridor. It was empty. No one had observed her discovery. Another deep breath and she entered the void.

She felt her way in the darkness until her foot struck against a solid object. A step. She went up. As she ascended the quality of light improved. Soon, she was passing lit torches, fixed to the stairwell by circular iron brackets, the design of which had fashioned the coils enclosing the torches into the sinuous shape of a snake's body.

The smell grew stronger as she climbed. She guessed she was somewhere near the west turret. And then the steps levelled off. She was faced with another obstacle, this time a conventional door. She hesitated at the threshold, pressed her ear to the wood. From beneath the door filtered a dim, greenish light. Freia felt her heart hammering. She pressed on the wood and gripped the handle. The door swung open and her eyes widened in amazement and disgust. She was in a large chamber lit by a strange fluorescence that pulsed from an unknown source. The smell was sickly, overpowering and Freia gagged as she took in the grim details of the interior. Bleached skulls hung from the ceiling on thread-like strands, rotating in the warm air. Elaborate tapestries were draped from the walls, each depicting a separate scene of cruelty or horror. One tapestry showed a tree in a garden, around whose branches were coiled a great serpent. Below the tree a woman stood looking up. The woman's hand was extended towards the tree, her hand reaching for the plump fruit that hung in tantalizing clusters before her. Another depicted a shocking scene where a young man or woman lay stretched out on a stone slab, while above them stood a snake-headed figure holding a long, curved blade. Previous victims lay in attitudes of death around the slab. Freia turned her head away towards the centre of the chamber. A giant cobra of bronze rose from the floor, its flat head angled back and frozen in a posture of attack. Its forked tongue flickered in the weird light and Freia found herself looking into its eyes, deep pools of green, drawing her in, soothing her distress. It was pleasant, just to look, to feel the warmth like a gentle cocoon around her body. Perhaps she would rest a while, sit and let the tension slip away.

As her eyes grew heavier the spell was shattered by the sound of a latch click. Freia's eyes flew open in time to see a small door at the rear of the chamber beginning to open. A shaft of daylight picked its way into the chamber. She turned and fled, throwing herself down the stairwell, tripping and stumbling the last few steps and landing heavily on the lower passage floor. Her breath was coming in short gasps as she scrabbled frantically for the hidden exit. She became aware that the green light of the chamber had invaded the stairwell and was now accompanied by the tap of advancing footsteps. Freia stifled a scream and her searching fingers closed around a long protrusion, a handle of some sort. She yanked it in desperation and felt the wall give outwards, depositing her on the stone floor of the corridor. Pain shot through her arm but the green light was bathing the flagstones. Freia picked herself up and, stifling a sob of terror, scrambled away, not daring to look behind her.

Chapter 23

Romanus warmed his hands by the regenerated fire. 'I don't think I've ever been so scared,' he said with a shudder.

Drufidius broke off from his perusal of the flatlands beyond, 'Well, that's an entirely natural reaction. N–nothing to be ashamed of at all.'

'It won't be the last time either,' Justina observed. 'Your chosen path will lead you into many dangerous situations.'

The novice nodded. 'Yes. I suppose you're right.'

'But I think you have a fine protector in Barnabas,' Drufidius said. 'He has much wisdom. And a strong arm.'

Romanus nodded again, apparently lost in thought.

'We need something to c–cook on this fire. The lady is hungry.' Drufidius beamed in a fatherly fashion. 'How are your foraging skills?'

Romanus grinned and dusted himself down. His hands were delicate, like a girl's. 'Adequate, I think,' the novice produced an object from his cloak.

'Ah, splendid,' Drufidius said, 'slingshot is not my specialty. And I'm a little old to chase rabbits with any hope of success.'

'I have kept Barnabas and myself in good supply,' Romanus said. 'And I improve with practice.'

'I will keep watch,' Justina offered, 'but please - do not be long.'

'We shall surprise you with the speed of our success,' Drufidius said, feeling positively cheerful at the prospect of food. 'Come, Romanus. To the hunt.'

Justina caught his arm. 'How well do you know this –Marius? He seems a good man. Tell me,' she hesitated, 'will he find Antonia?' Her eyes were filmed with tears.

Drufidius felt a stab of compassion. He took Justina's hand and squeezed it. 'He is a r–resourceful young man. I am quite sure your daughter will be reunited with you v–very soon.' He tried to maintain an optimistic expression, although realistically he didn't hold out much hope for Marius, let alone the girl. Being a parent must be a worrying responsibility. Drufidius had never given children much thought. He tried to imagine Bernicca in a maternal role; the idea was almost ludicrous.

'You are very kind. Thank you.' Justina's composure was commendable. She took a deep breath and stirred the fire, adding more wood in preparation for the proposed meal. 'You had best be on your way.'

Romanus led the way out of the enclosure. The woodland was sparse, but Drufidius was confident that a pigeon or two would soon find themselves in the cooking pot.

'You scan the treetops,' Romanus suggested. 'I'll cover the ground. Bound to be rabbit holes here somewhere, especially with the grassland just beyond. Maybe foxes too. Mind you,' he added, 'they're an acquired taste.'

Drufidius crept through the trees. In the back of his mind he still fretted about other, two-legged predators. But the area seemed quiet and unthreatening. He heard a commotion in the branches above and opened his mouth to alert Romanus as a large woodpigeon broke cover. His warning turned into a cry of pain as he felt a sharp blow to the back of his head, then the taste of dry leaves in his mouth. He realized he was lying face down on the woodland carpet. His head throbbed and lights danced before his eyes. Before the blackness overtook him he was vaguely aware of somebody scrabbling under his borrowed armour. Then nothing.

'Drufidius!' Someone was shaking him.

He moaned and opened one eye. That was a mistake. The pain was exquisite. He felt gentle hands beneath him, trying to turn him. He was slowly but firmly rolled over, his bulk completing the manoeuvre until he lay, spreadeagled beneath the woodland canopy. He opened his eyes again, and this time the pain was bearable.

'What happened?' Justina's anxious face looked into his.

'Something hit me. Hard.' He patted the back of his head and returned a hand covered with blood.

'Let me see.' Justina probed the wound. 'It's not deep. And the bleeding has stopped. Can you get up?'

'I'll try.' Drufidius used a sapling for support and rose unsteadily to his feet. Then he remembered. 'The stones.' He felt about under his tunic. 'Gone.'

'Romanus,' she said. 'One of the horses is also missing.'

'Which way?' Drufidius tried a few steps. His head ached but the pain was now a secondary issue.

'West. Towards the sea.'

Drufidius dug his heels into the bay's chestnut flank. Ahead, Romanus reined in his mount and briefly halted. Drufidius cared little whether the man waited or rode on.

He knew what he had to do and curiously it didn't scare him. Romanus wheeled about and bent low in his saddle, taking off down the sloping scrub with his cloak flying behind him.

Drufidius felt a strange elation, something he was quite unused to. His head had stopped aching. The land sloped gently down towards the Irish Sea and the wind whipping in his face bore the refreshing smell of salt. Romanus dismounted and walked quickly down a boulder-strewn path towards the sand. A northerly wind cut across the flat shoreline like a knife. Drufidius dismounted and as his feet touched the ground he paused, suddenly unsure. He hesitated, feeling the keening wind against his bare forearms. Romanus was standing on the beach. He held a sword in his right hand, and something else in the other. A bag. Drufidius walked down the path. The elation that had fuelled his ride had subsided into a flat calm. He advanced towards Romanus, his sandals making soft sucking noises as the wet sand plucked at his feet.

'Drufidius,' Romanus called to him, 'it was nothing personal.'

'I have some questions for you,' Drufidius called back – they were separated by no more than a hundred paces.

'Such as?'.

'Where is Barnabas?'

'Where I left him.'

'In the t–tomb,' Drufidius said. 'Of course. It was you I heard.'

'Yes.'

They were face to face on a narrow strip of sand between two small reservoirs, like miniature seas. A shoal of tiny fish darted to and fro in the water at

Drufidius' feet as the wind rippled the surface. The air was crisp and clean, the bay deserted but for the two men. It was as if they were the only humans alive, the only sentient beings in an otherwise empty world.

'Theft is a sin according to your Christian scriptures, I believe. And m–murder – ,' Drufidius took a step closer. He had never felt such anger. 'H–Have you forgotten your god?'

'I had forgotten myself. Why should I waste my life trekking around this miserable country after that dull ascetic?' Romanus hefted his sword. 'I didn't kill him, though. Just a tap on the head.'

Drufidius grunted disdainfully. 'And what of your calling?'

'This is my new calling.' Romanus waved the bag of stones.

'Do you know how much trouble they have c–caused? They are not your property.'

'They are now.' Romanus threw himself forward, aiming his blade at Drufidius' midriff. Drufidius stumbled to one side and brought his own weapon round in a clumsy effort to parry. Romanus fluidly sidestepped the thrust and immediately sank up to his waist in liquid sand. The surface bubbled and sucked around his body like a pair of puckered, oversized lips. Romanus cried out in surprise and flailed with his arms, attempting to find a solid purchase. The more he struggled, the more the sand increased its grip. Drufidius stood rooted to the spot, at once fascinated and then horrified by the outcome of his actions.

'Please– ' Romanus begged, terror-struck.

Drufidius sheathed his sword and took a careful step forward. 'The bag. Throw me the bag.'

Romanus bit his lip. He sank another handsbreadth.

'The bag.'

The novice grimaced and tossed the bag. Drufidius caught it and tucked it into his tunic.

'Get a branch, anything, please– ' Romanus twisted but the sand's grip was absolute.

Drufidius scanned the beach. Apart from the dark trails of seaweed there was nothing solid within reach.

'For pity's sake– '

Drufidius backed away, careful to retrace the indentations of his footprints. He searched the sandy scrub around the path. There was only the odd bleached fragment of driftwood. Too short. He looked back. Romanus' head was a dot on the sand. And the tide was coming in. Drufidius hesitated, then turned and walked quickly to where his horse was tethered. He had secured the stones, the crime had been judged and sentence passed. As far as Drufidius was concerned there was nothing more to be done.

Chapter 24

Justina examined the contents of the bag. 'They're beautiful,' she said. 'I can see how they would turn a man's head.'

'Or a woman's,' Drufidius said, tucking into a leg of rabbit. 'Hm. Very good. I didn't realize you were a skilled hunter, my lady.'

'I was a girl once,' Justina said, 'I ran free in the woods and hills – before I was an emperor's wife.' Justina held an opal up to the light. 'The king of gems.' She watched the rainbow colours glitter. 'Hope, innocence and purity.'

'Did you hear something?' Drufidius stopped chewing.

Justina cocked her head to one side and listened. 'It's getting dark. Probably just a bird or rabbit. I'll check the snares.' She drew her hair into a ponytail and was about to step into the open when something checked her. She crouched and peered through the niche in the stone. A group of five mounted Irish had halted in the centre of the enclosure. They carried long war-spears and were clothed in heavy fur jerkins. Their approach had been so stealthy they had given only the slightest indication of their presence. Drufidius pulled Justina back from the spy hole and took her place. He squinted through the gap. Each warrior carried a rounded shield embossed with a curved geometric design. The leader, sitting astride his horse, turned his head this way and that as he surveyed the buildings. Justina squeezed his shoulder and whispered:

Faelan. The giant dismounted and walked casually around the enclosure. Justina backed away. Drufidius silently thanked the gods that the fire had burned out – but the smell would surely give them away. Faelan stopped scarcely a spear's length away, so close that, had the narrow aperture been wide enough, Drufidius could have reached out and touched him. The chieftain pulled his breeches aside and urinated, heaving a sigh of satisfaction as the stream of liquid splashed in a steaming arc against the stones of the hut. Drufidius felt Justina shaking with fear. When he looked again the chieftain was pulling up his breeches. Faelan belched and ambled away to rejoin his war band.

The other warriors sat easy in their saddles as the overworked animals snorted and foraged, nibbling at tussocks of frost-whitened grass. Faelan remounted and began a conversation with his horsemen. There seemed to be some dispute over their next course of action. Drufidius relaxed. They would be on their way any moment. He turned to convey this to Justina but dislodged a loose slab of limestone. It fell in slow motion onto a pile of rubble where it split with a crack. Justina froze in horror. Faelan and his men stopped their conversation. Drufidius heard a quizzical grunt, then the sound of heavy footsteps. Through the remains of the hut entrance, Faelan's bull-like head appeared. Drufidius cast about for a weapon. His sword was on the other side of the fire. He cursed himself for leaving it unsheathed. Justina had shrunk into the corner; it was only a matter of moments before he saw them. The chieftain let out a cry of triumph as he caught sight of Justina and climbed in to pull her out. He grabbed her by the shoulder, roaring with delight, and dragged her from the building. She screamed and fought. Drufidius picked up the nearest and largest stone and pitched it towards the barbarian where it bounced off his huge back and fell ineffectually to the ground. Faelan grinned. Throwing Justina down like a straw doll, he retrieved his axe and walked towards Drufidius, hefting the axe. Drufidius looked around for an alternative missile as Faelan's horsemen whooped and shouted, manoeuvering their horses to encircle Justina. One dismounted and grabbed her by the hair. Justina screamed. Drufidius dodged Faelan's first blow and out of the corner of his eye saw the warrior inexplicably release Justina and clutch his chest. The Irishman, his face twisted in agony, ripped his tunic aside to reveal the point of an arrowhead protruding through his skin. He lolled backwards and Drufidius realized that he was already dead. Faelan howled and turned to face the threat. He drew his sword and whirled it around his head, baying for blood.

Barnabas appeared, carrying a long Roman *pilum*. Behind came a dozen or more olive-skinned men wearing auxiliary uniform. *Archers*, Drufidius thought, hysterical with relief, *Syrian archers*. Faelan charged Barnabas. The bishop judged his moment. The lance left Barnabas' hand and slammed into Faelan's chest, ripping through his body like a skewer. The barbarian chieftain fell like an ox.

'May god have mercy on him.' The bishop pulled Justina her to her feet.

She swayed and almost fell. 'My husband is indeed a good judge of character,' she said, weakly. 'You have brought help.'

'Better than that,' Barnabas said. 'I've brought an army.'

'He left you for dead?' Drufidius asked the bishop.

'He left me with a very sore head. But he was young, inexperienced. Had the roles been reversed I'd have made sure.' Barnabas smiled, 'but as you have related, God's justice is meted out in mysterious ways.'

'Did you not suspect?'

'Perhaps. A little. But– '

'You didn't expect his fall to be as swift.' Justina finished for him.

Barnabas shook his head. 'I did not, but the boy had never been as close to a fortune in precious stones before.'

'Not many have.' Drufidius felt for the reassuring bulge under his tunic and allowed himself a satisfied smile. For the first time in many weeks he felt that things were taking a turn for the better. As far as his eyes could see he was surrounded by the comforting presence of the horsemen, heavy and light infantry, archers and yellow crossed shields of Valentinian's task force. He could see the plumed helmet of the commander, Jovinus, at the head of the column and it was his raised hand that ended the short ride to the straits separating the mainland from Mona. Barnabas helped Justina dismount and they watched the efficient preparations of Jovinus' troops as the task force readied itself for the short crossing.

'Should be p plain sailing from now on,' Drufidius linked his arm in Justina's, 'our troubles are almost over.'

Chapter 25

The sails of the recently arrived Irish ships flapped gently at anchor by the quayside and the shadowy figures of the Irish sentries could be seen pacing the battlements and exchanging an occasional word in passing. Otherwise the night was still. A flickering light from the east turret indicated that Paulus was in residence. The time was approaching. Marius thought of Barnabas' story; the serpent and the saviour; the prayer he had heard in the Calleva church. He recalled the words:

> *'God made man, then God became man,*
> *God saved us in Yeshua,*
> *Christos, who is God'*

Perhaps this god could help him. He thought of the crucified men at the straits – Paulus' work, no doubt, and of the Jewish rabbi who had suffered a similar fate. He had not turned from his destiny, and what a destiny to face, Marius thought with a shudder. To face your end with courage was one thing, but to face it voluntarily, knowing the outcome to be pain beyond human endurance. . . it was extraordinary. Whatever and whoever this man Yeshua had been, he had at the very least been a man of superhuman courage.

Marius prayed now for a measure of that courage. If he was to have any chance of success he was going to need it. Freia had been right; the father of the girl she had promised to look after was indeed an army commander.

A commander of *armies* would be a better description; her father was Valentinian, emperor of Rome and her name was Antonia, sister of Gratian, the emperor's heir. He took a deep breath. Success would bring accolades; failure its own reward…

'There'll be snow before dawn, I shouldn't wonder.'

Marius turned to see Caelius stepping onto the battlement rampart.

'You seem preoccupied, soldier.'

Marius relaxed. Caelius was merely showing a commander's concern for his men. 'I was just thinking – about my family.'

'Ah yes. I think of mine often,' Caelius pointed into the darkness. 'way over yonder, across land and sea.'

'In Gaul?'

'Yes, in the south. I have a villa, some land. Horses, cattle, a good wife. . . ' The commander sighed deeply.

Marius shook his head. 'It's a fair distance to be parted.'

'It is indeed. But when this is over I shall return. I have plans,' Caelius laughed softly, his breath forming a cloud in the cold air, 'and none of them involve war.'

'How long have you been garrisoned at Mona?' Marius asked. 'You were here before Paulus?'

Caelius nodded. 'Long before. I have looked out on this grey, miserable sea for nearly five years. With little prospect of relief.'

'And Paulus made you an offer you couldn't refuse?'

'Would you have?' Caelius rubbed his hands together and blew into them. 'This cursed weather. How long would you endure it? If all goes to plan I'll be home within days.'

'When I was posted abroad,' Marius said, 'I would have given anything for a blast of cold air like this.'

'This would be before the wall posting?'

Marius' heart lurched. Caelius was looking at him expectantly. Here was the man's talent. An easy chat and then the trap sprung. He cursed himself for letting his guard down.

'Yes, before then,' Marius said, trying to sound casual and confident. 'The wall was colder even than this.' He laughed and the sound rang hollow against the turrets and crenellations of the battlements.

'And what of Fullofaudes? How did you find working under his command?' Caelius pressed. 'Tell me, did he still wear his father's cloak, the lions's pelt?'

Marius hesitated. What had he heard about the *dux?* Was Caelius spinning him a false line?

'For all the good it did him,' a booming voice filled the ramparts. Scapulus appeared out of the shadows. 'Led us straight into the mire. But then, we were outnumbered ten to one; Fullofaudes was not to blame.'

'Was he not?' Caelius probed. 'And you defended him to the last?'

'To the very last,' Scapulus said testily, 'until all was lost.'

Caelius nodded. 'Well then, your loyalty is indeed commendable. Do the same here and your fortunes shall improve, centurion.'

'That's why we're here,' Scapulus said. 'Eh, Marius?'

'Indeed. You can count on our support,' Marius agreed, thanking the gods for Scapulus' intervention.

Caelius looked them up and down. 'Good. Well then; I am in need of a warming draught of wine. I'll leave you to your – reminiscences.' He saluted and made his way along the ramparts until the darkness swallowed him.

Marius let out his breath with a soft whistle. 'Good timing. Thanks.'

'The lion pelt is all Fullofaudes will be remembered for,' Scapulus said ruefully. 'I still can't believe he's gone.'

'Fullofaudes was of barbarian extraction,' Marius said with a smile, 'he must have been pretty special to win you over.'

'There are barbarians and there are barbarians,' Scapulus said.

'And Fraomar? Has he won your favour yet?'

Scapulus grunted. 'He'll do. I suppose.'

The hall was full to overflowing, the mood expectant, each warrior understanding the significance of a blood alliance between Ireland and the Saxon kingdoms. Crimthann's lords surrounded him, awaiting the woman destined to be his bride. A low murmur of conversation pervaded the hall, broken by bouts of raucous laughter as the men waited, some stamping their feet impatiently, others picking quarrels or playfully punching a consort. Marius bit his lip, his senses tingling. It would be during the high point of the ceremony that he would make his move, when the attention was on Crimthann and Lawenya. He felt a cold breath of air and turned to see Paulus enter the hall, preceded by Freia. But there was something wrong; she held herself as if in pain and her eyes were downcast. Silence fell over the gathering as the notary turned to address them.

'My friends,' he began, 'this is an auspicious occasion. And I am glad you are here to share it with us. This alliance joins two nations by blood. The union will squeeze the life out of the Empire's western provinces leaving the land to a more deserving overseer. Some have already benefited from the produce of that land.' There were nods of assent and agreement. A warrior banged his drinking vessel on the table and crowed a war cry.

'Yes, you shall have more, my friend,' Paulus replied to a chorus of approval from the Irish lords. 'And you shall inherit a second green and pleasant land for your children.' More applause.

'This will not be the end of our alliance,' Paulus continued. 'But the beginning of a fruitful relationship that will usher in a new era. Britannia will have one ruler, and one ruler only. We will repel Valentinian's legions, such as remain, and take possession of the rich southern lands. Your kinsmen will secure the north.' Here Paulus made an inclusive gesture to Crimthann. 'My lord, you now have both the opportunity and resource to enrich your people with the fat of Britannia's inherited wealth. Valentinian will trouble you no more. With the south under my overall control and the legions expelled, there is nothing left to threaten our dominion.'

'You are *wrong*.'

Marius gaped as Freia spoke up, her voice tremulous but audible to the entire gathering.

'My little sorceress has a problem?' Paulus took Freia's arm and gripped it tightly. 'Tell me, what is troubling you? Speak up so that we all can hear.'

A low murmur spread throughout the hall. Sorcery was something to take seriously, especially on such a groundbreaking occasion.

'Tell them, *Buitseach*,' Paulus slapped Freia's face hard. 'We have no secrets. Enlighten us all.'

'You will not succeed,' Freia gasped in pain, holding her cheek. 'Your enemies are upon you.'

The murmur rose to a babble of concern. Marius watched in fascinated dread as Freia pulled away from Paulus and flung her arms in the air. 'The island will run with blood, as in days past. The sea will turn red. It is finished.'

There was a commotion at the far end of the hall, voices shouting to be heard above the hubbub generated by Freia's outburst.

A moment later it was clearly heard: the alarm echoed around the hall portals, first taken up by one, then tens, then hundreds of voices. 'To arms! To arms!'

The effect was instantaneous. Crimthann led the rush to the exit. Marius' first thought was that Fraomar's patience had exhausted itself, but they were few in number and would hardly have provoked such a reaction from the fortress guardroom. What should he do? Where was Freia? Marius craned his neck but she was lost in the melee. He vowed to come back for her, but now he had to take his chance and find Valentinian's daughter.

The quayside was in a state of confusion. One of Caelius' men was struggling to carry a heavy sack up the wooden ramp. 'Are you going to help with this or what?' the soldier glared at Marius.

Marius jumped onto the ramp and took the weight of the sack as it slid perilously close to the edge. 'Don't let go of that, by Mithras,' the man shouted at him. 'Paulus will have your guts.'

The sack was a dead weight. Silver, gold or precious stones in all probability. 'Pull it over here.' The man indicated a hatch set into the floor of the deck. Marius heaved while the soldier opened the hatch. The ship pitched up and down in the high swell, hindering the operation. 'Weather's getting worse,' said the soldier. 'We've got to get out fast, or we've had it. Do you know what's coming?' He cocked his head to the south. 'A *vexillatio* from Legio 1 Flavia Martis - the watchtower detail clocked their shield insignias.' He spat and cursed. 'Vicious bastards. We haven't a hope in Hades now.'

'Best be quick then,' Marius agreed. He grabbed the side of the ship to steady himself as it yawed. The Irish crew was in position, men with arms the breadth of mastheads, preparing to wield the large oars to guide them out of the bay before the sails were unfurled. Marius could hear the prisoners below. He ransacked his mind for something to prevent the ship casting off. 'Hurry up,' his new associate prompted. 'There's more to get on board.' He gave Marius a shove and followed him down the ramp.

'Leave what you're doing,' a voice bellowed. 'All of you!' Caelius stood on the wharf. 'Front of the fort, now! That's an order!'

Somewhere beyond the fort walls a horn sounded. Marius' new friend took off after Caelius and vanished through the fort gate. Marius looked around. The Irish on the second ship were preparing to raise the ramp. Apart from these, the quayside was clear.

'Wait.' The men stopped what they were doing and looked at him suspiciously. 'I have been tasked to check the hold. For illness.' Marius did an impression of an ailing prisoner, unsure if they understood. 'If they are too weak they will not survive the voyage.' His words were rewarded with blank stares. In desperation he said, 'Do you want to take living slaves to your homeland or corpses? It's your choice. You'll have to sail with the stink.' He gave them another impression and this time they appeared to get the message.

The first warrior shrugged and moved aside to let Marius pass. He made his way down to the hold, heart pounding. He moved deeper into the ship, which groaned and strained beneath him. The air in the hold was already stale; the gods alone knew what it would be like during the voyage to Ireland. He moved down the narrow walkway between the slave berths, peering into the shadows as his eyes adjusted to the half-light. An Irish was seated at the end of the hold. Marius held his breath. The man looked up and carried on with what he was doing, adjusting some fixture or knot Marius couldn't tell. He passed berth after berth. A dog barked, but the noise was muffled, from another corner of the ship. Where was she? Was he in the wrong ship? And then in the last he found her, curled against the deck head. She turned and his finger was on her lips. He lifted her gently and carried her to the hatch, past the man still engrossed in his nautical task. The stevedores had moved to the deck and he passed unchallenged down the gangplank. Once on the quayside he made for the stone steps leading into the fort, the emperor's daughter limp in his arms. Inside the fort, chaos reigned. The stamp of feet on stone reverberated around the building as the mobilization continued. Scapulus appeared at the south entrance. They met half way up the internal staircase. 'An army,' Scapulus was incredulous. 'Valentinian has sent Jovinus, no less - with an army.' He reached out his hand to touch the child's cheek. 'You found her!' The lopsided grin flashed. 'This'll mean a cosy retirement villa for me.'

'If we get out alive,' Marius said, 'I'll buy you one myself.'

Scapulus grasped his arm. Marius turned.

Caelius was watching them from the hall below, his hand on the hilt of his sword. He hesitated, torn between the urgency of battle preparation and his curiosity that was rapidly turning to suspicion. He placed a foot on the staircase and called up: 'Where are you taking her?'

Scapulus descended two steps.

Caelius drew his sword. 'I cannot let you pass.'

Marius shouted: 'She is but a child. She needs medical attention.'

'Just a child?' Caelius questioned. 'Then why such interest? Tell me, or you shall not pass.'

'This says I can.' Scapulus brandished his *gladius*.

Caelius thrusted. Scapulus twisted away but although the action saved his life, the blade drew blood from his side. His balance lost, Scapulus stumbled and, finding no purchase on the open stairway, crashed to the flagstones below.

Marius retreated up the staircase, placed the girl gently on the floor and drew his sword. Caelius advanced in a fury, attacking Marius with such violence that Marius' back was forced against the wall. The man fought as if possessed. The blade slid down the edge of Marius' *spatha* and he felt a shock of cold as it touched his exposed throat. Out of the corner of his eye Marius caught a glimpse of a figure watching their struggle from the shadow of the tower. Caelius had seen it too. The figure appeared to nod in affirmation. At that moment, the girl screamed.

Chapter 26

The landscape leading up to the fort at Cunedum was flat and featureless, with only wild hedges and a few isolated trees to break the monotony. It was possible, on a clear day, to command not only a good view across the bay from the harbour, but also across the island to the east for many miles. But today was not one of those days.

Jovinus, commander of the task force, had not worried unduly about secrecy. He was confident, from the intelligence provided, that he had more than enough at his disposal to take on the army of the barbarian alliance. He moved amongst his command, keen to engage the enemy before the weather gained the upper hand. The snow had stopped for the time being, the ground dusted with a thin layer of white, not yet deep enough to prove a problem for the infantry or cavalry. He looked at the sky. There would be more to come. It had been the god's blessing which had given them safe passage across the channel, avoiding the Frankish and Saxon vessels in a providential mist which had enabled them to glide through and make land at *Rutupiae*. His mission was simple: to destroy Paulus' forces and push them into the sea. Clearing the rest of the country could be dealt with later – that job belonged to another.

He signalled for the trumpets to be sounded. Ahead lay the fort at Cunedum; already he could see the Irish deploying their warriors. And there were the horsemen on the right flank, whose valour in battle was legendary. The battlements of the fort were busy with scurrying troopers taking up position along the ramparts. Jovinus wondered if the fort had *ballistae*. He doubted it. It was but a small fortlet, more of an early warning outpost for the main garrison at Segontium. His mouth set in a grim line. They had witnessed the remains of Segontium the day before. The barracks were a charnel house and the outskirts not much better. The auxiliaries had evidently fought bravely but, as Segontium had suffered the usual depletion of troops over a long period of time, they had been too few to defend against the concerted barbarian attacks. Well, now it was time to make amends. Jovinus raised his arm and silence fell across the ranks, from the auxiliaries at the head of the van, cavalry and archers, slingers and foot soldiers to the disciplined formations of regular infantry with their oval yellow shields, the sun reflecting coldly on their armour. The first centurion called out in a loud voice that rang across the flatlands and bounced off the fort walls, striking fear into the hearts of the bravest. '*Men of Rome! Are you ready for war?*' As one man the task force army raised spears, shields and swords three times in slow, deliberate succession. '*Ready! Ready! Ready!*' With shields slung over their shoulders and weapons drawn the formations advanced on Cunedum.

The lithe Syrian archers darted forward and at a fresh command the sky was darkened with flying projectiles. The two *ballistae* Jovinus had insisted upon had been quickly assembled and soon the *thwang* of their catapults sent the first of a shower of heavy rocks directly into and onto the fort's battlements. The walls exploded with each hit, sending huge chunks of masonry flying, scattering the troops from the ramparts like saplings. The cavalry wings rode in for the first skirmish, swords sheathed in shoulder-slung baldrics, harrying the barbarian flanks with their lances. The barbarians battered them as they flew past, bringing horses down with spear thrusts at close quarters. After the cavalry assault another rain of arrows came from the archers as the Cretan slingers moved in behind them and chose their targets. Heads split open under the assault of lead missiles as the Irish roared their defiance, moving forward into the next hail of arrows, shields raised in a protective roof.

Barnabas rode to join Jovinus from the rear where he had left Justina behind the baggage train, the safest place on the battlefield. Jovinus raised his arm in acknowledgement. 'Salve, Barnabas.'

'Salve. The Irish infantry will soon charge, d'you think?' Barnabas asked the commander.

'No. They will wait until we make the move,' Jovinus shouted above the tumult. 'And in the meantime they will try to break up our line.'

'They are outnumbered. They cannot prevail,' Barnabas shouted back. 'By the way, I have some additional help for you.'

The commander looked round to see a wild figure leading a group of twenty auxiliaries. Fraomar, his long hair gathered and knotted, reined in his mount and gave Barnabas a wave of acknowledgement. Barnabas returned the wave. 'He's a good man,' he told the commander. 'Use him.'

Jovinus waved his assent and Fraomar led Scapulus' men towards the fray. Barnabas galloped towards the auxiliary horsemen regrouping to the left of the throng. As he rode he allowed himself a wry smile. This was not how he had planned to begin his ministry in the West. But who was he to question the will of God?

Chapter 27

The girl's scream was enough to distract Caelius from his assault. Marius ducked under the blade. Caelius' arm followed through, ringing on the wall behind Marius' head.

Marius jabbed and Caelius backed away. Marius pressed home his attack, forcing Caelius against the east turret's heavy door. Marius swung his blade under the centurion's guard and knocked the sword from his hand in one swift motion. *Thank you, Saturnus,* Marius muttered under his breath. *I knew that move would come in handy one day. . .*

Caelius let his arm fall. 'Finish it,' he said.

Marius lowered his weapon, picked up Caelius' sword and sheathed it. 'Do what you have to do, Caelius, but leave us to ourselves.'

Caelius opened his mouth to reply but dropped to his knees, stabbed from behind. He pitched forward, eyes bulging in shock, and collapsed full length on the flagstones.

Marius darted to one side, but Caelius' killer had disappeared. The tower door was ajar, casting a narrow swathe of light down the passage.

'Someone is in there. I *saw* him.' Antonia clung to Marius, shaking with fear.

Marius spun as he heard a noise behind him then let out his breath with relief. Scapulus was climbing the staircase, grimacing and holding his side.

'You're a hard man to kill,' Marius said.

'Hard as a sandal hobnail, boy. Besides, I'm not planning to die yet,' Scapulus forced a laugh, ''til I get that villa you promised.'

Marius gave Antonia's hand to Scapulus. The centurion patted her head and the girl shot Marius a fearful look.

'It's all right,' he reassured her, 'Scapulus isn't as scary as he looks.'

'Ha. So you say,' Scapulus made a face for the girl's benefit and was rewarded with a tentative smile.

'Take her along the shoreline, away from the battle,' Marius told the centurion. 'There's a track that leads to a coastal path directly from the beach, Follow it. You can work your way to the rear of the task force.'

Scapulus nodded, 'I've sent my men that way already.' The big man cocked his head. 'And you?'

Marius' expression was answer enough.

'Don't hang around,' Scapulus advised. 'You know what'll happen to anyone those *Flavia Martis* heavies find when the walls come down. . . '

Marius nodded grimly and briefly gripped Scapulus' shoulder. Outside, the noise of the fighting seemed to intensify. A roar of tremendous volume shook the building as the Irish horsemen made another futile and suicidal charge against Jovinus' heavy infantry. Scapulus led Antonia away and Marius turned back to the turret. Gripping the knurled iron handle, he pushed the heavy door open.

Freia opened her eyes. A muzziness filled her head and she drew a hand weakly across her forehead. She was lying on some kind of stone bench. The sickly, sweet smell came to her nostrils and she knew immediately where she was She tried to move but her body felt so

236

weak; Paulus had done something to her. Somehow he had known that she had trespassed and looked into his forbidden chamber. Since then she had felt a terrible weakness, as if her body had been drugged by some dreadful potion or worse still, some dark incantation. Now Paulus had imprisoned her in that same chamber but for what purpose? Freia was conscious of the din of battle somewhere close by. This gave her hope. She had to break free of whatever curse Paulus had used to paralyze her. She heard a furtive movement. A door closed somewhere with a dull clunk. Then she heard voices – Paulus and a more familiar accent. *Marius*. Freia pushed herself to the edge of the bench and collapsed onto the floor. Fighting back tears of pain she began to crawl.

The spiral stairwell echoed to the tread of Marius' boots. He took each step cautiously, Caelius' sword in one hand and his own in the other. He reached another door and pressed his ear against it. All he could hear was the constant clamour of the battle being waged. He opened the door. At first he thought the room was empty but then realized that there was someone standing by the slit window overlooking the harbour. A high-backed chair stood in the centre of the tower room, a small rectangular table to its side. Apart from these, the room was bare.

'Paulus,' Marius said. Now that he was here, he felt curiously detached. Here was the man responsible for his parents' death. Paulus. *Catena*.

'Fighting is a tiresome business, is it not?' The voice was soft, reasonable. 'Have you come to kill me?' The question was posed as if the answer were of little consequence.

'I – I don't know,' Marius said. He could feel a heaviness creeping into his limbs, a torpor. 'I want to talk to you.'

'How intriguing. What about, I wonder?'

'You're finished here,' Marius said with an effort. He wanted to sit down, take the weight off his feet.

'Please,' Paulus indicated the chair, 'be my guest.'

Marius sat. He felt very tired, 'Your commander. You killed him.'

'Caelius?' Paulus gave a sharp laugh of disdain, 'He was a weak fool. I have no tolerance for sympathetic soldiering.'

Marius' eyelids were heavy. He placed both swords carefully on the floor. He couldn't remember what they were for.

'That's right,' Paulus said, 'you won't be needing those. Someone might get hurt.'

Marius' eyes closed. He needed to sleep. It was warm, he could see a fire, a blazing wheel of fire turning round and round. He stretched to feel the warmth. It was good. He would go into the fire. It would be safe there. But someone was calling him back. At the edge of the flames a cowled figure held a wooden cross high above its head. The cross seemed to glow brighter than the flames; it propelled him away from the fire. Marius opened his eyes. Paulus stood above him, the blade of Caelius' sword plunging towards him. He tried to raise an arm, to ward off the blow but knew before he tried that it would be impossible. And then a figure flung itself between the descending blade and Marius' paralyzed body. Freia's scream broke the spell and Marius hurled himself to one side, sprawling on the floor. Freia collapsed, a crimson stain spreading over her breast. Her eyes flashed a warning as Paulus raised the sword again. Marius caught the notary's wrist and twisted. The sword clattered to the floor. He rolled and found his feet. At the same moment Paulus saw the other sword lying beside the fallen chair. They both lunged for the weapon but Paulus was quicker. With a cry of triumph he flourished it. Marius backed towards the window, casting this way and that for something to defend himself with. Paulus struck, cutting Marius below his shoulder armour. The pain was instant and intense. He felt a warm trickle running down his arm and grabbed the table, holding it out like a shield. Paulus attacked again, chopping the blade down the centre of the table, sending splinters of wood flying. Cursing himself for a fool Marius remembered the dagger hanging from its baldric under his cloak. He fumbled for it. Seeing the knife, Paulus hesitated and advanced with greater caution.

'You murdered my parents,' Marius said.

'Did I?' Paulus affected concern. 'But there were so many– '

Marius threw himself at Paulus. He was under the notary's guard and felt the sword swish above his head. He had the knife in his hand, plunged it up and twisted. He rolled over, panting with exertion. The room was empty but for Freia's still body. He conducted a frenzied search. Paulus had vanished. And then his eyes were drawn to the green slat of light falling across the flagstones. He followed the light to its source and threw back the flap. He took a step back in horror before he realized that the snake in the chamber was a statue. Gagging at the smell he retreated into the tower room and slammed the aperture shut. His head cleared and he crouched beside Freia's still body, cradling her head in his arms. Her eyes opened and she smiled. Marius pressed his cloak against her chest to staunch the flow of blood but she coughed and pushed weakly at his shoulder with her hand. 'No.'

'Why?' Marius asked her gently. His eyes prickled. '*Why?*'

'Tell my brother,' she whispered, 'that I love him. And I would have loved you too, Marius of Corinium, had circumstances been kinder.'

Marius nodded and held her, rocking her gently. Time stood still. He was unaware of the thud of Jovinus' missiles striking home, the shuddering of the building as the battlements slowly collapsed. Neither was he aware of the shouts and cries of the rebels as they fought bravely but hopelessly for their lives. All that mattered was Freia, this moment in time. Marius bent and kissed her gently. Their eyes locked and she gave him one last smile before her soul slipped silently into the afterlife.

Marius stepped into the courtyard like a man in a dream. The noise outside was cacophonic. It was snowing heavily, large flakes adding to the drifts which had formed during the earlier fall. He ducked instinctively as a hail of slingshot hurtled over his head. *Come on Marius, wake up,* he told himself grimly. *She's gone. There's nothing you can do...*

The courtyard was littered with bodies. A handful of rebels still held the west tower, ducking and loosing arrows between the salvoes of return fire. As he looked up one of the archers fell soundlessly to join the other corpses, an arrow embedded in his eye. The dead rebel's helmet bounced and rolled towards him. Marius snatched up the soldier's shield and rammed the helmet onto his head. He crouched low and looked out to sea. Was it his imagination or was something moving, rising above the swell. Could it be? He caught the swirl of a dark cloak, the raising of an arm. Marius stared, rubbed his eyes. There, again. This time he was sure. Someone was walking on the surf. He strained to pick out the detail but the figure was enveloped in mist. Marius shivered. *Flesh and blood?*

Another hail of missiles fell around him, arrows this time, and he turned to find better cover but as he did so he caught in his peripheral vision, too late, a rock spinning over the crumbling battlements. Marius dived to one side but the rock caught him a glancing blow on the side of his helmet and the light went out like a snuffed candle.

Jovinus' heavy infantry continued their inexorable progress towards the fort, swinging their shields as if to some pre-ordained rhythm. The barbarian cavalry, hindered by the deteriorating condition of the ground lost many horsemen as the hooves of their mounts slipped on the slush created by the snow and constant pummeling of the earth by both foot soldiers and cavalry. Fraomar rode hard amongst the Irish flank, flourishing his sword to left and right among the press, seeking out the exposed flesh of the enemy and wreaking terrible damage. The rearguard of the alliance, Caelius' mercenaries, deployed in a semicircular formation in front of the beleaguered fort, fought hard against Jovinus' auxiliaries and light infantry, who attacked and regrouped constantly leaving the exhausted rebels little time to regain their strength. Time and time again they rushed from both flanks, the slingers firing a salvo in unison then the infantry following through by first casting their shield-piercing spears then wading in with the *spatha*. The ground became a quagmire of mud, slush and blood. Fraomar, taking a rare break from the action sought out Jovinus, seated on his chestnut bay on a slight rise to the left flank. Fraomar's face was wild with the heat of battle. 'One last push, Roman, and they are finished,' he told the commander. 'There is a coastal path to the rear of the fort where the horses may not go but on foot it is possible. If I take twenty men with me I may be able to prevent the Irish ships casting off.'

Jovinus assessed Fraomar's suggestion, letting his tactical eye sweep across the battlefield. 'Go to it, barbarian, with my sanction. They will retreat into the remains of the fort at the last.' He surveyed the building and grunted 'It will not deny us the victory; it will merely buy them a little time. But, Roman or barbarian, every last man within will die.' Jovinus drew a hand across his throat. 'This place will be razed to the ground.'

Scapulus accepted a draught of wine from one of the reserves guarding the baggage train. As the welcome liquid coursed down his throat he caught sight of Fraomar leading a group of men at a brisk trot towards the coastal path he had recently taken to carry Antonia to safety. Scapulus returned the wine jar and hailed the familiar figure covering the tail end of the group.

'*Hoi!* Fabius!'

Fabius turned briefly, signalling haste. Scapulus sprinted to join them, keeping a wary eye open for stray arrows. For a big man he could move quickly and was soon trotting abreast of his second in command.

'We're after the Irish,' Fabius panted and pointed. Two ships had already cast off and were now well out of bowshot range. 'With any luck we'll stop the last or at least give them something to take home.' Fabius grinned.

Scapulus ran on and caught up with Fraomar, noting as he passed along the column that most of the men were Flavia Martis auxiliaries, half their number archers, the remainder infantry. Fraomar grunted a greeting and the column slowed a fraction as the path narrowed. Rounding a corner they ran straight into five of Caelius' rebel detachment coming the other way. Fraomar's borrowed *spatha* swung in a hissing arc. The soldier had his own sword half way out of its scabbard before Fraomar's removed his head. The helmet went spinning, clattering off the rocks below. Scapulus booted the head after it and rammed his *gladius* into the next man's face. The blade entered the rebel's mouth; blood gushed, he fell. Three were left. They hunched, weapons raised, feinting, waiting for them to make the first move. Fraomar obliged; he stepped to one side and signalled. Arrows whistled, finding their unshielded targets. Fraomar and Scapulus stepped over the bodies and trotted on, the Flavia Martis contingent following hard on their heels.

The dockside was emptying fast. Scapulus saw immediately that the last of the Irish ships was about to slip the net. Oars were in motion, the deck alive with frantic activity as the seamen strove to put distance between themselves and the doomed fort. Another command from Fraomar and the archers loosed a fresh volley, this time drawing return fire from the departing vessel. Scapulus brought his shield up and braced as two arrows tore through the reinforced wood, their barbed points protruding a finger-length from his face. A cry to his left as one of the Flavia Martis infantrymen took a missile in the leg. Scapulus peered cautiously around the oval shield. The ship had slipped further away, the prow turning, pointing across the water to its distant homeland.

And there, on the deck was Crimthann, feet planted firmly on deck, his braided hair flowing over his cloak. He raised a hand in farewell. Fraomar scooped up an abandoned *pilum*, hefted it and released. The shaft sped towards its target, dipped and buried itself in the decking at Crimthann's feet. The Irish king didn't move a muscle.

An arrow skittered along the jetty and came to rest beside Scapulus' sandal. He turned and brought his shield up. The rebel archers were firing on them from the fort ramparts. Fabius raised an eyebrow and Scapulus nodded. 'Clear those battlements. Kill everything that moves.' Fabius quickly selected five infantymen, evil looking thugs with vacant, murderous eyes, plus three archers.

'And everything that doesn't–' Scapulus advised as an afterthought. It was always best to be sure.

'Consider it done,' Fabius said with a grim smile.

Scapulus watched them climb the steps and disappear into the fort. That would give the rebels something to chew on, the centurion thought with grim satisfaction; with any luck the defenders would think the unexpected attack from the rear comprised of more men than there actually were and panic accordingly. Perhaps Caelius' men had recognized the vulnerability of the coastal path and the troops they had recently encountered had hoped to see off precisely the sort of tactic Fraomar had so successfully implemented.

When Scapulus turned his attention back to the fleeing ship he saw that Fraomar had arranged the archers into a three forward, three back rapid fire phalanx. Significantly, the Alamann had also ordered them to dip their arrows into a vat of pitch which had been set ablaze by some stray fragment of burning wood, possibly from one of the *ballistae* missiles. Triads of flaming arrows sped out through the snowflakes towards Crimthann's ship. Some fell short; others buried themselves in the ship's wooden frame. Very soon an orange blossom of fire spread along the deck. Black smoke whipped skywards in the breeze. A minute later the entire vessel was engulfed in flames. Scapulus watched in fascination as Crimthann's warriors made their choice, either throwing themselves into the water, disappearing under the spume as their armour dragged them down, or remaining on deck, waiting to be claimed by the fire. Scapulus hoped that there were no prisoners below deck but as far as his memory served, this particular ship had been laden only with cargo – booty from the inland raids. The centurion sighed regretfully. What a cursed waste. But then he recalled Marius' assertion that, as of this morning, the fort still contained sackfuls of stolen goods which he doubted the rebels had had time to load. Excellent. When Fabius and the Flavia Martis savages had finished clearing out the courtyard he would have a look for himself. Then with a sick jolt he realized what he had forgotten: as far as he knew, Marius was still in there.

Marius opened his eyes. His vision blurred, then slowly cleared. He could feel the roughness of the fort wall on his back. Something was pinning his legs. A body. He heaved the dead man aside. Blood oozed from the soldier's mouth. The noise of battle was still shaking the air. Steel clashing; voices yelling; the sound of trampling cavalry. Marius looked up to the ramparts. They were devoid of life. A movement to his left. Infantrymen were moving amongst the dead and wounded. There was an occasional cry, a death rattle as the *pilae* found those still clinging to life. They were getting closer. Marius found that he was too weak to move. His leg was numb where the corpse had been lying on it. He started to inch along the wall, dragging his rebellious legs after him. The movement was noticed. Someone was standing over him. He looked up and saw only the red shield insignia of Flavia Martis, the wicked point of the *pilum*. The face that looked into his bore no trace of recognition nor compassion. The arm went up, the *pilum* poised to strike. Marius tensed for the end. The pilum came down, but a handsbreadth from Marius' chest it was knocked aside by the edge of a *gladius*. Marius knew only one person stubborn enough to prefer the old-fashioned *gladius* over the *spatha*. He could have cried with relief. Scapulus loomed overhead. 'Not this one,' he told the infantryman, who moved onto his next victim with a shrug and a growled curse.

'So,' Scapulus winked. 'I leave you on your own and what happens, eh? You take a catnap while the rest of us do the dangerous stuff.'

Marius accepted Scapulus' outstretched arm and allowed himself to be pulled upright. The blood was returning to his legs and, despite his pounding head, he seemed to be in one piece.

'Ready to fight, boy?' Scapulus asked him with a grim smile. 'Welcome to the army. There's a battle going on out there, in case you didn't know, and I'm missing it.' He tossed Marius a *spatha*. Marius hefted it. It felt good. Fraomar appeared at his side, his whole expression an unspoken question.

Marius shook his head and raised his eyes to the east tower. 'I'm so sorry, my friend. There was nothing I could do . . . nothing . . .' it sounded so inadequate. But what more could he say? Marius braced himself for the reaction. His fingers curled around the *spatha's* comforting solidity.

The Alamann had trusted him with his sister's life; how would he react?

After what seemed an age, Fraomar nodded and simply asked: 'Who?'

'Paulus,' Marius told the gladiator. 'Freia gave her life for mine. She wanted you to know that . . . that she loves you.' He swallowed hard. Later, he would weep with Fraomar and speak of Freia's bravery. Now was not the time. To his credit and Marius' enormous relief Fraomar asked no further questions, but his deep-set eyes darkened under his brows and his cheeks reddened with repressed grief and anger. *The gods help anyone who stands in the Alamann's way now,* Marius thought to himself as he relaxed his grip on the *spatha*.

'Some good news,' Scapulus shouted above the escalating din. 'That reptile, Nipius, has fled and the Lady Justina is still in one piece.'

'And Antonia– ?'

'Is safe with her mother behind the lines,' Scapulus said tersely. 'We need to get going – Fraomar's sprung twenty good men from the stockade – your Callevan lot. They're weak but willing.'

'Right, we'll join them, head back along the coastal path and make our way to the front line,' Marius suggested. 'Does Jovinus know we're here?'

Fraomar nodded. 'Yes,' the Alamann replied, 'but we must be gone before his troops take the fort . . .' He hesitated and glanced up at the east tower.

'Leave her be, Fraomar,' Marius said gently. 'The fortress will be ours before the day's end and we will honour her.' He gripped the Alamann's wrist and two men's eyes met in a silent bond of loss.

At the rear of the stockade Fraomar's new allies fell in and they took the path along the coastal ridge to emerge at the rear of the regrouping Irish horsemen. Marius watched them anxiously. If they were spotted the Irish could run them down. But the barbarian attention was on the right flank of Jovinus' infantry and they passed unscathed to the west of the battle, joining Jovinus' men by their own formation of *ala*.

The noise was deafening, making his head hurt all the more. Marius saw the yellow Roman shields of the frontline infantry studded with projectiles as the Irish archers let off another volley. Then came the charge. As Marius waded into the press sword raised, he felt an arrow thrum past his ear. Bending low, he rammed his way into the melee of whirling men and horses. Fraomar was with him, thrusting this way and that, as if endowed with the strength and endurance of ten men. Marius saw a warrior dive towards him, axe held aloft. He piled into him and cut him down with a stabbing stroke; the next moment, another had flung himself onto his back and wrapped his arms about Marius' neck. Marius tried to prise the arms away. He felt himself dragged down by the weight of the barbarian. He fell heavily, jarring every bone in his body but rolling as he did so. The action dislodged his assailant who leapt to his feet and lunged towards him again. Out of the corner of his eye, Marius saw Fraomar drive his sword into an Irish chest, then move towards him, crouching low. An auxiliary staggered with his hands pressing a gaping neck wound. The man fell gasping to the ground. Marius scrambled for his sword which lay on the bloodstained gorse an arms' length away. As his hand closed on the handle he twisted the weapon around and up feeling it sink into the barbarian's stomach, the man's dying weight pushing it deep into his body. Fraomar's face loomed. He rolled and Marius saw him kick out at a fresh assailant. The Irish dodged the blow and thrust his sword, seeking to run Fraomar through. Fraomar turned with amazing speed and Marius realized that the Alamann held a short sword in each hand. The arms scissored and the Irish head flew. But another appeared behind the Alamann and brought his axe high, ready to sink it into Fraomar's exposed back. Marius knew a warning would come too late. Finding his feet he allowed his bodyweight to carry him forward, his sword arm at full stretch. The *spatha* sank into the axeman's side and the Irishman went down, gasping. Fraomar spun on his heels and, signalling his thanks to Marius, finished the man off with a thrust to the heart. He withdrew his sword and shouted, '*Move!*'; Marius realized the warning was for him. He ducked his head as a horseman barged through, his deathblow missing Marius by a whisker. The rider rode on to find his next target. The press was thinning, the number of fallen outweighing those still fighting. A strong hand pulled Marius to his feet. Fraomar had leapt onto a riderless horse and was fighting to control the terrified animal. The horse reared up, the hooves missing Marius by the narrowest of margins. Marius needed no further encouragement. He hoisted himself up behind Fraomar, and for a split second the circumstances, sounds and smells of battle recalled the fight by the road to Corinium. But this was no mere skirmish; all around, men were locked together, sword biting into sword, sparks flying. Marius caught a movement behind and whirled, parrying an axe blow that would surely have split his skull in two. The axe rebounded off his helmet, stunning him with its force. The man was coated in blood and grinning maniacally. The axe swung again but as the axe descended his head was removed cleanly from behind by the sweeping cut of a Roman *spatha*. The man fell like a sack of corn, his detached head spinning on the ground before it was kicked aside by another pair locked in deadly embrace. The Irish began another charge, but Jovinus' cavalry were waiting. Before the Irish horsemen had gathered speed they were cut off by a reciprocal onslaught of mounted men from the left flank. Fraomar and Marius disappeared into their midst as the cries of battle rose and fell with the swell of the waves and the gusting snow spiralled, settling onto the battered turrets and gables of Cunedum like a shroud.

As dusk fell, the remnants of the Irish force had fled south east towards the straits. Jovinus let them go. His reserve units waiting at the pontoon bridges would deal with them.

Those who had retreated into the fortress fought on. Jovinus admired them for their bravery. He briefly considered terms of surrender, but rejected the thought on the grounds that prisoners were difficult to manage in winter. By the gods, this was the latest campaign he had ever fought. Valentinian had not exaggerated when he had told Jovinus he had an unusual job for him. Even the emperor had given up hostilities against the German tribes for the winter. And that was due to rain, not snow.

The battle had been a straightforward affair, in Jovinus' estimation. The flat contours of Mona provided no easy retreat for the barbarian alliance except the sea, the escape route he knew the Irish leadership had taken. Jovinus wondered if the rumours were true, that the great

Irish High King, Crimthann himself had been here. He hoped to find out when the leaders of the conspiracy were brought to account.

The heavy infantry had finished the surviving Irish. A remnant was fleeing west towards the sea in disarray. Jovinus raised his arm to signal the auxiliary *turmae* to pursue and cut them down. He then turned his attention to the fort. It was time to join the fray. He began to pick his way through the battlefield. The air was filled with a familiar sound; the groans of the maimed and wounded. Infantrymen were moving from body to body, finishing off casualties with quick thrusts of their spears. Jovinus reached the fort gates as they were forced open and his front-line troops entered like the wrath of the gods. There was no sadder nor more fearsome sight than when Roman took the life of Roman and Jovinus knew his troops would show no mercy. He had no sympathy for any rebels who may yet be lurking inside the fort. They had gambled and now they would pay the price of failure. Jovinus guided his horse through the ruined gates into the courtyard.

Chapter 28

They stood silently, each lost in their own thoughts. Barnabas finished his prayer and Fraomar, Marius and Scapulus moved forward to shovel cold earth onto the simple wooden casket. The Alamann paused at the graveside, unbuckled his sword and placed it on the box. 'She was a warrior in spirit. Now let her take this into the afterlife, so that all may know her valour. May the earth rest lightly upon her.'

Barnabas took his arm. 'She has the sword of the spirit with her already,' he said. 'Her Lord has already welcomed her into the afterlife. But let it be as you say.'

'I will always remember,' Marius whispered. 'Always.'

Justina and Antonia stood beside him, their faces clouded with sorrow. 'She helped us,' Justina said, 'and so many others.'

A group of soldiers were standing at a respectful distance. One stepped forward. He held his right arm awkwardly, but extended his left in salute. 'My name is Gaius Rufrius Pavo,' the soldier paused. 'I can tell you much about your sister and what has taken place in these last days.'

Pavo looked down at the casket and drew a weary hand across his eyes. He faced Fraomar and raised his chin. 'I crave your pardon. And if, having heard me out, you are unable to give it, then my life shall be forfeit.'

Fraomar nodded and placed a hand on the man's shoulder. 'I will hear what you have to say. But I will have no more blood shed on my sister's account.'

'Marius.'

Marius looked up. An auxiliary was calling from the fortress gate. 'Jovinus wants a word.'

Marius found the new fortress commander in the west tower. Marius hesitated on the threshold but whatever evil had dwelt there had long since departed. He could feel the change in the air.

'Ah. Marius. Sit down.' Jovinus indicated a chair. The commander stood by the wall and rapped the entrance to the hidden room with his knuckles. 'You've seen this – what's behind here?'

'Yes. That's where Paulus went. It leads to the lower floor.'

'And the contents of the chamber?' Jovinus stroked his chin.

'The snake? Who knows? Some questions are best left unanswered.' Marius thought of the green light. The smell.

'I'm going to have it destroyed. The whole lot. Unless you think Valentinian– '

'No. I expect he'll just want Paulus.'

Jovinus grunted. 'And you have no idea where he might have gone? No bodies have been found matching his description.'

Marius thought of the dark figure riding the waves. Perhaps he had imagined it. 'I have no idea,' he replied. 'Perhaps there is another way out–'

'Nobody will get off this island via the straits without my knowledge,' Jovinus said abruptly. The sea is the only remaining option.'

Marius surrendered to the logic. 'Perhaps. He may have fled with Crimthann's ships at the last.'

'And what of the Irish king?'

Marius sighed. 'Probably drowned or burned alive. But even so I'm certain of one thing.'

Jovinus raised his eyebrows.

'Paulus will return. This is a mere setback.'

The commander cleared his throat. 'Well, that being the case I could do with a stable garrison here. Can't just abandon the place. We have to hold these shores and hold them firmly.'

'I know someone who may be willing to repair and man the fortress temporarily. His men have been through a lot. They could do with the respite.'

'Ah. The *dux* remnant. Scapulus isn't it? Send him along would you?'

Marius left the commander to his paperwork and went to find Scapulus.

Scapulus rubbed his hand over his stubble. 'Could be worse I suppose,' he said to Marius. 'And you're right. The lads could do with a break. They have a roof over their heads here – of sorts–' the centurion surveyed the rubble-strewn courtyard. 'And plenty of supplies.'

'And something for their retirement too, by the look of things,' Marius grinned.

Scapulus returned the grin. His men were sorting through the abandoned cargo on the quayside. 'Well, some of it'll be returned to the owners I expect,' he said, 'but not *all* of it.' The big centurion shouted a caution to one of his men, who had slipped and almost dropped his precious load into the sea. The centurion looked out into the bay. 'I can think of worse places to be,' he said, 'but a few months'll be enough.'

'You'll be relieved by then; Jovinus is a man of his word.'

'Seems so,' Scapulus said. He lowered his voice. 'How's Fraomar? Taking it all right, is he?'

Marius sighed. 'As well as anyone could expect. I fear he blames me for what happened.'

'No,' Scapulus said, 'he knows the score. You did more than anyone could have done. Don't hold yourself responsible.'

'But that's just it,' Marius said. He thought of Freia's beauty, her selfless sacrifice and hung his head. 'That's just it; I always will.'

Chapter 29

Calleva seemed unusually quiet as they arrived at the west gate. For a moment Marius feared the worst. Had some disaster befallen the town in the preceding weeks? Perhaps the Irish had paid it a visit after all. Or maybe the Saxons had sneaked an opportunity. He called to the duty sentry. 'What's happening? Where is everybody?'

'Public holiday,' the sentry replied, 'everyone's at the amphitheatre.'

'Lucius has evidently been enjoying himself in our absence,' Barnabas commented.

'Hello,' Marius turned in his saddle at the sound of marching behind them. 'What's all this?'

A rigid column of soldiers, two abreast, entered through the gate. Marius could see the plumed helmet of authority at its head

'Who is in command here?' the *centenarius* enquired.

The sentry scratched his head and stepped forward. 'Well, the commander is at the baths this morning. Can I help?'

'Tertius Favonius Pictor. Londinium *vicarius* command. I'm looking for a Lucius Septimius, governor of *Britannia Prima*. We have orders for his arrest.'

Marius looked at Drufidius, whose expression conveyed something between puzzlement and elation.

'Well?' the *centenarius* said. 'He's not at the amphitheatre. We've already been there. I understand he's resident at the inn?'

The sentry nodded. 'That's correct, sir.'

Marius called Barnabas and Fraomar over. 'Something's up,' he told them. 'They're after Lucius – and he's not at the games.' To the *centenarius* he said: 'I can show you the way.'

'And you are?'

'Marius Appius Scaevola. Councillor of Corinium.'

Tertius Favonius Pictor looked him up and down. 'Looking a little travel-worn, councillor? You know Septimius?'

'I do,' Marius said.

'Very well.' Pictor signalled to his men.

A thought occurred to Marius. 'Drufidius – I think you'd better find Bernicca and bring her along, don't you?'

Drufidius gave him a strange look. 'G–good idea, Marius. Don't w–wait for me – I'll catch you up.'

The inn courtyard was deserted but for a few slaves grouped around a black mare. One of the men was inspecting the animal's hoof, pointing to a loose nail that seemed to be causing some disagreement. They looked up as the military procession entered the courtyard then continued with their debate. Whatever was going on was not their affair and they were used to the inn's endless stream of visitors.

'Which way?' the *centenarius* barked.

'To the left and then straight down the corridor,' Marius said.

'Is this wise?' Fraomar whispered tersely. 'Septimius will have me thrown into jail.'

'He won't,' Marius promised. 'I have a feeling he won't be able to do anything any more.'

They followed Pictor down the corridor. There were footfalls behind: Bernicca and Drufidius hurrying along to meet them.

Pictor banged on the door of Lucius' quarters. No response. He put his shoulder to it and it flew open.

'Gods of my fathers,' Pictor said, 'what a mess.' He stood to one side and opened his hand to indicate the interior of the governor's quarters. Marius could smell the blood before he saw it.

Barnabas entered the room and made the sign of the cross as he took in the chaos. Two bodies lay in a congealing pool of blood.

Marius pointed to the prone body of the Praeses. 'I think he's beyond arrest now.'

Pictor shook his head and blew air out of his cheeks. He approached the other body and turned it over to reveal a bloodstained face. 'Recognize him?'

Marius shook his head. There had clearly been a titanic struggle. Not one piece of furniture was intact. The room looked as if a herd of cattle had been driven through it, scattering all fixtures and fittings in wanton disarray.

'He was a strong man, by the looks of it,' Pictor said, examining the Praeses' body. It was covered in deep cuts, particularly about the arms. 'Defense wounds.' Pictor lifted an arm and let it fall. 'Looks like he was unarmed.'

'I wonder,' Marius said. He bent over the body of the unknown assassin, lifted the dead hand.

'What are you doing?' Fraomar asked suspiciously.

'Just a hunch,' Marius said. He rolled up the sleeve of the man's tunic and made a small noise of satisfaction in his throat. 'Ah. As I thought.'

Pictor stooped and followed Marius' pointing finger. On the arm was a small tattoo. 'A snake?'

Marius nodded.

'Well, whatever. It makes no difference to me I'm afraid. This is out of our jurisdiction. The local authorities will have to deal with it.' Pictor signalled to his men.

'Wait,' Marius said. 'What was the charge?'

'Treason,' Pictor replied. 'Sensitive documents were found in Septimius' quarters relating to matters of internal security. They were leaked to Saxons at the coast. I can't say any more.' The *centenarius* repeated the order and his men prepared to file out of the building.

'I, I – um– don't think that's quite correct,' Drufidius stepped forward.

Pictor groaned and slumped his shoulders. 'Gods. Who are you?'

'Drufidius Sextus. C–Councillor of Calleva.'

Pictor drummed his fingers on the well-worn hilt of his *spatha*. 'Well? What is it?'

'The offence was not committed b–by Lucius Septimius.'

Bernicca stepped forward, 'Please excuse my husband, he has–'

'Quiet, woman!' Drufidius shouted. Bernicca's mouth opened and closed.

Pictor found an undamaged chair. He upended it and sat down with a sigh. 'Continue.'

'I think you'll find that this woman, Bernicca Crispina, is the instigator of the affair,' Drufidius went on. 'You see, we were offered a bribe. My wife was keen, but I, well, I'm not saying I wasn't tempted, but, anyway– '

'Drufidius!' Bernicca glared. She moved towards him.

'Restrain her,' Pictor said.

Drufidius continued haltingly, watching Bernicca squirm in the arms of Pictor's soldiers. 'We visited

Londinium on business and I believe, the er, *vicarius*, was led astray by my – wife – it has happened before, once or twice, I believe–' Drufidius trailed off. Then in a louder voice: ' – and I also believe her to be responsible for the theft of the original documents for which the Praeses stood accused.'

'It's a lie!' Bernicca shrieked.

'She then arranged for the information to be copied and sent our slave girl– ' Drufidius moistened his lips, ' – Freia, to meet the agent and deliver it. Of course she then had to bring the reward back, a. . . considerable reward – but she, well, she never– '

'Stop him!' Pictor shouted as Fraomar launched himself at Bernicca.

'Fraomar, no!' Marius got behind Fraomar and wrapped his arms about the muscular torso. Barnabas pitched in and between them they managed to drag Fraomar away from the drawn swords of Pictor's men. The Alamann's eyes scorched the air between himself and Bernicca. 'This is all your doing,' he glowered.

'Forgive him – please.' Marius appealed to Pictor. 'His sister was killed in Mona as a consequence of what Drufidius has just explained.'

Fraomar brushed their restraining hands aside. His eyes bored into Bernicca's.

'This can be proven?' Pictor asked.

'You have my word,' Drufidius replied. 'I can v–vouch that she confided her intention to plant the original scroll in this very chamber. And there's this, of course.' He produced a bag from his tunic, untied its leather thong, extracted several large opals and offered them for Bernicca's inspection. 'Your reward, my dear. Take a good look and ask yourself if they were worth the lives that have been lost.' Drufidius replaced the stones in the bag and passed it to Barnabas. 'Here's a t–trustworthy man. He can decide what happens to them.'

'Once a fool, always a fool,' Bernicca snarled, 'and you are an eternal fool, husband.'

'Well,' Barnabas said. 'I suggest a split between your municipal funds deficit, Drufidius, and the church. That's what Freia would have wanted. Anyone disagree? Good.'

'Then our business is finished,' Pictor said. 'We have the traitor we came for.'

'Goodbye, my dear,' Drufidius said. 'Enjoy the company of the *v–vicarius*. I'm sure you have a lot to t–talk about.'

After Pictor and his troops had taken Bernicca away and the Callevan military had completed their inspection of Lucius' quarters, Marius and Barnabas found themselves a quiet corner of the inn and sat reflectively in the company of a large pitcher of wine.

'The tattoo,' Barnabas said, 'you were expecting to find it?'

Marius took a draught of wine. 'Yes. I thought he might have had a visitor.'

'There is a link with Paulus, then?'

'Marsallas' doing, I'd guess.' Marius smiled at the bishop's thoughtful expression. 'No loose ends. Rejecting his offer meant that we were potentially hostile to his intentions. And he didn't want me or Lucius letting the cat out of the sack.'

'Ah. But Drufidius rejected the offer – and so far he has not been targeted.'

'But Bernicca– '

The bishop nodded. 'Of course. Her compliance probably saved him.'

'And the fact that he wasn't here.'

'And neither were you,' Barnabas said. 'Fortunately. Watch your back, Marius. Even though the barbarian threat has been weakened Paulus may still have *Areani* in the area to carry out his dirty work.'

'I will take care, rest assured,' Marius said. 'But now, Barnabas, it's time to come clean.' Marius jabbed his forefinger at the bishop accusingly. 'I have met officials of the Christian church before and none are quite like you.'

Barnabas smiled into his wine. 'Hmm. Is that so?'

'It is,' Marius confirmed. 'So, out with it. Who are you?'

'I am genuinely a bishop,' Barnabas smiled again, 'but a little more too. I served with Julian in Persia as an *optio* to begin with, then as centurion.'

'I knew it.' Marius shook his head wryly. 'Your skill with a sword owes more to army experience than to prayer.'

'They go together for me,' Barnabas laughed. 'Prayer for protection before and thanksgiving for my spared life afterwards.'

Marius grinned. 'That makes sense. Go on.'

'I then served under Valentinian before his elevation to emperor. He was a fine soldier.'

'I have heard as much,' Marius said. 'And I'm guessing that you too made a favourable impression on the emperor to be?'

'I did,' Barnabas replied thoughtfully. 'And since I took holy orders he has seen fit to honour me with the occasional …undercover assignment.'

'I see.' Marius drained his wine. The innkeeper plonked a new jug on the table and Barnabas filled his cup.

'Thanks. So, let me guess,' Marius pressed on, intrigued. 'You were tasked not only to ensure Valentinian's family came to no harm but also that Nipius did not get up to any mischief whilst in Britannia?'

'It is complicated,' Barnabas said. 'Nipius has long been seen as a danger. He has supporters, both here and in Gaul. He was also building support in Germania, so Valentinian wanted him out of the way, yes, but at the right time and in the appropriate place. Terricula let the cat out of the sack, as you would say, with his rather clumsy attempt on Nipius' life.'

'And that was all?' Marius said. 'What about Fraomar?'

Barnabas nodded. 'You are an astute young man, Marius. Valentinian also wanted me to keep an eye on Fraomar to ensure that he came to no harm.'

'So you let him take a leading role in the battle for Cunedum?' Marius asked with a straight face and a twinkle in his eye. 'Safe as a walk round the Forum.'

Barnabas shot him a self-conscious grin and shrugged. 'Could I have stopped him?'

Marius laughed. 'No, I suppose not.'

They sat in companiable silence and Marius reflected on the journey from Mona. It had been a dangerous one, despite the protection afforded by Jovinus. Although the battle at Mona had destroyed the nerve centre of the invasion there were still bands of marauders at large, acting independently of the defeated forces of Cunedum. Now that Jovinus had returned to Gaul, Marius hoped that a major task force was on Valentinian's priority list. He didn't wish to spend more time than was necessary at either

Calleva or Corinium although he blessed the gods for their fortitude in defense.

'So, what will you do now, Marius of Corinium?' Barnabas broke the silence.

'Do? By the gods, who am I to disappoint an emperor?' Marius held up his hands and laughed. 'Valentinian wanted an audience with Fraomar; now I am also able to reunite the emperor with his wife and child.'

Barnabas smiled. 'I know what you're angling for, Marius. As I have to file a report with Valentinian I would be glad to accompany you, if you'll have me?'

Marius grinned and held out his hand.

Epilogue

The Rhine frontier, winter 367AD

'The emperor will see you two now,' the *seniores* officer said, 'you haven't got long – physician's orders.'

Marius glanced at Barnabas, who returned a gesture of encouragement. Fraomar, as usual, wore his unreadable expression. Marius and Fraomar ducked under the tent flap to find a thick set man reclining on a purple couch, propped up at one end by a packing case. His complexion was pasty and his forehead was covered by a linen cloth, which he removed as they came in. 'So. Fraomar of the *Alamanni* arrives at last,' he said, wringing the cloth into a small basin.

'It is an honour to greet you, Caesar,' Marius said with a bow.

'Honour? Yes, I suppose so – Marius isn't it?' Valentinian reapplied the cloth with a groan and lay back on the couch. 'You find me not – at my best,' the emperor said. 'But I've heard the news from Jovinus.' He peered at Marius from under the cloth. 'Some people will do anything to evade curial service, eh?'

Marius opened his mouth to defend himself but Valentinian waved him into silence. 'I jest, Marius, I jest. You are to be congratulated for your efforts councillor, not reprimanded. And I have to thank you as a husband and father for the safe homecoming of Justina and Antonia.'

'It is an honour to receive your thanks, Caesar but I must also report that the leader of the barbarian alliance escaped,' Marius said. 'I–'

'Ah yes. Paulus.' Valentinian levered himself up on one elbow. 'What an irritation he's proving to be. But I think you do yourself a disservice, Marius. You successfully infiltrated his command centre and got within striking distance. Had conditions been more favourable you may well have put an end to him once and for all. No, no,' the emperor shook his head, 'it was a fine effort, and performed under the most trying circumstances according to Jovinus. For the time being the threat is over. The barbarians no longer have a controlling authority. That was your success. They can now be swept out of Britannia – as long as we employ the right tactics.'

'Does Caesar plan to send a larger task force?' Marius enquired.

'Certainly,' Valentinian shuffled himself into a sitting position and took a deep breath, 'you know, the physicians bled me yesterday. It fair takes it out of you. But they know best, I suppose.'

'I am glad to see you making a recovery, *dominus*,' Marius said, 'but will you be well enough to lead the task force?'

Valentinian looked up. 'Me? Good God, no. There's more than enough going on here to keep me occupied. And our friend may be able to talk some sense into his people over the next week or so.' Valentinian acknowledged Fraomar with a small inclination of his head. 'I've arranged some meetings. Let's hope– ' The emperor rose stiffly to his feet, 'they do some good. And quickly, because–' he grimaced in pain and sat down again, 'I have a job for you, should you wish to accept it.'

'For me?' Marius asked.

'For both of you. And for our clerical friend. Where is he, by the way?'

'Waiting outside, Caesar.'

'Get him in here,' Valentinian snapped at the attending officer.

Barnabas appeared under the tent flap. 'Caesar.'

'*Must* people call me that?' The emperor swung his legs back onto the couch. 'Right. Let's take Fraomar first.' He motioned to Fraomar. 'Come forward. Now, yours are a stubborn people. But I am prepared to be lenient on two conditions: One; that you talk them out of this ridiculous notion that they are hard done by. I have been more than generous under the terms of our earlier agreements. And two: that you are prepared to lead such Roman units as I designate to bring our friend Nipius to justice. Yes, it will mean a return to Britannia, but under slightly different circumstances. And then, I will ensure that you are repatriated with a suitable level of compensation. Subject to your success, of course.'

Marius watched for Fraomar's reaction. The Alamann returned the emperor's gaze for a moment and said: 'You will leave my people in peace? I have your word?'

'If you can persuade them to see sense, my word shall stand.'

'I would bring another to justice. *Alamanni* justice.'

'I am aware of your loss and you have my sympathy. But Paulus can wait.' Valentinian blew his nose and inspected the contents of the rag. 'Our immediate concern is the stabilization of Britannia. And Nipius is a less than stabilizing influence.' He lay back on the cushion. 'If you sort out the Nipius thing, then you may turn your attention to Paulus.'

'If Caesar pleases, I would like the opportunity–' Marius blurted.

'Yes, Marius. I'm sure. But what ought we to do with you? You've just begun your career on the council. We need men like you in the provinces. And now that Septimius is no longer with us there's a vacancy for a governor. I'd say you fitted the bill.'

Marius was horrified. 'But Caesar, I–'

Valentinian held up his hand and laughed, 'All right. All right. I was just testing the waters. What is it you really want, Marius? Well, it's not hard to guess.' Valentinian smiled and raised his thick eyebrows.

'Then you will grant me a commission?'

'It is *highly* irregular. But, under the circumstances–'

Marius was elated. 'Caesar is most generous.'

Valentinian looked at each of them in turn. Marius, Fraomar, and Barnabas. 'You make a good team,' he said. 'If I can persuade my holy agent–' here he gave Barnabas a knowing look, 'to postpone his heavenly pursuits, you may continue to work together. Now I must involve Count Theodosius in our plans. He is to be the task force leader. A good man – you'll like him.'

As the emperor finished the tent flap rippled again and a boy of perhaps seven or eight years of age came in. In his arms he carried a pile of writing tablets, which threatened to topple at any moment. He stopped when he saw the three men standing before the emperor. 'Ah, Gratian. I wanted you to meet these three and learn a lesson.' Valentinian ruffled the boy's hair.

Marius looked at Fraomar, wondering what the lesson could be. The smile returned was the smile of friendship and forgiveness. Marius felt an upsurge of emotion, a lump in his throat which he quickly swallowed. He moistened his lips and waited for the emperor's words of wisdom.

'The most unlikely combinations,' Valentinian said at last, wagging his finger to get Gratian's attention, 'often prove the most effective. Remember that, lad. It may come in useful one day.'

Latin Glossary

Ala	Cavalry wing
Alamanni	Federation of Germanic tribes
Comes	Count as in *Comes Litoris Saxonici (count of the saxon shore)*
Dominus	Lord, master
Familia	Family - including slaves
Focus	Fireplace, associated with an altar
Genius locii	Household gods
Gladius	Short, stabbing sword
Lanista	Master of gladiators
Legio	Legion (infantry)
Pilum(ae)	Spear
Praeses	Governor
Spatha	Infantry-issue sword
Turma(ae)	Cavalry unit
Vexillatio	Unit of Roman troops (usually detached from main Legion)
Vicarius	Senior official

Irish Glossary

Buitseach	Witch, endowed with magical powers

Author's note

The dilemma when writing in this genre is that one desires to stick as closely as possible to proven historical fact whilst also introducing the 'what if' element to an acceptable and believable level. Such introductions may well fly in the face of what is considered by historians to be historically verifiable and therefore admissible. To any objections raised in this area, I have but one defense. And that is to point out that 'Catena' is primarily an invention of my own making based *loosely* on the events of 367AD. Hence, there *was* a Paulus. He *was* known as '*Catena*', and was certainly a very unpleasant character. Valentinian *was* the emperor of the West at the time and an invasion *did* occur in 367, as described by the Roman author Ammianus. Historians surmise that such an invasion would have required a coordinator of some stature; someone familiar not only with the structure and strength of Roman military deployments but also which political issues were likely to affect the emperor's judgement. Paulus C certainly fits the bill and it seemed rather a waste to allow the man known as *The Chain* to rest in peace after his execution in Africa. In summary I am not trying to play 'fast and loose' with verifiable history but to entertain, and I apologize if by reading this novel you are in any way led astray from accepted historical boundaries.

In terms of the 'look and feel' of fourth century Britain, I have tried to paint as accurate a picture as possible. The provinces were divided as described, Corinium being the capital of *Britannia Prima*. Interestingly, there was indeed a fourth century governor by the name of Lucius Septimius, although I cannot claim that the character described in 'Catena' bears any resemblance to the original, save the fact that the real Lucius was also a dedicated pagan. We know this because he is noted as making an 'almost aggressively pagan dedication at Corinium' by Peter Salway in his excellent work, 'Roman Britain'. Fraomar also has a real counterpart in an Alamannic chieftain who was sent to Britain in 372. Salway confirms this to be a known fact and I quote: 'Fraomar was in fact sent to Britain as a deliberate act of Imperial favour by Valentinian 1 as a military tribune to command a normal Roman unit of Alamanni already stationed in the island'.

Religion

The fourth century was a time of religious change. Constantine had legalized and formalized Christianity during his reign in the early years of the century but there was still a strong pagan tradition, particularly amongst the civil magistracy. The short reign of Magnentius whose tolerance, even encouragement, of pagan worship caused many to 'come out' and resume their old ways of worship led directly to the Pauline persecutions when Constantius gained control of Britain. No doubt there were many who simply continued their pagan practices in secret. Valentinian himself was of Christian persuasion, although I suspect that he, like so many others, could best be described as having a 'nominal' rather than a 'life-changing' faith, such as demonstrated by the character of Freia. Many slaves, the downtrodden members of a corrupt society, embraced the new religion as being one that offered hope, salvation and equality. What more could a slave wish for than this? Small wonder then that many found the answer they sought in the person of the humble rabbi from Galilee, Jesus Christ, the chosen one of God.

The Roman Army

The army saw many structural changes during the 3rd and 4th Centuries. The legions were redeployed and reabsorbed into two distinct groups, the *limitanei*, operating on the frontiers and the *comitatenses*, originally stationed with the emperor, but later becoming more of a mobile field army to be deployed as the need arose. The thinking behind this change was based on the premise that a reasonably well maintained border force combined with a high quality mobile army would be the most effective way to deal with the many and varied threats to the empire. Britannia did suffer from a degradation of troops as demand across the channel became more pressing, but the double defeats in 367AD of the Saxon Shore Count, Nectarides, and the *dux Britanniarum,* Fullofaudes, left the country vulnerable in the extreme to the invaders. Many Roman troops deserted after the defeats and took to wandering the countryside, no doubt undertaking a little plunder and pillage themselves. In 'The Serpent and the Slave', the character Scapulus and his men had awarded themselves 'leave of absence' from the army, and this is indeed what many of the army remnant actually did. It was only when Count Theodosius arrived late in 367AD and offered free pardon, food and supplies to any renegade troops wishing to give themselves up that the Britannic army began to reassemble itself into some sort of order. For the hapless ordinary folk of Britannia, particularly those living in the countryside, it must have been a very unpleasant and trying time to have lived through.

Part 2 in the Chronicles of Britannia will follow as :

"Rebels of Valentia"

www.ingramcontent.com/pod-product-compliance
Lightning Source LLC
Chambersburg PA
CBHW020347180626
46812CB00001B/371